Readers love TA MOORE

Skin and Bone

"…this book checks all my boxes. I could not put it down."

—Love Bytes

"I would totally read the next book in the series given the quality of writing and emotional engagement I had with the first two books in the series."

—Gay Book Reviews

Every Other Weekend

"It is nicely twisty and fun, with lots of excitement and unexpected elements that kept this one very engaging."

—Joyfully Jay

"Ms Moore has written an interesting story, a great mystery, with a great deal of suspense."

—Paranormal Romance Guild

Wanted – Bad Boyfriend

"This was a twist on an enemies-to-lovers trope that was quite entertaining."

—Jessie G Books

"This was a fun read, and I totally enjoyed it! You guys should definitely check it out!"

—The Novel Approach

By TA Moore

Every Other Weekend
Ghostwriter of Christmas Past
Liar, Liar
Take the Edge Off
Wanted – Bad Boyfriend

DIGGING UP BONES
Bone to Pick
Skin and Bone

WOLF WINTER
Dog Days
Stone the Crows

Published by DREAMSPINNER PRESS
www.dreamspinnerpress.com

TAKE THE EDGE OFF

TA MOORE

Published by
DREAMSPINNER PRESS

5032 Capital Circle SW, Suite 2, PMB# 279, Tallahassee, FL 32305-7886 USA
www.dreamspinnerpress.com

Trade Paperback ISBN: 978-1-64405-180-1
Digital ISBN: 978-1-64405-179-5
Library of Congress Control Number: 2018914540
Trade Paperback published June 2019
v. 1.0

Printed in the United States of America

This paper meets the requirements of
ANSI/NISO Z39.48-1992 (Permanence of Paper).

To Mum, who always knew I could do it,
to the Five, who convinced me I could,
and to Gran, who loved a good romance.

Twenty-Five Years Ago

FROM NOWHERE the fire spluttered to life on the hood of the wrecked car—like a burning bush, like God had given a pass on this one.

Then the baby started to cry. It was shrill and hiccuping, the inconsolable wail of something that had never gone uncomforted, never known more than passing pain.

No.

One step forward, off the road and onto the wet grass. Later the lie would be that they would have tried if they had the chance. The truth they could never quite escape was that they took that one step to get a better view. That strange, sick moment.

A big silver car swerved off the road and onto the hard shoulder. Chips of gravel spat up from under the tires as the driver scrambled out, half-tangled in a seat belt.

"Jesus Christ," the man spluttered, his voice almost reverent with horror. "What happened? Is there anyone in there?"

The baby screamed again, a throttled screech that cut like razors.

"Oh God." The man pulled his jacket off and wrapped it around his hands. He yelled back to the car. "Call the police. The ambulance. Tell them there's been an accident."

In the vehicle the woman, tarty-looking thing with ratty hair and a muppet-skin coat that didn't match the nice car, fumbled with her phone. Her voice was so shrill it cut through the crackle of the fire. The man wrenched at the door with coat-mittened hands. When that didn't work, he picked up a rock and smashed the window.

God gave one last wink, and the car flared with an almost solid *whoomph*. The man fell back, arm raised to shield his face. The baby cried, and the car burned.

Later the lie would be that they'd done all they could. The truth would be that it would have been easier if the man had given up then.

Some people just had to be heroes.

Chapter One

CAL TOOK a drink of his piss-weak beer and listened with half an ear as his date bitched on about his day. It was easy enough to keep up. The guy was a doctor, nurses didn't respect him, and had he mentioned he was a doctor? That left Cal free to focus on other things.

Like what the *fuck* was the guy's name again?

"… but enough about me." The doctor tucked his napkin into his collar and smoothed it down over his tie. He was a compact man with wiry forearms and a nervous mouth. "I'm here to get away from work for a bit. What do you do?"

Cal ran his finger around the inside of his collar. It was too tight, and it still smelled of prison starch. It had been months, but he didn't wear shirts often.

"I'm a driver."

The doctor nodded as though he cared. Cal doubted it. A poke in the back of his brain reminded him he was supposed to actually try to make a good impression. He shifted on the skinny wooden seat and took another drink of whiskey.

"It's a family business," he said. "Limos and stuff."

"You'll have to give me your card." The doctor chuckled and took a sip of his wine. "It would make a hell of an impression if I had you drive me up to the next big fund-raiser at the hospital."

Not as a date, then, Cal thought dryly as he glanced toward the kitchen. If they'd gone to McDonald's, he could have had something to eat already, and he was pretty sure the doc would be a lot less irritating facedown on a bed. The guy looked like he had a nice enough body under the tight shirts and fussy manners. If nothing else, Cal could give him something to do with that mouth other than talk.

Make an effort. He heard El's voice snap in the back of his head. *Act like you'd rather have a second date than sex.*

"It's not cheap," Cal said. "But people always seem pretty impressed when we pull up."

Of course that probably had more to do with who was in the car than the low-slung Bentley itself. Evade Inc. wasn't in the top tier of the UK's close-protection industry, but they were the solid middle-of-the-road option. Soap stars and Japanese businessmen might not need—or be able to afford—a bodyguard, but they could appreciate a driver with muscle and evasive-driving qualifications.

"It's for charity," Doc protested light-heartedly. "Surely you can volunteer your services for that."

The beer was gone. Cal rolled the glass in his fingers and wondered if another IPA was a good idea. It usually wasn't. Another beer was how he'd gotten half the scars on his knuckles. Of course, he got the other half when he hadn't drunk enough beer and he had to listen to someone run their mouth.

Swings and roundabouts, that's what his dad had always said.

Cal swapped his tumbler for the iced glass of water on the table. It tasted like tap, that tinge of pipe and limescale.

"Let us know," he said with a lazy grin. Someone who knew him better than Doc would have known that wasn't a good sign. "We'll see what we can do."

Doc looked smug, as if he'd scored something in some game only he was playing. He took a drink of wine, and an awkward silence fell. It felt louder, somehow, against the background lilt of conversation and cutlery.

"So, ah." Doc reached up and rubbed his thumb under his ear. "I see you've got some ink there."

"You do," Cal said. He didn't want to talk about his tats. It was too fucking hard to talk about them and not get stuck in his past.

The waiter finally brought their plates out—white china too hot to touch and a pinwheel of steak Cal could balance in the middle of his palm. Doc had gone for some sort of broth with flakes of fish floating in it.

"Is this like the wine?" Cal cracked. "We swill it around to see if we like it and then order a full plate?"

Doc looked embarrassed for him. He adjusted his black-framed glasses and leaned over the table.

"No, it's haute cuisine," he said sotto voce. "This isn't Wetherspoon's."

Cal caught the waiter's eye and raised his glass to show he needed another drink. He took a bite of his rolled steak and heard the familiar deep-bass twang of his ringtone.

"Work," he excused himself as he wiped his hands on a napkin and reached into his jacket pocket. Not just work, he realized as he fished his phone out. It was El's number.

"What?" he asked gruffly as he swiped his thumb to take the call.

"Date going well?" El asked.

Cal glanced over the table at Doc. He had his napkin pinned to his chest with one hand as he lifted the broth to his mouth. Gran used to eat soup like that. She'd fancied herself classier than the rest of them.

"Okay," he said. "What?"

"Well, I'm sorry to cut it short," El said. "But I need you to come in. One of our legacy clients. How much have you drank?"

"A beer." Cal nudged his chair back from the table. "Where do you need me?"

"Hold on."

There was a beep as El shifted to the other line. While he dealt with the client, Cal glanced over the table at Doc.

"Sorry, I gotta go and make nice with a client," he said as he stood up. "Can't be helped."

Doc frowned. "A limo emergency?" he said skeptically.

Cal plucked his leather jacket off the back of the chair and shrugged it on. The leather settled over his shoulders like an old friend. "Yeah, if I wanted to leave, I'd not bother with an excuse."

"Well," Doc said reluctantly as he stood up. He blinked nervously behind his glasses. "Maybe another time."

"Sure," Cal said. "Call me."

He tucked the phone back against his ear as he wove his way through the clutter of small overpopulated tables. The door jingled as he nudged it open and stepped out into the chilly evening air. His breath smoked as he headed down the road to where he parked his bike.

"Renaissance at St. Pancras," El's voice broke the silence on the phone. "Don't be a dick. Do your job. Make an effort."

He hung up before Cal could growl at him. Cal clenched his fist around the phone until it bit into his fingers and then shoved it into his pocket. This was what he'd asked for—a chance to clean up his act, even if it did mean that his brother constantly reminded him to get to it.

With that in mind, Cal supposed he should have learned what Doc's name was. Too late now.

RAY WAS already at the hotel when Cal got there, parked on the gray swoop of drive outside the gothic fairy-tale castle of the Renaissance. The doorman on duty watched suspiciously from under his bowler as the squat middle-aged man in the expensive suit handed over a folder on the client—Cal didn't know why El bothered; he knew Cal would never read them—and keys to the Bentley in exchange for Cal's bike.

"El said he was legacy," Cal said as he tugged his helmet off and tossed it to Ray. "You know him?"

Ray shrugged as he slung a leg over the bike. "El just said to keep him happy," he said. "Don't think he's been around since the old man's time."

Evade Inc. had been their grandad's business. Not that it had a name back then—it had been a rotation of cars far too fancy to be parked outside their council house and pocket money for El and Cal if they detailed the smell of cigar, whiskey, and sometimes blood out of the leather. Grandad wasn't a crook. He was an incurious man with a lead foot and two kids to feed after his son was sent to jail.

"Coulda been anything," he'd told Cal once after Cal found a tooth in the boot. "Some novelty shite. Bastard didn't eat enough fruit. I don't know, because I didn't see anything."

He'd flicked the tooth into the drain and then cuffed Cal around the back of the head. "Neither did you."

After Grandad died, El had taken the company legit. They had a website. Invoices. The back seat still reeked after a job, but it was weed and champagne instead of fear and the occasional puddle of piss.

Well, usually.

They still owed the old guard, though. Or the old bastards thought they did, and that was basically the same thing. Most of them were out of the business now, retired to Spain, full of complaints about gangs, Russians, and kids with no fucking respect. But they liked to be squired around in style when they came home.

"Oh," Ray added as he thumped the helmet down over his ears. He stretched over and gave the corner of Cal's collar a sharp tug. "El said to keep the tie on. Make a good impression."

He revved the bike and pulled off before Cal could give him a message to take back to El. Probably for the best.

"Fucker," Cal muttered under his breath.

He fished the crumpled tie out of his pocket and strung it around his neck as he headed into the hotel. Inside, it was all gentle music, glass ceilings, and artfully scattered leather chairs. A few people had wandered out of the bar to sit and chat in the lobby over glasses of wine and expensively crossed legs. Their pointed relaxation contrasted to the nervous businessman hunched over his tablet in a corner as he pecked out a presentation. The watery whiskey on the table at his elbow had obviously had a few refills.

Behind reception one of the clerks popped up like a meerkat to give him a dubious look. Life wasn't as simple as it had been in his grandad's day. Back then a guy who looked like Cal, from the close-cropped head to the neck tattoo, could be assumed not to belong in a nice place like this. Now she had her suspicions, but she couldn't be sure.

"Can I help you, sir?" She hedged her bets. "Do you need a room?"

Cal gave her his best bad-boy grin as he walked over to the polished wooden counter and leaned on it. It didn't soothe her suspicions any, but it did make her cheeks go pinker under the blush.

"Evade Inc.," he said as he pushed a card over the counter. It was black and minimalist, with muted gray letters stamped onto the card as though even the contact details were evasive. "I'm here to see Joseph Bailey?"

The girl glanced from the card to Cal's face and back to the card. Her eyebrows creased together, and a narrow wrinkle grooved crookedly into the skin between them.

"Mr. Bailey is expecting you?" she asked as she reached for the phone.

"What I was told," Cal said easily. He leaned farther over the desk to nod at her phone. "Check with him?"

She scooted her chair back from him and punched a number into the phone.

"Mr. Bailey," she singsonged. "This is the front desk. I'm sorry to disturb you, but there's someone here who says you're expecting him?"

There was a pause, and she pursed her lips as she visibly got the wrong end of the stick. "Oh. Of course, Mr. Bailey. Yes. I'll send him down now. Immediately."

She hung up the phone and swiveled her chair to the side to fish a key card out of the dispenser. As she slotted it into the computer, Cal wondered idly what she thought he was there to do. People used to think he was a rent boy, but he was over thirty now and the market for middle-aged rough trade was limited.

That was why he had worn a shirt and tie on a Friday night, after all. Signed up for fucking Tinder like he cared more about what someone liked to do than what their cock looked like.

"Here you go, sir," the receptionist said. She plucked the card out of the computer and held it out to him. "This will give you access to the lifts and all available floors. Mr. Bailey is currently in the spa. He said you should go and meet him there."

Cal plucked the card out of her fingers with a rough "thanks." Great. He got to watch some poor sod rub wrinkly old flesh. That was how he wanted to spend his one night off.

He knotted his tie on the way down in the elevator and smoothed the black ribbon down over his chest as they reached the spa. The doors bounced open to reveal a minimalist space of steel, glass, and pale wax-smoothed wood. A tall, gray-haired man with a face that looked as though someone had chiseled it from pissed-off granite stood on the other side. He looked Cal up and down, from cropped blond head to boots, and grunted.

It was hard to tell if he was disappointed or had gotten what he expected.

"You're Elijah's brother?"

It actually took a second. No one called El by his given name, probably because it made him sound like a Mormon who had gotten lost on the wrong side of town.

"Yeah." Cal stepped out of the elevator before the doors could close again, and he stuck out his hand. "Cal Tate. Evade Inc."

There was a pause, long enough to make the point that Chisel could fuck with Cal if he wanted to. Then he grabbed Cal's hand with his rough, scarred mitt.

"Edward," he said. "I knew your grandfather. He was a good man. Didn't talk much. I always admired that about him."

Cal scratched the back of his neck as he weighed his crappy bank account—for the work he did Cal made okay money at Evade, but he'd never saved anything in his life—against the fact that even his long-suffering brother would wash his hands of him eventually if Cal kept fucking up.

"If the police flag us down," Cal warned, "I'll pull over."

Edward smiled as though someone had drowned his dog and then told him to say cheese. "That side of the business stopped being profitable a while ago," he said. "Come on. Mr. Bailey's waiting for us."

He turned on his heel. There was a precision to the movement that Cal recognized. El moved the same way sometimes. The military trained that into you. No surprise there. Most of the good close-protection pros in the UK had a military background. There were a few ex-cops in there, but it was mostly the forces. Edward had probably been something a bit more specialist than a squaddie like El, though.

Cal fell in behind Edward as they walked through the curved tiled halls of the spa. It felt mostly empty. Most of the doors were open to reveal leather beds and smooth cream-plaster walls. Soft music and gentle voices leaked from under the few doors that were closed, and the air smelled like jasmine and oil.

He heard the sound of water before they reached the pool. It was tucked away down a low, black mirror-tiled tunnel, and the sound of the two men's footsteps was loud off the bare walls. He tasted salt against the back of his throat instead of chlorine as the tunnel opened out into a low, dimly lit room, tiled in a small rust-red pattern. The irregularly shaped pool was the brightest lit space in the room, as underwater lights made it glow a flickering sapphire blue. The dark shadow of a body cut through the water like a knife, with strong, impatient strokes.

"Wait here," Edward told Cal.

He walked over to the edge of the water and crouched down as the swimmer's head, slick and dark as an otter, broke the surface.

"The driver from Evade is here," Edward said as he jerked his thumb over his shoulder. "Do you want to speak to him?"

"Why not," the man said dryly as he pushed wet hair back from his face. "You've done everything else, after all."

He pushed off the side of the pool and swam over to the steps at the side. Water streamed down his long body as he climbed out—all tight muscle and pale skin. A ribbon of black fabric cupped his balls and stretched over the curve of his ass. His face was all sharp bones and elegance. He belonged on the cover of a magazine.

So much for old and wrinkly. Joseph Bailey looked like he was in his twenties, and Cal could see enough of that lean, wiry body to tell there were no wrinkles there. It wasn't such a good idea to look. All of a sudden, Cal's collar wasn't the only thing that felt too tight. He should have read the client file, he supposed, because this wasn't one of the usual perma-tanned, gold-chained old gangsters who usually rocked up.

Edward picked up a white toweling robe and walked over to hold it up for the wet Joseph to shrug on.

"So, what are your qualifications?" Joseph asked as he tied the robe shut and walked over. He looked Cal up and down. "Military?"

"No."

Joseph lifted one dark groomed eyebrow. There was a birthmark on his forehead, a patch of faded pink skin that dripped down to the corner of his eye and wrinkled with his curious expression. "Police?"

Cal smirked briefly. "Not exactly." He felt El's glare on the side of his head and made himself straighten up. "I've accreditation in advanced evasive- and defensive-driving courses. I've been in a lot of brawls, and I know what I'm doing. We're drivers, not bodyguards."

Joseph considered him for a second. Finally he shrugged.

"Fine. If I need a driver," he said as he cut a sharp look toward Edward, "I suppose you'll do. I don't care what you do when you're not driving me, but I expect you to be on call 24/7 for the next month. If that costs extra, I'll pay it. I've a suite here in the hotel. You can have one of the rooms. Any questions?"

Cal shrugged.

"It's your money," he said.

"Well, I'm glad someone realizes that," Joseph said. He shrugged his robe back off, tossed it over a chair, and then turned his back on Cal. "Edward will show you up to the suite. Give him your number. I'll call when I need you."

He paused on the edge of the pool for a second, and Cal took a second to admire the view of lean muscled back and tight ass. Then Joseph dove into the pool, and when Cal looked up, he caught Edward's eyes on him across the water.

After a second, Edward unclenched his jaw. "I'll show you up to the room," he said stiffly and stalked out.

It was a silent trip up in the lift. Edward didn't say anything until they reached the suite, where he fished a card out of his pocket and swiped the door open.

"You aren't his type," he said coldly as he unlocked the door. "Don't get your hopes up."

"Or what?" Cal asked. "What you going to do, Eddie, if I get my hopes all up in Joe's business?"

It was surprising how many hard men would stumble when you put them on the spot about their threats. Most people wanted an excuse to let the red mist descend, not to actually explain it ahead of time. It made the whole "I didn't know what I was doing" front later a lot harder to pull off.

Edward was confident in his violence. He gave a thin smile that didn't reach farther than his cheekbones.

"You can take the small bedroom," Edward said as he pushed the door open. The suite opened out from the doors in muted blues and browns, all leather chairs and sepia-tinged maps mounted in waxed-ash frames on the walls. It was probably bigger than most people's houses; it was definitely bigger than the converted flat Cal rented three streets over from his childhood home. "Third door down. Here's your key. Don't steal anything, Mr. Tate. With your record…."

He didn't need to finish. The point was that he knew. Cal acknowledged the answer of "or what" with a brief nod.

"Mr. Bailey will need you early in the morning," Edward said as he tugged the cuff of his shirt back to check his wrist. "So you should get a good night's sleep. We can go over the schedule in the morning."

Cal shrugged and stepped into the suite. He was halfway down the hall when Edward cleared his throat.

"Mr. Tate? I recommended your company for this job because I had nothing but respect for your grandfather," he said. "I hope I can say the same about you at the end of this month. If I can, you'll find this contract a lucrative one. That's the carrot. I do prefer it to the stick."

Cal didn't bother to turn around. He shrugged. "I'm here to drive the car, mate," he said. "Like you said, with my record I need to keep my nose clean."

He let himself into the room Edward had pointed out to him. It was small and white with an undersized double bed and a large bay window that looked down into St. Pancras station itself. Cal stripped his tie and jacket off. The back of his neck was itchy with the unfamiliar chafe of the stiff fabric, and he watched the few people out this time of night shuffle through the station.

It hadn't been a lie. The last thing Cal needed was trouble. He didn't want to end up like some of the old lags in prison—in for stealing a packet of fags and no real desire to get back out. Nothing left but stories of the old days and a hooker on the outside who'd give them a pensioner's discount, and they called her their girlfriend.

What he needed was to get this job done, a nice, dull man like Doc to come home to, and to sort his life out.

The problem was that Cal wanted what he'd always wanted—fast cars and men who were no good for him.

Chapter Two

JOE SCRUBBED one of the hotel towels over his head as he stepped out of the suite bathroom. "I still don't see why I need a driver," he said from under the jasmine-sweet folds. "Unless you've forgotten *how* in your old age."

He heard Edward grunt.

"I'm used to American roads," he said. "Evade Inc. has a good reputation, and if Tate drives you, then I can concentrate on protecting you."

Joe slung the towel over his shoulders and pushed his hair back from his face with both hands. A trickle of gritty cold water ran down the back of his neck. "You're overreacting, Edward." He sat down on one of the low leather chairs in front of the window and poured himself a glass of whiskey. "It's hardly the first time someone has threatened to kill me, yet here I am."

"Hmm," Edward said noncommittally. He clasped his hands behind his back and tilted his head to the side. "Have you ever given any thought to why so many people want to see you dead, Joseph?"

Joe put his feet up on the ottoman and tilted a sardonic toast in Edward's direction. "Jealous of my wealth, good looks, and charm?"

"They don't help," Edward said with a flicker of amusement. He unbent enough to sit down on the edge of the bed. "Joseph, you need to take this seriously. These aren't your dad's old enemies running their mouths, or empty threats some accountant wrote on his pink slip. I think you should go back to LA. Sort things out with Kristen before it's too late. Whatever happened, it doesn't have to be the end of the world, and whatever business you have here, I can handle it for you."

That *was* what Edward had always done. Joe took a drink of whiskey—sour rye on the back of his tongue. When Dad had been busy, it was Edward who took Joe to the birthday parties of kids who didn't actually like him and whose parents were scared of his Dad. It was Edward who'd paid off the headmaster at his first school and the one after that.

Edward had been more like a father to Joe than Harry Bailey ever had time for. And like Harry, Edward thought that all Joe needed to settle him down was the love of a good woman. Joe supposed that, in a way, they might have been right, although not in the way they thought.

"It's not the end of the world," he said. "It's just the end of me and Kristen. And you're my chief of security, not my boss. I don't need you to handle my business. Handle your own and make sure the letters stop."

A muscle jumped in Edward's jaw, a trapped jiggle under grooved skin and a scruff of graying five-o'clock shadow.

"Of course, sir," he said, a frosty bite to his words as he stood up. "I'll get on that right away. All I have to do is find out which of the many, many people who dislike you actually want to see you dead. And what about Tate? Do you want me to let him go? Since you don't think you need him after all."

Joe licked his lips and took another drink of whiskey as he thought about Cal Tate and, more specifically, Cal Tate's full, ridiculously pretty mouth. He imagined his fingers hooked in the wonkily knotted tie as he pulled it loose from the overstarched white shirt and his mouth against a sweat-salty neck as he chewed his way around the spray of ink under Cal's ear.

Joe could feel the flush of heat up the back of his neck, and his cock ached under the sweatpants he'd pulled on for the commute between the suite and the spa.

"No," he said casually, almost dismissively, in an attempt to disguise that raw flash of reaction. "Since you don't feel up to the job, he can stay. As long he doesn't screw up."

Edward inclined his head in stiff acknowledgment and turned to leave, but he paused in the doorway and tilted his head slightly toward Joe. "Whatever this is," he said, "you need to at least tell me, Joseph. There's only so much I can do if you keep me out of the loop."

That was true. It was also the point. If Edward knew what Joe was doing back in England, then what he'd do wouldn't be inclined to help. He'd worked for Harry Bailey for over twenty years, and his loyalties weren't going to change now. Neither of them could stop Joe from doing what he wanted, but they could impede him.

"I'm not keeping you out of anything, Edward," Joe said. "It's not your business."

"Yes, sir," Edward said quietly. "It's your choice. I have some things to do this evening, but I'll see you in the morning."

He walked out and closed the door behind him. It wasn't slammed—Edward didn't believe in shows of temper—but it closed behind with a firm click. Joe grimaced and leaned his head back against the chair. There was a knot of sour regret in his stomach and nothing to do about it. He could apologize, but he wasn't going to change his mind, so it would just be empty words.

More empty words. Joe smiled wryly as he took a drink of whiskey and held it on his tongue to feel the burn. Those were what he was good at, after all. He doled out assurances to the executives of failing companies and promises to lovers. Sometimes he even bought into his own patter… until it all collapsed under its own weight and everyone had to face reality. No wonder there was a file full of death threats in Edward's office.

That made Joe think of Kristen for a second, of her honesty and her expectations. He didn't want to.

Joe drained the whiskey and thought about his new driver instead—the taste of him and the heavy, muscled bulk of his shoulders under his shirt. He cupped himself through his sweats, thin fabric slick against his cock, as he imagined all that muscle sprawled out and… accessible. His undecided imagination painted ink all over the expanse of tanned skin he hadn't seen and then erased it again until the only ink was the ghost of lines that peeked over Cal's collar.

It was hard to decide what he preferred. Either way he liked the idea of being the only one who knew what was under that shirt as he watched Cal go about his day.

Joe squeezed his cock roughly and felt the dull throb of it all the way back into his ass. His breath caught hotly at the back of his throat, and he chewed on his lower lip as he tugged on his cock with short, impatient jerks of his fist.

In his head he saw the flicker of Cal's eyes again, the quick once-over that lingered at Joe's thighs.

Before he could think better of it, Joe reached for his phone and flicked through his contacts until he found the Driver details Edward had input earlier. He hesitated for a second, his thumb poised over the screen. His mouth was dry, and the awareness of what he wanted was clear and distinct in his head. It wasn't the one glass of whiskey that made him feel drunk as he jabbed in the message.

"I said 24/7," he muttered aloud as he hit Send and then tossed the phone aside. "Let's see if he knows what that means."

It wasn't one of his better lies. The truth was in the hot twist of want in his balls, the eager, dizzy edge of anticipation that fizzed in the back of his brain. He poured himself another glass of whiskey—an amber excuse in a crystal glass—and waited.

The rap on the door came a couple of minutes later. Joe pushed himself up out of the oversoft embrace of the chair, adjusted his cock so the hard bulge of it wasn't obvious, and walked over to open the door.

"Whiskey?" he offered as he held out the glass.

Cal looked at the whiskey and then at him. "I don't drink and drive."

"No one is asking you to drive," Joe said with a crooked smile and waited.

There was a pause, and then Cal took the whiskey from him. There were scars on the backs of his hands and calluses over his knuckles. He hadn't claimed a martial-arts qualification, but he obviously knew how to fight. His hands were messed up, but his face wasn't.

The thought occurred to Joe that if he was wrong about that brief once-over, he could end up on the other end of that scarred fist. It strung the hot wire of lust tighter in Joe's balls. He liked to be in control—in business, in bed—but there was something heady about the threat of being out of it.

"Sit down," Joe suggested as he waved to one of the chairs. "If you're going to work for me, I suppose I should know a little bit more about you."

Cal gave him a sidelong look and then leaned against the post of the bed instead. That—Joe decided as he sat back down—actually worked better. He poured himself a whiskey and admired the view as Cal took a sip of his drink. There was nothing elegant about Cal's body, no gym-sculpted muscle or narrow waist, just heavy muscle and long legs. His face looked like something you'd see carved in a museum, with heavy, broody bones and a lush, soft mouth.

"So what do you wanna know?" Cal asked.

Joe spread his hands. "Entertain me," he said.

"I expected to get laid tonight." Cal took a sip of whiskey and chased a stray drop over his lower lip with his tongue. "I was on a date when my brother called me in."

"You're being paid well for the inconvenience," Joe said. "I'm sure you can make it up to your… girlfriend?"

Cal smirked. "First date."

"And you were going to get laid? It must have been going well."

Cal glanced down at himself and then back up at Joe with a cocky tilt of his mouth. He gave a one-shouldered "well, come on" shrug that pulled his shirt tight over his chest.

"So, is that it?" Cal asked as he pushed himself off the bedpost. He walked over and bent down to put the barely touched whiskey at Joe's elbow. "Or are you going to cut to the chase?"

He smelled of cologne and a hint of fresh sweat—a mixture of cedarwood, salt, and musk. The heavy bulk of his body was angled over Joe's, one arm braced on the arm of the chair.

"You have somewhere else to be?" Joe asked.

Cal kissed him with a rough, eager pass of soft lips and sharp teeth. The aftertaste of whiskey lingered on his tongue, a hand-me-down sting of liquor on Joe's tongue. Cal chewed Joe's surprised breath off his lips and then pushed himself back away from the chair.

"Bed," he said as he stepped back and unbuttoned the collar of his shirt. The flash of ink and the tight lines of tendons in Cal's throat quivered heat all the way down Joe's nerve endings. He shifted in the chair and tried to will the tight bulge of his cock back under control. "Yours or mine. It's no skin off my nose."

Joe tilted his head back against the chair, wet hair cold against his scalp, and slowly ran his tongue over his lower lip as he tried to adjust his plans. He wasn't often wrong-footed. His career as a troubleshooter might have been rooted in nepotism, but he'd kept it because he was good at it. If he hadn't been, Harry would have given him a stipend and sent him to Monaco or somewhere to be decorative and useless. Even if they'd been close, which they had never quite pulled off, Harry was never a man who'd let sentimentality get in the way of money.

Cal had managed to do what dozens of real estate lawyers and site supervisors had never quite pulled off—throw Joe off script so abruptly that he hadn't even seen it coming. The reality of not being entirely in control of an encounter, the reins yanked from your grip, was a lot less pleasant than the possibility of it.

"You know what they say about assumptions," Joe said as he watched Cal tug the tails of his shirt out of his trousers.

Cal shrugged and paused with his fingers on the buttons of his shirt. "You really the type of guy who gives a crap about his employees' lives?" he asked. "I mean, if you're *real* interested, I can tell you all about my hopes and dreams."

"Which are?"

The grin wasn't what Joe expected. It was wide and goofy and plastic to the point of reshaping that brutally pretty face into something awkward and oddly charming.

"Get laid," Cal said. "Drive fast. I'm a simple man."

Joe put his tumbler down, close enough to Cal's that the glasses clicked together. He tilted his head curiously to the side.

"Do all your customers get this sort of hands-on service?" he asked.

"Yeah," Cal said. He undid the last button on his shirt and let it hang open as he tucked his hands into his pockets. "There's a customer-satisfaction survey, and with an iTunes gift card on the line, I like to go the extra mile. Look, if you want to pretend you had to seduce me into this? We can pretend you've threatened my paycheck if I didn't comply with your deviant desires."

"Deviant?"

"In for a penny, in for a spanking," Cal said. He pressed the back of his hand to his forehead and heaved a fluttery sigh. "Oh no, sir. I'm a good man. What of my reputation?"

Joe snorted as he stood up. The dull ache of lust clenched in his balls, a sharp, immediate need that shouldered the mess of everything else aside. He didn't need to think about it. All he needed to do was grab both ends of Cal's wrinkled tie and twist.

"A good man?" he asked as he pulled on the makeshift leash.

For a moment Cal didn't shift, his jaw set as he leaned back against the twisted collar. Then he gave in and took a step forward. Joe had the edge on him in height, if only by an inch or so, and Cal had to tilt his head back to look at him.

"Good enough," Cal said. He brushed his hand over Joe's crotch in a quick taunt of a caress that pinched pleasure deep in Joe's balls. His hand drifted up to Joe's hip, and he twisted the waistband of the loose black sweats around his fingers. "Good enough at some things."

Joe kissed him. He wanted, for a second, to take his time, to explore Cal thoroughly and to coax something like a plea from that smart mouth. But that wasn't what this was about—there was accepted practice for nearly anonymous hookups, the same as there was for anything else—and Joe didn't have the patience for it anyhow.

He bit Cal's soft, ripe lower lip and then slid it from between his teeth. "I guess I should take you for a test drive, then," he said as he stepped back. The tie slipped from between his fingers, the wrinkles set with sweat now. "See if your 'good enough' will… satisfy."

Amusement played over Cal's face. "You wanna kick the tires?"

"I want to fuck you," Joe said bluntly. The words felt rough in his mouth and as salty-sour as sex. "Finish taking that shirt off. Leave the tie."

Cal considered that for a second, his eyes hooded and amused. Then he did as he was told. Ink was scrawled over his broad shoulders and down his upper arms in bold, black lines. There was no theme or style to them. An elegant raven, shadow etched in soft gray, shared his bicep with a messy-edged tribal dragon. A rose bloomed in heavy red on his ribs, the only piece of color on his skin, and the edges of the petals scuffed down to pink where it curled over his ribs.

It worked like graffiti on a beautiful building—the rough edges of it drew attention to the lean muscle and long bones underneath.

"Custom paint job," Joe said. "I like it."

Cal smirked and grabbed his cock through his trousers. The gray fabric outlined the heft of it, half-risen to the occasion. "You should see what's down here."

"That's the plan."

Cal's eyes tracked appreciatively down the hard line of Joe's stomach to the obvious line of his erection under his sweats. He dabbed a damp line with his tongue over his lower lip, and he flexed his fingers lazily around his cock. "You first," he said.

Something dark and hot twisted low in Joe's stomach. He wasn't sure if he felt smug at Cal's obvious interest or thrown by the shift in the balance of power. Joe was—even if not on his own merits—a wealthy man. He didn't *try* to be a dick about it, but the weight of all that money had its own gravitational field.

"See, I'm supposed to be the one taking advantage of you," he said as he hooked his thumbs into the waistband of his sweats.

Cal shrugged and watched, his eyes hooded with lust, as Joe slid the black cotton over his hips and down his thighs. His cock stood proud from between his thighs, the skin taut around the thick jut of his shaft. He wrapped his hand around it and passed his thumb over the head. Slick precome smeared under his fingers.

Was he really going to do this, he wondered with a flash of something almost panic. It scraped the back of his throat as he took a deep breath. No excuses this time. No Kristen to pretend she didn't know *something* as she took him back to her straight, white-linen bed. No Edward to discreetly not notice anything as he waited in the car.

Hell, it was the first time since he was fifteen that he'd fucked someone whose name he was 100 percent on.

Some sober little part of his brain—sober or scared—dug its heels in. It was an awful idea, and it wasn't too late for second thoughts. Joe decided he didn't care… not enough, anyhow.

"Who's the rose for?" he asked.

Cal looked surprised for a second. He reached over and rubbed his ribs were the ink splashed. "It's… I wanted to feel pretty," he said, the brief stammer covered with a smirk.

It turned out Cal wasn't a good liar. Joe let it go. It was hardly important to the next half hour.

"Your turn," he said as he glanced pointedly down at Cal's trousers. "Unless you've changed your mind?"

Cal chuckled with a low, dark sound in the back of his throat as he unbuckled his belt. "I don't really do second thoughts," he said. "Ask my brother. Half the time I don't even think about it once."

He hooked his thumbs into the waistband of his trousers and pushed them down over his hip bones. The striptease had been Joe's idea, but he didn't want to wait anymore. He stepped forward and pulled Cal into a rough, eager kiss.

No second thoughts for either of them, then.

He bruised the kiss onto Cal's lips with sharp teeth and eager mouth as they stumbled backward a step. Cal grabbed a handful of Joe's ass and squeezed the tight curve of muscle. He dragged Joe closer, until Joe's cock rubbed against Cal's hip, the gray fabric of the trousers rough against tender skin. It made Joe squirm with the hunger for more contact.

He thrust roughly against Cal, and his cock rubbed against fabric again and then slid over the waistband to brush against tight, warm skin. He groaned into Cal's mouth, over the slick muscle of his tongue, and ran his hand down Cal's broad back. He traced over the heavy bands of clenched muscle to the vulnerable dip of Cal's spine.

He pulled his mouth away from Cal's and chewed his way down the alcohol sting of aftershave on his jaw to the skull-and-smoke ink on his throat. A guttural "fuck" scraped up out of Cal's throat, and Joe felt the growl of it against his mouth. A hard jolt of interest twisted the nerves in his balls as he wondered what it would like to feel that noise around his cock.

"Well?" Joe asked as he pushed Cal back against the bed. "Still wish you got to second base with your date?"

Cal leaned back against the bed, his arms braced behind him against the mattress and his hips caught on the carved edge of the baseboard. He stood with his legs spread shoulder-width apart and his trousers slung low enough to show the scruff of dark curls that led down to snug red briefs. The tight cotton toned with the tattooed rose *and* trapped the hard curve of Cal's cock.

"If I wanted to fuck the doctor that bad," he drawled, "I'd have told El to shove the job and send Ryan."

Joe grazed his thumb down Cal's stomach, from his belly button to the elasticated cuff of his briefs. He traced his fingernail along the border between skin and underwear, a teased caress that made Cal grimace and tilt his head back. The pulled-taut line of his neck was wet and shiny with Joe's spit. "Ryan? Am I missing out?"

Cal frowned.

"He got higher marks on his accreditation courses than I did, but I finished faster. I think I'm a better driver, but he never breaks the rules, so it's hard to tell."

It sounded like he took that question more seriously than he had anything since he came into Joe's room. Joe moved his hand down and gave the hard rise of Cal's cock a rough squeeze through his briefs. Cal's gasp was a harsh scrape of breath between his teeth as he thrust up against Joe's hand.

"I meant was I missing out down here," Joe said.

Cal licked sweat off his upper lip. "Oh, yeah. Naw, Ryan's too fucked-up to fuck. I was definitely your best bet not to end up with a black eye."

"Lucky me."

Joe pushed Cal's trousers and briefs the rest of the way down Cal's thighs. His mouth went dry as he saw Cal's cock for the first time. He had a nice cock—long and solid as it lifted up toward the flat of his stomach.

"You want a taste?" Cal asked as he reached down to pull his foreskin back. The exposed head was flushed and slick, and Joe could imagine the taste of it on his tongue. It tightened his balls up between his legs, but he could imagine something better.

"You first," Joe said.

Cal glanced down at Joe's cock and folded his lower lip between his teeth.

"So polite," he said as he went down on his knees, his trousers still tangled around his calves. "That's what you get when you fuck the rich."

Joe snorted. "It seemed like you needed something to do with that smart mouth other than run it," he said.

Then the words dried up and caught in his throat as Cal wrapped his mouth against the head of Joe's cock. Pleasure pulsed down into his balls and crawled back along the tight cord of nerves to tickle his ass with the promise of "later." He cupped the back of Cal's head. The hair was too short to dig his fingers into. It was cropped down close to the skull until it napped like velvet, but he flexed his fingers against the heavy skull.

Full lips stretched wet and tight around Joe's cock as Cal sucked his way down the shaft. He grazed rough hands up Joe's thighs until his thumbs settled into the fold of thin skin at his groin. He pushed up firmly with the flat of his tongue against the underside of Joe's cock as he pulled back. Then he reached the head and sucked on it, the tip of his tongue suddenly clever as it traced the thread of the frenulum and then lapped eagerly at the slit.

Cal let the head slip lewdly from his mouth and ran down the side of the shaft with lips and tongue and the occasional ball-wrinkling brush of teeth. Joe chewed on the inside of his cheek as he breathed raggedly. His muscles twitched and trembled under his skin as his nerve endings overloaded. Cal cupped Joe's balls in his hand and squeezed them gently.

The scrape of practical calluses against tender skin made Joe spit out a ragged "fuck" and pull Cal back up to his feet.

When Joe slanted a kiss over Cal's mouth, he tasted himself on Cal's tongue, flat and metallic, the taste of brine from precome and his swim. Joe's cock was pressed against Cal's stomach, spit-wet shaft pressed against the tight skin, and he could feel the wet nudge of Cal's erection against his thigh. Cal kicked his trousers off between sharp-bitten kisses and rough caresses and nearly tripped over the tangle of fabric as Joe pushed him back up against the bedpost.

The idea of it had crawled sticky and eager into Joe's brain earlier, the cocky tilt of Cal's body against the carved, white-washed pole fuel to all sorts of dirty thoughts. He cupped Cal's face in both hands and kissed him hard enough to press his head back against the post. The scruff of stubble on his jaw, pale gilt compared to the darker hair he'd cropped short over his skull, itched against Joe's palms.

"Turn around," he rasped against the damp seam of Cal's mouth.

Cal paused and looked slightly taken aback. "You wanna fuck me?" he asked. "Most people want my cock in *them*."

The thought of it made Joe's ass tighten with a wet pulse of sensation like a heartbeat between his legs.

"Is that a problem?" he asked. His balls throbbed heavily, the hint of the ache he was going to have to wank out if Cal decided it was. He ignored it.

Cal thought about it for a second as he ran his tongue over his teeth behind his lip. He shrugged and pulled Joe in close, their bodies pressed together from chest to balls. Cal grazed his lips along Joe's jaw and bit gently at the hinge of his jaw. "Not if you've got a condom."

"Turn around," Joe told him.

Cal sighed, his breath warm against Joe's throat, and lifted his head. "This isn't a porno. If you stick your cock in me without a raincoat on," he said, "I will lay you out."

Joe snorted and stepped back. "Do it," he said. "And lean on the bedpost."

Cal gave him a dubious look but then turned and did as he was told. He lifted both arms to head height and gripped the arm-thick bar of wood. His fingers slotted into the carved grooves and the long straps of muscle in his back tensed visibly under the skin as he leaned forward.

His ass was Irish pale and tight, all hard muscle and unmarked skin. It was Joe's turn to nearly trip over his own feet.

It was still an awful idea, but he didn't think he'd regret it.

Condoms were stashed in the bedside drawer, along with lube. Joe pulled one out and fumbled the rubber out to roll down the length of his cock. The tight rubber and pressure of his fingers as he smoothed it down his shaft made the heavy ache of arousal flutter in the pit of his stomach. He stroked himself again, tip to root, and then looked up. Cal had twisted around to watch Joe over his shoulder.

"Didn't trust me?" Joe asked as he walked back over. He kicked Cal's trousers out of the way before he tripped over them again. "I'm hurt."

Cal snorted.

"You're a pretty fucker," he said. "I like watching you move, that's all."

The casual compliment, nearly more backhand than offhand, caught Joe off guard. He felt heat crawl under his skin and tried to ignore it.

"Yeah, well, I don't look as good as you in a tie." He smeared lube on his hand and ran his fingers across the hard curve of Cal's ass. It was wet and shiny against white skin. "You ready?"

"Since about nine o'clock," Cal rasped.

Joe pushed his hand between Cal's cheeks and rubbed his finger over and around the puckered hole. It tightened under his finger and then loosened again so he could slide his finger in. Long, slow strokes worked Cal slippery and open until he growled under his breath and pushed his ass back against Joe's hand.

There. Joe's fingers were deep enough inside that he grazed the smooth nodule of Cal's prostate. The brief touch made Cal twitch and rasp out a ragged breath. So Joe did it again, harder this time. Cal swore, a breathless, trailed-off "fuck," as the nerve-rich bundle reacted to the rough stroke.

"You want me to fuck you?" Joe asked as he leaned forward to nuzzle the skin under Cal's ear. He smelled of sweat and a splash of sharp, musky cologne. His cock pressed against Cal's hip and his balls were heavy and tight with hunger, but he wanted to hear Cal say it. He stroked his fingers into Cal and pressed his finger down on the tight node of nerves again. "Well?"

"Fuck," Cal muttered. He leaned forward to rest his forehead against the wooden post. "Yes. Jesus, Bailey, please. Fuck me."

Joe kissed the hinge of Cal's jaw and shifted back. He slid his hand free of Cal's ass and pulled his cheeks apart. The wet slick of his ass was open and eager, and Joe pressed the head of his cock against it. The tight pressure of Cal's ass squeezed at his cock like an eager hand as he slowly pushed inside Cal.

He felt the hot flare of satisfaction that he had what he wanted, and then it was lost in the sticky hunger for more.

Joe rubbed his hand up Cal's back, along the tight patterns of muscle, and gripped the heavy bulk of his shoulder. Slow, short thrusts spread Cal's ass around his cock until he was buried inside him. He leaned forward and kissed his way along Cal's shoulder blade, sweat sharp and heady against his tongue.

"Would you have done this with your date?" he asked against skin.

"Naw," Cal said after a second. "He definitely wanted fucked."

Joe rocked his hips against Cal in slow, hard thrusts. His muscles clenched tighter with each stroke and twisted around the hot core of pleasure. He reached over Cal's hip and wrapped his fingers around his cock. Each time he thrust into Cal, he stroked back on the hard, curved jut of his cock. The skin was thin and velvety under his fingers, wet with lube and come. He could feel the pulse of it against his fingers as he squeezed tighter at the base.

"He has no idea what he's missing," Joe said. "Your ass feels like it was tailored to my cock."

Cal snorted. "You could have said tight, mate."

Joe dug his fingers into Cal's shoulder and thrust roughly into him, hard enough to jolt him against the support of the bedpost. It creaked, and Cal tightened his fingers around it as he sucked in a sharp breath.

"Tight," Joe said. "So fucking tight."

He shoved into him again with hard, eager thrusts in time with the rough strokes of his hand around Cal's cock. Sweat slicked their bodies, each thrust noisy as wet thighs slapped against a sweat-and-lube-glazed ass.

Under him Cal swore and pushed against each thrust, his cock tight and swollen under Joe's fingers. He came first, come hot as it dripped between Joe's fingers and onto the floor, and he staggered for a second as his legs trembled under him.

Joe pulled out, the sudden absence of hot pressure around his cock an ache, and tumbled both of them onto the bed. He sprawled out on top of Cal, stripped off the condom, and thrust against the flat, hair-rough plane of his stomach. Cal cupped the back of his neck and kissed him, his soft lips almost tender against Joe's mouth.

Joe twisted the—by now ruined—tie around his fist and pulled him into something rougher. He wanted sore and bitten lips, for the track marks of tonight to still be visible in the morning. Cal obliged him, his hand rough on the back of Joe's neck as he bruised hard kisses into his mouth and down his throat.

The clenched muscles finally gave, and Joe came against Cal's stomach. Come smeared between their bodies, against their skin, as he lay on top of Cal's long, sweaty body. He panted raggedly against the crease of Cal's throat. His raw lips stung as sweat coated them, a reminder he probably wouldn't think bruises such a good idea come morning.

Cal stroked a rough hand up his back, his fingers gentle against the long line of Joe's spine.

"So," he growled in Joe's ear. "About that satisfaction survey?"

Chapter Three

THE EASY, post-fuck endorphin rush spread through Cal's body like warm honey as he stretched out over the empty, sex-musky bed. His joints felt loose and his skin the right size for once. The only body part that wasn't in on the feel-good love-in was his brain.

Fuck sake, he thought sourly as he folded his arm behind his head. He really couldn't help himself, could he? Less than forty-eight hours after his big resolution to clean up his act and here he was in bed with some cocky rich kid who wanted to slum it with the staff.

Okay, the whole arrogant "come here, bend over, suck my dick" thing worked for Cal. It always had. That was the problem. He was supposed to have arranged a second date with Doc, not fucked his employer two hours into the contract.

Cal scowled at the flawless plaster ceiling. His brother was right. He was fucking feral.

"What?" Joe asked as he came out of the bathroom.

Cal glanced over. "What what?"

"You look like the ceiling did something to you," Joe said as he tucked a too-small-for-the-job towel around lean hips. His eyes were cautious as he rested his shoulder against the bathroom door. "Regrets?"

Cal scratched the back of his neck and cast his gaze over Joe from knees to those cool, near-black eyes. It was a nice view, but the guy was pretty obviously not second-date material. With the come washed off his stomach and the bruises Cal had left on him yet to stain past red, Joe looked like he belonged on a spread in a magazine, not in bed with an ex-con who'd already been on thin ice with his employer before his latest fuck… up.

That was okay. Cal knew the script. This wasn't the first time he'd been someone's bit of rough. It didn't bother him. He *was* rough, and he liked to fuck. Nervous men in grotty bars, whose suits were worth more than the monthly wage of anyone who drank in there, appreciated that.

And until about a week ago, Cal had appreciated that they were nearly as glad to get rid of him in the morning as he was to go.

People like Joseph Bailey didn't take people like Cal out for dinner and the opera. The only way he'd take Cal to either would be so he didn't have to wait for valet parking.

That didn't bother Cal. He'd known the score from the minute Joe offered him the whiskey. It just pissed him off. When he'd been twenty, his parade of screw-ups and living down to everyone's expectations of him had been funny—and fun, to be honest. Now he had to wonder if that hadn't been a choice, if he was shitty at being a person.

None of which, he reminded himself, was Joe's problem.

"Regrets aren't really my thing," Cal said. He stretched out on the bed and let himself enjoy the way Joe watched him. Why not? Once you'd nicked the car, you might as well turn the radio on. The ache between his hips was dull and weirdly pleasant, like the satisfying ache in his abs after a workout. Although, hell, it really had been a while since he'd been fucked. "You?"

Joe tilted his head to the side. A dark curl of wet hair fell over his forehead and half hid the thumbprint of red on his brow. He looked surprised at the question… or maybe at the answer.

"No," he said. "Not this time."

The quiet statement invited questions. Cal figured they'd both be happier if he didn't ask them. He was not the guy for a heartfelt conversation about, well, anything really. Certainly not about coming out. Cal had fucked that up so badly that El hadn't spoken to him for a year, so about the only advice he could give was "don't fuck your brother's best friend and let his wife find out."

Not exactly universal.

"I should go and get some sleep," Cal said as he sat up. He scratched his stomach. The short scruff of hair was matted under his fingers. "Unless there's anything else you want to know about me?"

Joe crossed his arms and shrugged. "I'm fairly confident I got to all your hidden depths," he drawled, amusement in the crooked curve of his mouth. "I'm not throwing you out, by the way. It's a big enough bed, and it hardly seems worth the walk of shame down the hall."

The tie dangled around Cal's neck as he stooped to grab his trousers and then pull them on. The wrinkles would take a visit to the laundry to press out, but thankfully he knew El would have stuffed a spare set of clothes in the boot of the Bentley.

"Probably not a good idea," he said as he hitched the trousers up over his hip bones. "Your head of security already warned me off."

The muscles at the hinges of Joe's jaw clenched visibly under the skin. There was nothing amused about the tight smile he pulled back from his teeth. "Sometimes Edward oversteps," he said. "He worked for my father since I was a kid, and sometimes he forgets he isn't my father."

Cal shrugged and hung his wrinkled shirt over his arm. "To be fair," he said, "I *am* the bad company people fall in with, so you can't blame him."

The tension loosened around Joe's mouth as he snorted. "Didn't I seduce you?"

Cal winked at him. "That's what I wanted you to think."

"Really?" Joe pushed himself off the bathroom door. The towel gave up its precarious grip on his narrow hips and dropped to the floor as Joe walked over. He grabbed the tie and twisted it around his hand until the fabric was tight around Cal's throat and Joe's knuckles nudged up under his chin. The pressure made Cal tilt his head back, and Joe teased a kiss across the corner of his mouth. His lips were soft, and his breath was sharp with mint. "So you wanted me bad enough to come running?"

The answer to that twisted a hot and hard "yes" in Cal's balls. He bit that admission off the tip of his tongue. It was never a good idea to admit anything—not to the cops, your lovers, or yourself. Cal scruffed the nape of Joe's neck instead, pressed his fingers down against tight muscle and tendon, and claimed his mouth in a rough slash of lips.

His cock stirred lazily, not quite ready for round two, but up to being coaxed. Cal entertained the idea for a second and then quashed it with the mental image of Edward's face when he brought breakfast in the morning. He assumed that was part of the old git's duties.

"You did the running," he told Joe as he leaned back. "Hell, I hardly had to do any work, but…."

Joe's fingers tightened for a second, and then he relaxed them to let the strip of abused fabric slither free. A rueful smile tilted his mouth.

"Maybe another time," Joe said as he stepped back.

It would be a bad idea. Cal knew that. He was on his last, thin chance with El—brother or not—and he didn't exactly have the kind of résumé that would get him a job without the security net of a long stay in prison at the end of it.

He folded his lower lip between his teeth as he looked Joe over. Broad shoulders arrowed down into lean hips and long legs. There was muscle there, tight and defined, but it ran to long legs and elegance instead of bulk. Cal had never really had a type—unless you counted "trouble"—but there certainly wasn't anything about Joe he objected to.

"Probably," Cal admitted wryly. "Don't make it a good idea. See you in the morning, Mr. Bailey."

This time Joe let him leave without protest. Cal closed the door behind him and stood in the dark as he took a deep breath to clear his head. It didn't work. He could still taste sex and salt on his tongue. Cal's skin was sticky with both.

Fucking feral, he cursed himself as that lazy twist of interest stirred again. He really was.

A soft click echoed down the hall, and the lights flashed on. They weren't that bright, but it was unexpected enough to make Cal squint and blink spots from his vision. He turned and looked down the hall where Edward stood stiff and straight next to the light switch. The hard-faced man was still dressed in his nondescript black suit. Either he hadn't gone to bed yet or he'd slept in it.

"You're not a man to take advice, are you, Mr. Tate?" Edward said quietly.

Cal shrugged and shook his shirt out to shrug it back on over his kiss-bruised shoulders. He scratched his stomach again. Edward glanced down, grimaced in distaste, and looked away quickly. Cal walked down the hall to him.

"You've seen my record," he said. "You think nobody ever told me it would be a good idea to knock that shit off?"

Edward's mouth tightened into a grim line. "Joseph isn't…"

"Yeah, well, that's his problem," Cal said. "I am. If you don't like it, well… looks like I'd be the only one doesn't have a problem."

A cold light flickered in Edward's eyes, and he leaned toward Cal. "I could change that," he said.

Cal shrugged. "Be an asshole, then," he said. "No skin off my nose."

That took the wind out of Edward's sails. Sometimes an instinct to self-destruct could work to your advantage, but not often. Cal waited for a second. When Edward glared at him in confused frustration, Cal shrugged and went back to his room.

He thought about a shower. In the end he shrugged and stripped back down. Often enough he'd crawled into bed when he stunk of worse than Joe. The bed was soft, the pillows fat, and the linens smelled a helluva lot better than the ones at his place. If he was going to get fired in the morning, he might as well take advantage of clean sheets with no laundry.

It felt like he'd only closed his eyes when the alarm went off.

HE WASN'T fired.

In fact, based on Joe's cool demeanor when he came out of the bedroom the next morning in a tailored gray suit and his hair dry and styled in a loose quiff, it was possible Cal had dreamed last night's encounter. But he hadn't. The dull sting of the night—tender like sunburned skin—was evidence of that.

Three days later the ache had faded and Joe hadn't mentioned it again, not even late at night when Cal hitched up a knee in his rented bed and grabbed his cock while he wondered if Joe'd want to be fucked this time. Not that Cal would mind if he didn't.

Parked outside a narrow, gray office building in the Bentley, Cal dangled his hands over the steering wheel and passed the time with an attempt to remember how long it had been since he'd had someone else's cock in him. A few years, at least. He hadn't forgotten what it felt like, but he'd forgotten how… fuck, he didn't know. Cal stretched his fingers as he fumbled at the feeling.

Exposed, he supposed, but not in a way you wanted to stop. Like he didn't have to front it out—whatever the hell it was this time—for once.

He glanced in the mirror at the traffic warden who had worked her way down the road toward him. Usually playing chicken with a parkie would usually not be his idea of a good time, but he was still on his best behavior. Sometimes the universe *didn't* put the boot in after you fucked up, but even Cal knew not to push his luck. So he had stuck to the speed limit, not poked at Edward, and the only thrill he had to look forward to was a close call with a ticket.

She stopped next to low-slung, two-tone BMW and pulled her pad out. A pink-faced man with a yolk-stained napkin tucked into his collar burst out of a restaurant as she worked. His keys jangled in his hand as he waved them about angrily. The traffic warden heard him out as she finished the form and then slapped it on the car before he could object further.

Cal chuckled. He'd be the first to bitch if he got a ticket, but Napkin guy looked like a dick, and he drove a dick mobile with red accents. So couldn't happen to a nicer guy. The scene as the woman faced off against Napkin guy bought Cal a few more minutes before he had to move.

He kept a casual check on the rearview mirror. Parkies could be deceptively light on their feet when they saw a chance to ticket you, and besides, Napkin was a dick, and even if they were a traffic warden you didn't punch women.

Granddad had always been firm on that. You didn't punch girls, you only talked to the cops if it was pervert related, and he didn't care what anyone else said, Mrs. Smith wasn't from Pakistan, and even if she were, you never called anyone *that.* Whenever El got on Cal's case about being a fuckup, it was some comfort to remember that, by Grandad's moral standards, he was still on the straight and narrow.

A woman who'd worn a cream pantsuit to breakfast, her hair pin straight and matte, stormed out of the restaurant. She shoved her purse back in her bag and marched over to snatch the napkin out of Napkin guy's collar.

"Now what am I going to call him?" Cal wondered out loud.

"Call who what?" Joe inquired as he got into the back of the car, with a lockbox under his arm. His lean, elegantly suited frame impinged over the drama on the pavement. He pulled the seat belt across his body and clicked it into the anchor.

"Nothing, Mr. Bailey," Cal said. Company practice was to call the employer "sir" or "ma'am" unless instructed otherwise, but Cal had never been able to wrap his tongue around that. In his mouth, "sir" always sounded sullen. He started the engine and glanced in the mirror, his attention split between Joe's lean, handsome face and the tail end of the confrontation as the woman threw the eggy napkin at the traffic warden. "Where to next?"

So far it had been a round of banks, law offices, and the Bailey Property Trust's London office building. Most of the time Cal waited in reception and cadged a cup of tea from whoever seemed amenable. The clerk at the last lawyers had thrown in a plate of cookies and his number.

It was in Cal's wallet. He was, after all, supposed to be on the lookout for a nice boy with a good job and a domestic streak.

In the back seat, Joe laid the lockbox over his lap and tapped his fingers on it. His dark, straight eyebrows were pulled down in an expression a twist of the mouth away from a frown. Cal waited for directions while the engine idled quietly under his foot.

"Mr. Bailey?" he repeated. When Joe didn't react he tried again. "Joe?"

Dark eyes—still close as dammit to black in the sunlight—flicked up to meet Cal's gaze in the mirror.

"Do you know where there's a good florist?" he asked. "I need a wreath on short notice."

Cal raised his eyebrows at Joe in the mirror. "Flowers aren't really my thing," he pointed out dryly. "But there's a place we use when a client wants to surprise someone with a car full of flowers. They're usually pretty good."

Joe gave him a quelling look in the mirror. "I don't need a résumé," he said witheringly. "Just some flowers."

"Flowers, she can do." Cal twisted around, his arm hooked over the back of the seat. "It'll be about a half hour?"

Joe shrugged and leaned over to set the box on the floor. He sat back and lifted his tablet from the seat. "I pay you whether you're driving or drinking tea."

It might not have been a joke, but it made Cal laugh anyhow. Joe looked amused for a second, with a half-smile and a shrug that briefly reminded Cal of the other night. Then he shook his head and went back to work.

Cal straightened up in the driver's seat, checked the road, and pulled out. Old habits made him clock the nondescript Volvo parked opposite, its muted navy paintwork and tires so new and shiny the edges weren't even scuffed. He dismissed it a second later. Even if it was an unmarked car, it was no skin off his nose. He wasn't doing anything wrong and didn't even have any plans to in the foreseeable future.

A SWEATY man in misjudged yellow workout gear power walked between the gravestones. The sound of Taylor Swift on repeat was loud enough to hear through his headphones. Disapproving looks followed him as the people who were there to actually mourn registered his presence.

Cal leaned against the front bumper of the Bentley and thought about whether he should stick his foot out to trip the guy. Probably not, but it was tempting.

He dragged his attention away from the exaggerated jiggle of the guy's ass—not a bad ass, as it went, but nothing looked that good as it pistoned up and down in acid yellow—and back to the phone tucked against his ear.

"… have you talked to Jane?" El asked. Casually. As though that weren't the whole reason he'd interrupted Cal's day.

"Nope."

El cleared his throat. "When you do, could you tell her—?"

"Nope."

"Cal, you owe me."

"I know," Cal said. "Doesn't mean I am going to pick sides in your divorce."

"You're *my* brother."

"And Jane has never tried to bury me in the backyard," Cal said. "So you aren't coming out ahead there."

El snorted but didn't argue the point. They loved each other—they had to; they were all the family they had left that was worth shit—but that didn't mean they always got on… or had ever gotten on in the traditional sense. Their childhood had been spent alternately at odds or allied against any outsider who thought they could put their oar in. As kids, El had never quite gotten over Cal being born, and Cal had never quite gotten over not being El.

"Fine," El gave in. "How's the job going? Any problems?"

Cal rubbed the back of his neck—*strong fingers dug into his shoulders, the heady weight of a cock in his ass, Edward's grim, harsh face as he killed the afterglow with threats*—and glanced up the hill to where Joe paced between the long, sunlit graves.

"Uneventful," he said. "Nothing an Uber couldn't have managed."

A sigh trickled down the line. "Tell me you didn't say that in earshot of the client," El grumbled. "If the man wants to pay over the odds to be driven around the block in a fancy car, don't put him off because you're bored."

Cal watched as Joe paused at the end of the row, the wreath of purple and blue flowers tucked in the crook of his arm. Joe looked around—it was too far to see his expression, but Cal imagined it was the same irritated pinch of his mouth from last night—and then turned to the left. It didn't take long for him to disappear out of sight behind a bank of spindly trees and shadows.

"Don't worry about it," Cal said. The taste of Joe was long gone from his lips, but he licked them anyway. "What else do I have to do?"

There was a pause, and then El said, "Do you have any friends who aren't criminals?"

"You?"

"I'm your brother. I have no choice."

"I miss the cars, not the assholes," Cal said. The acrid edge to his voice tasted like bile. He swallowed it. Last time he'd seen his best mate, the shithead sold him out on the stand. It had been a year, and it could easily have been worse, but it had been Cal's fucking year. Mick was lucky Cal had worked out that revenge wasn't worth another year. "Don't worry about me. He's put me up at the Renaissance for the duration. Guy's too rich for common sense."

"Do not."

"I don't plan to," Cal promised.

It wasn't a lie. He'd already done it, and despite the temptation, he didn't plan to revisit Joe's bed. That sort of thing got complicated fast, and Cal was already on Edward's bad side… assuming there was another side.

It might have worked on anyone else, but El had known Cal since he told his first lie, so he snorted.

"At least wait until the contract's up," El said. "And if you see Jane, tell her I need to talk—"

"No."

Cal hung up and tucked the phone into his pocket. There was no sign of Joe on his way back to the car. Who did an American have buried in a London graveyard, Cal wondered as he patted his pockets for a smoke. It was only when he came up with a strip of gum instead of a packet of Benson and Hedges that he remembered he'd given that habit up.

It had been a sort of sacrifice to his new, clean act. He'd quit the two vices most likely to kill him—smoking and stealing cars—so could anyone really hold it against him if he fell off the dangerous-men bandwagon every now and again?

The collar of Cal's borrowed shirt—retrieved from the garment bag in the boot earlier—rubbed at his neck. He scratched under it and wondered when El's last visit to Grandad had been. The abrupt blare of a horn cut through his distraction, and he turned around to see the yellow-clad power walker slap his bare hands angrily against the bonnet of a low-slung sports car.

"Watch where you're going," the man yelled as he threw his hands up in the air. He gave the bumper of the car a dent with his trainer. "Idiot!"

The driver gave him the finger out the window and veered around him. Cal started to turn back to the graves but stopped as a dull navy car, so nondescript it was memorable, caught his attention. It was stopped in the back corner of the car park, in front of two other cars.

It probably wasn't the same one. There were lots of navy cars, after all.

The passenger-side door popped open, and a lanky figure in baggy jeans and a baggier hoodie, skull and Slipknot logo half-peeled off the well-washed cotton, scrambled out. Despite the sun that beat down on the manicured, vibrantly green grass and pruned trees, he had his hood tugged up over his head and down nearly to the bridge of his nose. The scruffy figure loped between the parked cars and cut across, instead of around the sunken dips of the graves. Meanwhile the navy car gunned the engine and pulled away from its spot.

Cal gave in to the sharp-nailed prod of suspicion and tried to get the license plate, but between the distance and the dirt, it was impossible. It turned out the gate and disappeared from view, and when Cal looked back at the graveyard, the hoodie had disappeared from view too.

A kid, Cal tried to convince himself, dropped off to pay his respects. That was all. Even if it wasn't, Cal was a driver, not a bodyguard. No one had ever been exactly clear where he could toe up to that line, but this would be clearly over it.

"Shit," he muttered aloud as he pushed himself off the car.

Cal walked briskly up the narrow path between the carved, occasionally florid gravestones until he reached the turn Joe had taken. He looked around as he walked briskly along the road, eyes peeled for either Joe or the scruffy kid in the torn hoodie.

"This is what comes of not listening to El," he muttered to himself as he sidestepped some mourning old ladies. "I bet this doesn't happen if you date a doctor."

Gravel crunched under Cal's feet as he walked along the path. He scanned the green slopes at either side of the road as he looked for an expensive suit and stupid hair or Slipknot hoodie as he nicked a bunch of flowers from a grave.

He rubbed his ear as he took a left at a swooning angel, the crack her nose had taken at some point probably why she'd had to sit down, and followed the narrow, uneven lane trod between the graves.

At the top of the slope, shadowed by a thick spur of hedges, Cal finally saw Joe in front of a large, gray gravestone. His hand rested carefully, almost uncertainly on top of it, and his head was bowed. He didn't look like he wanted to be interrupted.

Cal paused next to Mr. and Mrs. Eddie Tanner and wondered if he could get away without being seen. Before he could make up his mind, the hoodie belted through the gravestones and grabbed Joe.

Fuck.

Cal sprinted up the hill as the hoodie tried to muscle Joe away from the grave. It didn't go as easily as the lanky man had expected, as Joe dug his heels in and jabbed an elbow back.

Chapter Four

JOE WAS a rich man. He'd been a rich kid. There had always been a chance someone would try to snatch him. For as long as he could remember, Edward had run him through drills about what to do if it happened—a checklist updated each time Joe shot up an inch or hit another useful milestone, like knowing his address or how to text with his phone in his pocket.

In practice, that all turned out to be nearly useless.

Instead of a carjacker with a gun and a clear plan, it was rough hands and the stink of fresh sweat layered over old body odor under a sweat-damp hoodie. He jabbed his elbow to the side and tried to hook his foot around the attacker's bandy, jean-clad legs.

"Get off me," he panted as he tried to pry gloved fingers off his arm. "Let go and I won't call the police."

The attacker snarled a muffled "Shut up!" and jabbed a short, vicious punch into Joe's back. The pain spiked into Joe's kidneys and then radiated out across his back. He staggered, and the attacker grunted in satisfaction as he muscled him between the graves.

Joe grabbed an old headstone. The granite was rough under his fingers, and he tore a nail as the attacker yanked him away. The small, sharp pain finally reminded him of something Edward had told him to do, so he let his legs go from under him and his attacker cursed as he tripped over his long, bony legs. The hard grip on Joe's arm loosened, and Joe managed to wrench himself free.

He fell onto his ass and kicked his heels into the grass as he scrambled backward. The attacker picked himself up and ran at him again. A skull leered out from under the hood—bare bones and tombstone teeth under the glitter of feverish blue eyes and rough skin. He swung a booted foot in a wild arc, and Joe caught it against his arm with a dull impact that his brain decided didn't hurt yet. The assailant lurched forward and stamped on him with heavy, frantic boots. The thick rubber soles connected with Joe's thighs and crushed one hand into the grass.

"Get away from him!" Cal's rough voice cut through Joe's confusion-fed panic. "Son of a bitch!"

At least, Joe thought with relief as he curled up to protect his head, if he got kidnapped, there would be a witness.

The attacker staggered to a stop and leaned down to grab a handful of Joe's shirt. A ragged, glass-gargled voice spat out, "Fuck off home, rich boy, and stop asking questions. Next time—" He grunted as he dragged him over the grass, and Joe groped behind him as he tried to find something to hang onto. He dug his fingers into the dirt and grass and then met cold, empty air. "I'll finish the job first."

Joe glanced around and saw a grave gaping open behind him—sharp edges of wet dirt and a long drop down to an old, dirt-scabbed coffin.

The panic washed back, outsized and incapacitating. Joe grabbed at the attacker with frantic hands, hooked his fingers in the musty hoodie, and clawed into the mask. It twisted under his fingers and slid down the man's face. He got a glimpse of a clumsy nose—broken so often it smeared out from the crooked bridge—and the man pulled his arm back.

Cal hooked his arm around the man's throat and wrenched him backward. The man's fingers clenched on Joe's shirt and then deliberately let go. Joe clenched his teeth on a scream as he dropped into the grave. He hit the coffin with a thud, and clods of dirt, dislodged from the dark, damp sides of the hole, fell in on top of him.

His chest squeezed painfully as though the throttled-back scream took up all the room.

Trapped. He couldn't move. His lungs hurt. Pressure on his shoulders and across his chest....

Joe took a ragged breath—he could *taste* the wet soil on the air—and shoved through the acrid wall of panic. It wasn't a box. He wasn't trapped. It was only a hole.

A *grave*, his brain corrected with icy precision. It was a grave, and the cracked, wet wood under his fingers was a coffin. Joe lurched awkwardly to his feet, dug his fingers into the soft dirt walls, and tried to scramble out. He managed to boost himself up to grab the edge of the hole, but it crumbled away under his fingers, and Joe dropped back onto the coffin with a thud.

"Cal!" He could hear the sound of a struggle overhead—the hard thump of knuckles on skin and the scuff of feet over grass. Joe clenched his hand into a fist and thumped it against the dirt wall. "Get me out of here!"

There was another thud, someone grunted, and a sharp voice screeched disapproval across the graveyard. "Show some respect for fuck's sake! I'm calling the police!"

Fuck. That was all he needed.

A second later Cal leaned over the grave. "Need a hand?"

Joe bared his teeth. "Get. Me. Out."

"That does it for me in the sack," Cal said as he reached down to grab Joe's wrist and hauled. "When you aren't fucking me, learn to say 'please.'"

For a second, Joe's brain glitched out as he tried to process the dregs of claustrophobia and the stark, flat fear that someone had heard Cal say that. All the old stars of the show jostled into his head—the lurid headlines, the tell-alls from his hookups, and his dad's closed-off, disapproving face—and screeched that everyone would think he was gay.

It shouldn't matter, for fuck's sake. His dad was his boss, but Joe was a grown man and he had his own money. He'd broken up with the only person who actually had a reason to object to who he slept with. But tell that to the paranoia that chewed on the back of his brain.

Joe scrambled up over the trampled edge of the grave, into the sunshine and the thick, green smell of cut grass, and fell into Cal's arms. Or at least, hung off Cal's broad shoulder for a second as he caught his breath. The sharp lemongrass and honey smell of the hotel soap caught on his tongue and spawned a dark, smug wash of possessiveness.

Stupid, he thought sourly as he pushed himself off Cal, took a step back, and then stumbled gracelessly sideways as he nearly tripped himself back into the hole. It wasn't *his* soap, and even if it were, last night had hardly been the start of anything.

"C'mon," Cal said as he grabbed Joe's elbow. "We should call the cops. Get you to a doctor."

Joe pulled his arm free and stepped back again. "I'm fine," he said coldly as he straightened his jacket and brushed fastidiously at the grass stain on the sleeve. "There's no need to make a fuss, Mr. Tate."

The bite in his voice made Cal's eyebrow twitch slightly in response, and he pulled his hand back to rub the bruise on his jaw instead. Joe bit the side of his tongue. He knew he was being an asshole, but with the last of the panic still hot in his ears, he couldn't stomach any… constraint.

He looked around. An old woman with a small black dog tucked under her arm and a phone up to her ear stood at the bottom of the road and frowned up at them. A few rows over, a couple murmured to each other as they curiously craned their heads.

"Did they see anything?" he asked.

"Not much," Cal said. "It happened pretty quickly. Look, if you don't want to call the police, we should at least call Edward. He's your—"

"No," Joe snapped. He swallowed and tasted the metallic salt of spent panic and anger. "Let's be clear, Mr. Tate. The other night changed nothing about our relationship. I'm the boss, and if I don't want to say 'please,' then I won't. You'll still do what you're told. If you can't do that, then I'll do what Edward wants and get your brother to send a replacement."

The minute Joe said it, he wished he could take it back. In his head it had sounded more of an unsentimental reinstatement of boundaries and less like a privileged asshole with control issues. He couldn't even blame it on the claustrophobia.

Reserve shuttered Cal's pale eyes, and he shrugged.

"You're the boss."

The apology was on the tip of Joe's tongue, but he couldn't bring himself to spit it out, probably because he *was* a bastard with control issues. Instead he pushed past Cal and stalked back down the hill.

"Spit or swallow?" Cal asked behind him.

The low, growled question reached down under Joe's good sense, palmed his libido in one callused hand, and flicked his temper with the other. Joe felt heat prickle up the back of his neck as he turned around, but he couldn't swear whether he wanted to punch Cal or kiss him.

Split the difference, a wicked little idea suggested, *put him on his knees and make him show you what he does.* The mental image was easy—paint his memory of the hotel bedroom with sunlight and Cal's mouth around Joe as he came—but that didn't mean it helped.

"What did you say?" he asked.

Cal held out a handkerchief. "Spit or swallow," he said as he gestured at his own lower lip. "You're bleeding."

Joe touched his mouth, and his fingers came away wet and red. He hadn't noticed before, but now he felt the sting of a split lip under the hot static of panic that had filled him.

"Thank you," he said after a second. "I didn't hear you right."

He took the handkerchief, wiped his fingers clean, and then dabbed it carefully against his lip. It hurt now that he knew it was there.

Cal smirked at him with a slow, cocky slant of his mouth that said he knew exactly what he'd said. "Did ya?" he asked. "That's a shame, but you should mind that lip."

He headed on down the hill. Joe pressed the folded cotton against his mouth and watched him go. There were grass stains on the white cotton shirt pulled tightly over his shoulders and mud on the trousers that weren't quite tight enough to show his ass off to full effect. The wicked little thought nudged back into his brain to note, *"He's not that cocky when he's under you. If you...."*

Joe shoved it back into its box for later, when he was alone between fresh hotel sheets, and limped after Cal.

"I need a drink," he said instead and then glanced down at himself with a grimace. He'd dripped blood all down his shirt, and there was grave dirt worked into his trousers. "And some new clothes. I don't want to explain this to Edward."

"HERE," CAL said as he set a glass of whiskey in front of Joe. He sat down on the other side of the table with a bottle of soda and straddled the low chair with his long legs. "Try that."

Joe picked it up and took a drink. The liquor stung the cuts inside his mouth and burned on the way down. He ran his tongue along the inside of his lip and tasted the dull-penny taste of fresh blood.

"Thank you," he said.

"You paid for it, Mr. Bailey." Cal shrugged as he lifted the soda. "I did as I was told."

There was, probably, nothing particularly lewd about the pucker of Cal's lips when he drank, but Joe had to shift uncomfortably in the booth and look down into his whiskey. He rubbed his thumb over the sharply cut corner of the square glass.

"What I said," he said stiffly. "It might not have been called for. I'm not used to my personal and professional lives being quite so… connected."

Cal swallowed and wiped his mouth on the back of his hand. "Don't usually sleep with the help?"

"You make it sound sleazy."

The first smile since the graveyard curved Cal's mouth. It didn't slide into goofy, but it touched his eyes. He slouched back in the chair and idly rubbed his thumb around the lip of his bottle.

"I kinda like it sleazy," he said. "But I get it. You don't want anyone to know you banged me."

"That doesn't make it sound any better."

Joe glanced over Cal's shoulder to see if any of the people at the bar could hear them. The bartender was slouched at the far end, his attention on the TV. A couple of businessmen were two beers past insufferable as they boasted about money and leered at the woman at the table by the window, red curls scooped atop her head and her attention pinned to a laptop.

The slow wash of relief annoyed him. The only people who could justify commentary on his sex life were either dead or, finally, cut loose to actually be happy. He didn't know why he was still… scared. Unless it was the habit of it.

Cal shrugged and leaned forward, his soda held out for a toast. Condensation dripped down the side of the bottle as he tilted it. "I'll mind what I say," he promised. "You say please."

He waited as Joe picked up the whiskey glass and held it loosely between his fingers. "And if I don't?" he asked.

"I'll do what I'm told," Cal said. His smile sharpened. It was a small change in expression—a tightness at the corner of his mouth, a hint of sharp, white tooth—but it stripped the easy humor out of Cal's face. "But you'll know that I think you're a dick."

"You'd have plenty of company," Joe said. He touched his thumb to his lower lip and winced at the ache of it. "Our friend at the graveyard among them."

There was a zip file full of death threats on Edward's computer to send to the police "in the event of," and those were only the ones that wanted Joe harmed. That didn't include the people, the ones he'd grown up with, worked with, and dated, who didn't like him that much. Why should the opinion of one pretty contract worker with a tight ass matter more than all of those?

The answer was probably in the question, Joe thought with a flutter of wry humor.

He reached forward and clinked the base of his glass against the bottle.

"Deal," he said. "I'll say please… in public."

Cal snorted at him, but a hint of interested color flushed his cheeks and the sharp bones of his temples. He sat back and lifted the bottle. This time Joe glanced away before he got distracted by Joe's mouth, and his eyes caught on a blotchy, irregular stain on Cal's torn sleeve instead.

"Is that blood?" he asked.

Cal looked blank and then glanced down at his arm as though he'd just remembered. "Oh. Yeah." He put the soda down and rolled the sleeve back up his arm. The raw, red line scraped through a set of crooked initials inked onto Cal's arm and then curved down and around to nick the top bar of the crucifix on the pale underside of his forearm. It was scabbed roughly at the corners and raw-looking along the rest on the length of it. Cal clenched his fingers and rolled his fist to move the muscles under the sliced skin. "Turns out your friend in the graveyard had a knife."

A minute ago Joe would have said he'd spent too many chemicals on fear today to muster any more. He'd been wrong. It caught in his chest like cold, wet rags as he remembered the attacker's desperate energy and the venom in his voice as he threatened to finish the job next time. He'd come equipped to do it too.

"I didn't know you were hurt," Joe said. "I'm sorry. If you want to go to the police, I won't stop you."

Cal shrugged and rolled his sleeve back down. "It's a scratch," he said. "I've had worse."

There was a pause as he took a drink. Then he grimaced and leaned his elbows on the table as he leveled a serious look across the table at Joe.

"Look, it's not my business. You made that clear," he said carefully. "But are you sure you don't want to tell Edward? This is his job, and, to be honest, it's not mine. I'm only a driver."

"And get laid," Joe said, in a halfhearted try at humor. The echo of the other night's claim made Cal's mouth twitch.

"That's more of a hobby," Cal said.

Joe finished the whiskey, but it didn't do anything to squelch the guilt. He set the empty glass down on the table with a click and steepled his fingers against the rim.

"This was my call. I'll take the consequences," he said. "I don't expect you to put yourself in harm's way, not any more than you already have. What I do expect is for you to respect my wishes, and I do *not* want Edward to know."

Joe knew the drill. The minute Edward found out the stalker had escalated from empty paper threats to physical action, he'd want to institute new security measures that would curtail Joe's ability to move around freely. Under normal circumstances the ability to run to McDonald's without an escort would be a small sacrifice to make in return for not being thrown into a grave.

Right now, it would ruin everything.

"Are you close with your parents?" he asked. "Your mother?"

Cal looked askance for a bit, but after a second, he visibly decided to play along. "Not really. My dad's a junkie. He's really good at it but useless at anything else, like being a parent. Mum's married to some lawyer, lives up in Newcastle. She likes to pretend me and El don't exist." The flat honesty caught Joe off guard. That must have shown on his face, because Cal twisted his mouth into that sharp-edged, unamused smile and shrugged. "It's their shit, not mine."

That sounded like a good philosophy. Joe wished he could follow it, but his family's "shit" was hard to scrape off.

"My mother died," he said. It was habit to try and sound sad about that—half because people always seemed to think he should be, and half to see if he could wring the emotion out if he said it often enough, plaintively enough. A sort of emotional muscle memory. "It was tragic and sudden. She had a heart attack one day, and that was it. She died. People do."

He paused and shifted uncomfortably. The conversation usually ended at "tragic and sudden," a one-two of bad luck that no one ever wanted to question. Even when it was Joe who said the words, he could hear Harry's flat, uninviting delivery in the words.

"We never talked about her," he said. "I asked, but… Edward always said it was too painful for Dad to talk about."

Cal reached over the table and stole the glass from under Joe's fingers. "I'm guessing this is a two-drink conversation," he said as he stood up.

He wasn't wrong. Joe licked his lip and tasted the diluted salt of blood. The hangover from his panic attack in the graveyard sat like a stone in the back of his skull, his stomach and arms ached dully from the beating he'd taken, and the whiskey he'd downed hadn't even touched the edges of it.

"Get me a beer," he said. Then, since he'd promised, "Please."

Cal pointed his approval with one finger as he headed back to the bar. He leaned on the counter and waited for the bartender to drag himself away from the TV. Three stools down the two rowdy businessmen switched their attention briefly away from the redhead to Cal.

"Charge by the hour, mate?" one of them cackled as he nudged his companion in the ribs. "What's the going rate?"

Joe tensed.

Cal turned and looked the man up and down. Whatever the expression on his face was, it made the businessman flush and look worried.

Shit.

"Sweetheart, if you could afford me—" Cal said. His voice was pitched lighter than usual, the roughness that made Joe's balls clench stripped from under the words. "—you'd know it without having to ask the price."

The businessman's friend laughed and punched him in the arm while he crowed, "That's true. He's got you there, Ned."

The flush on Ned's cheeks darkened angrily. He tossed back the dregs of his wine and curled his lip.

"Who do you think you are, you fuckin—"

"Think it through before you finish that," Cal interrupted him, "because I will knock your fucking teeth down your throat if I don't like what comes out of your gob."

Whatever Ned had been going to say crawled back off his tongue and down his throat. He blanched, muttered something under his breath, and turned his back. His friend laughed harder and refilled both their glasses.

The confrontation, at least, inspired the bartender to leave the TV for a minute as he came down the bar. He popped the top off the beer and another soda and handed them over the bar along with a soft-voiced comment.

Whatever he said made Cal shrug at him before he took the drinks and came back to the table.

"Does that happen often?" Joe asked as Cal sat down.

Cal glanced back over his shoulder and shrugged. He slid the beer across the table.

"It used to happen more," he said. A wry smile curved his mouth as he waved a hand at his face. "When I was a kid, I was pretty as fuck."

He said it like it would be news to Joe, as though he weren't… well, the sort of man someone would call to their room to seduce five minutes after meeting him. The pretty had faded, that was true, but it had been replaced with heavy bones and brooding sensuality. Cal apparently had no idea.

"You aren't exactly hard on the eyes now," Joe said.

Cal shrugged. "I do okay," he said dismissively. "So what? You think your Dad…."

He trailed off expectantly. Joe faltered as he was faced with filling in the blank. It had been his idea to start the conversation, but this would be the first time he'd actually said it out loud to anyone. There was a possibility that the minute he did, the whole construct of suspicion and circumstantial evidence would collapse into wishful thinking.

Joe had seen it happen often enough. Some executive would get up to present his foolproof plan to save his company, every supplier sourced and line of income double-checked, but all it took was one previously unconsidered question to scoop out the foundations. It was usually Joe's job to pinpoint and ask that question, so it would be ironic if someone did it to him.

Better now, he supposed, than in front of Harry.

"My dad doesn't like publicity," he said. "No fancy parties, no sex scandals, no celebrity friends. He always said only idiots court publicity, that if people see you on the news with a gold-plated Bugatti, the first thing they'll think is you don't deserve it and they do."

Cal laughed and crossed his arms, his elbows braced on the edge of the table. "It's like he's met me."

"As a little kid, I thought he'd found some life hack that none of those other rich people understood," Joe said. "It wasn't until I was a teenager that I worked out that part of it was that Dad had skeletons in the closet and some very dangerous associates he didn't want anyone to know about. By then, though, I had my own secrets."

Sixteen years old and his cock hard in the barman's mouth, caught between the realization that *this* was the missing piece and flat terror that *this* was another cock in the equation. His dad, who boasted about what a lady's man his son was and joked—or "joked"—about dynasties, would never understand.

"Then I got—" Joe hesitated on the *engaged* and took a drink of beer to cover his stumble. He looked over the table at Cal, who was straightforwardly into cars and guys, and wondered if he'd understand Kristen, if he'd get that Joe had really thought he could make it work if he liked her and pretended that he hadn't fucked some guy in a club. Probably not. Joe wasn't even sure he ever thought so himself, not really. "I had my picture taken at a few nightclubs, ended up in a couple of gossip magazines. A few weeks later, I started to get some weird emails."

"Threats?" Cal asked.

"Not then," Joe said. "Odd. Angry. They weren't threats, though. They just accused me of lying."

Over and over again. There was no way to read personality into a computer font, but the uncompromising, all-caps repetition of LIAR, sporadically misspelled, still conjured rage and angry, jabbed keystrokes.

"About what?"

"I didn't know," Joe said. He'd thought it was a lot of things, from a threat to out him to an angry ex-employee, but he hadn't known. "Not at first. Then they emailed me that we both knew the truth about my mother, and that if I kept lying, they'd *make* me stop. To be honest I thought it was this vlogger who was obsessed with an actress friend of mine. He'd ambushed me outside of a bar when I was with her and tried to antagonize me into something… newsworthy. One of the things he asked was if my mother would be proud, and I said she would. It was the only thing he did that got a reaction, so at first I figured he wanted to see how good of a goad he was."

"But it wasn't."

Joe shook his head. "No. It was like that broke some sort of dam, and they started to send emails and letters. Then they started to mail stuff to our offices in LA. That's why Edward is involved. Once it escalates into real life, it's a lot harder to keep it off people's radar."

"They're some nut, though," Cal pointed out. He took a swig of his soda and then gestured with the bottle. "Maybe they think your mum's, like, the Virgin Mary or something. People make weird connections sometimes. They think they're real, but that doesn't always mean they are. You don't—"

"I didn't take it at face value," Joe said impatiently. He wondered if the people with their company-saving plans, laid out in action points and diagrams, felt this irritated at being questioned. Probably. Maybe it was a wonder he didn't have more death threats. "I made inquiries. I talked to people who'd known her before I was born. No one knew anything. Her and Dad had been living half the year in England. She was from here, and then one year, Dad came home with me and told everyone she died. Suddenly and tragically. No details, no records."

"So, what?" Cal asked. "Do you think something… bad happened?"

"I don't know. I think my father lied about what happened to my mother. I don't know why he did it, or when he started, but he did," Joe said. He took a drink of beer and decided not to add the last level to his blueprint, in case it collapsed under its own weight.

I think she might not be dead at all.

That sounded too stupid to risk saying out loud, like a child's fantasy in a grown man's mouth. The thing was, Joe still couldn't shake the conviction it was true.

His mother should have been buried in that graveyard today, with her parents. It was one of the few details his dad, drunk and maudlin, had ever given him. But the only names etched on the stone had been his grandparents.

Chapter Five

THE BLOODIED shirt lay in a tangled ball on the black-and-white tiled floor as Cal stepped out of the shower. He'd scrubbed the scrape on his arm open again, and blood dripped, pink and diluted, down his arm to his fingers and then onto the floor.

Cal grimaced and grabbed a washcloth to sop up the blood. He held it against the cut while he unzipped the first-aid kit he'd grabbed from the car. A quick application of an alcohol swab made him hiss, and then he stuck a square of gauze against his forearm. The ends of the cut peeked out from under the bandage, but it would do. He fumbled one-handed with a roll of tape and tore papery lengths of it off to clumsily slap it down on his arm.

The final result wasn't pretty, and he was going to lose some hair later, but it would do. Cal gave himself a quick rubdown with a towel, head to balls, and then glanced at his reflection in the mirror. The asshole at the cemetery had thrown an elbow that caught Cal in the jaw and rattled his teeth. He could feel the ache of it in the bone, but the bruise hadn't come up yet.

Cal rubbed his jaw, the scruff of stubble that had grown back in since he'd shaved that morning rough under his fingers, and wondered idly how Joe would feel about a beard. He caught that thought and grimaced at himself. Sex might always be on the table for him, but he was pretty sure that, as far as Joe was concerned, that itch was scratched.

Besides, he probably had other things on his mind than Cal's ass—things like complicated feelings about his mother, and nobody enjoyed that in bed. Like El and his soon to be ex.

Cal hung the towel off the hook on the back of the door and padded naked into his bedroom. He grabbed a fresh uniform from the wardrobe—washed, pressed, and ready for wear before Ryan dropped them off—and got dressed mechanically while he wondered what he should do about Joe's complicated feelings.

He should *probably* still spill his guts to Edward. Standard operating procedure was to cooperate with their client's security teams. Little Ms. Bouncy Popstar might appreciate that you sneaked her out to KFC at midnight, but when her security team blacklisted the firm, she wouldn't fight them.

Problem was—Cal shrugged the shirt on last and rolled the sleeves back, remembered the giveaway slash on his arm and rolled them back down again—that Edward was a prick, and Cal liked Joe. Even though he was a high-strung brat… with an out-there theory that he still needed to explain.

Cal took a quick look at himself in the mirror. The close crop had grown out enough to stick up at odd, short angles. He scrubbed his hand over his head to flatten them down and headed out into the suite. The faint sound of bubbling water led him down the hall and into the large, country-house-styled study, with a heavy wooden desk in one corner of the room and two oversized leather-and-tweed armchairs in front of an empty hearth.

There was a coffee maker on the desk, wreathed with steam as it spat milky coffee into a round glass cup. Joe stood in front of the bookcase with his attention halfheartedly focused on the rows of hard-backed books. He'd changed out of his scuffle-damaged suit and into black jeans and a fitted black jersey shirt, the sleeves pushed up to his elbows. His hair flopped over his forehead, more curled and less styled as his gel wore off.

Cal bit his lower lip with sharp interest. It was something about the juxtaposition between the intimacy of casual wear and the fact that Joe's casual wear was what most people would wear on a date. Hell, if Doc had looked like this on their date, he'd have told El to shove it when he called.

"Anything good?" he asked.

Joe glanced around at him. "Pretty sure they were bulk bought for their bindings. There's a copy of *Robin Hood* here, though, that seems up your alley."

"Not really a reader," Cal admitted with a shrug. "Look, this thing with your mother…."

"You think I'm crazy?" Joe said.

"No. Maybe," Cal said. "I mean, it sounds a bit weird but people do stuff. My mum pretends I don't exist, that the life where she had me and El never happened. People rewrite themselves all the time. They even believe it sometimes. I'm not saying it's right, but it seems more important that someone is trying to kill you."

The last drops of coffee drained from the spout into the cup. Joe picked it up by the handle and cradled it gingerly in his bruised hand as he stared into it.

"It's not," he said quietly. "Not to me."

Cal snorted. He spread his hands when Joe looked at him. "That's the sort of thing I say," he said. "Now that I'm on this side of it, I can see why it pisses my brother off."

Joe raised one dark, straight brow. "What happened to minding your manners?"

"I don't expect *you* to say please in private," Cal said.

Something dark and heated flickered through Joe's eyes. "Good to know," he said softly. Then he blinked, and the moment was gone. He took a drink of coffee, grimaced in distaste, and set the cup back down on the desk. "I'm not stupid, Cal, and I'm not putting myself at risk. Today was the first time this guy's gone further than threats. In future I'll be more careful."

He said it as though he were being reasonable, all his cool self-possession back in place after it had slipped earlier. Cal scowled at him in frustration, because it wasn't fucking reasonable.

"Why not talk to your dad?" he asked. "Now you know he's lying, maybe he'll come clean."

Joe snorted. "You clearly haven't met my father," he said. "Confession, like publicity, is something for idiots. And to be clear, I don't need your permission. A few hours in my bed doesn't give you a say in my life."

Cal rolled his eyes.

"I don't want a say in your life," he said. "I don't want a front-view seat to your death."

Joe snorted. "It was a thug with a penknife," he said. Apparently he'd forgotten how badly shaken he'd been earlier or maybe he didn't want to admit it anymore. "I wasn't in any real danger. Cal, I don't expect you to get involved. In fact, I'm telling you not to. You said it yourself—you're a driver, not a bodyguard."

YEAH, CAL was sick of his own words being used against him. Frustration pushed at the inside of his skull with a rattled pressure that needed a release. *Use your words*—that's what the therapists always told him—*not your fists.* Cal had never been good at that.

He took two long steps across the room and into Joe's space—close enough to floor him, close enough to kiss him. The wary flicker in Joe's eyes suggested he wasn't sure what way Cal was going to go either. His throat bobbed awkwardly as he swallowed and looked down at Cal. There wasn't much space between them. Cal licked his lips slowly and leaned in until their bodies touched from shoulder to thigh.

"You got it," Cal said. His lips grazed Joe's throat as he spoke. The skin was freshly shaved and sharp with soap. "Next time I'll leave you to get the shit kicked out of you."

He reached past Joe and grabbed the cup from the table to take with him as he left. The coffee wasn't as bad as Joe had made out.

THE DOBBINS'S front door was locked, and a heavy length of chain was doubled through the handles to underline the point. It didn't mean it was closed.

Cal cut around the side of the building, past drifts of old food wrappers and drained, crushed beer cans discarded against the wall, to the door at the back. He heaved it open with a grunt, and the corner of the heavy, metal-cored door scraped the existing groove in the old, concrete a millimeter deeper.

It was dark inside. The windows were papered over, and only a couple of the gas-yellow neon strips were lit. Cal stood for a second to let his eyes adjust and wondered how much of a fuckup he was about to make. In the boxing ring, a kid, all sharp bones and ragged jeans hanging off his bony hips, bounced off the ropes and cursed in a sharp, clear voice.

"Mind your fucking tongue," Malcolm said as he tossed a towel in the kid's face. He veered over toward the side of the ring and lifted his chin in Cal's direction. "You want something, mate? Cos… fuck me!" Surprise and delight spread in a wide, gleeful smile over Malcolm's face as he saw Cal. "Holy hell. Cal? Is that you?"

Well, Cal thought wryly, too late to slink out now. He shoved his hands into his pockets and headed toward the ring as Malcolm ducked between the ropes. The rest of the bar had turned around to check out what was going on. Most of them shrugged and went back to their beer and conversations. A couple of Cal's old mates downed theirs and slunk off to the bogs. Behind the bar, Gwenie, who'd managed the place with her tits jacked up to her chin in defiance of time and gravity for as long as Cal had been coming there, grabbed the phone.

Malcolm jumped down off the ring and threw his arms around Cal in an enthusiastic hug. He roughly thumped Cal's shoulders as he rocked them from side to side. His exuberance squeezed a laugh out of Cal, despite his reservations about whether this was a good idea or not. Malcolm had always been a hard guy to resist, whether he wanted to cheer you up or talk you into jacking a car from outside a dickhead lawyer's house.

When Cal told El he didn't miss any of his old friends, he'd lied, the same way he lied to Joe when he said he'd stay out of his business. Still, what they didn't know wouldn't come back to bite Cal in the ass.

"Where the hell have you been?" Malcolm asked as he grabbed Cal's shoulders and took a step back.

"Jail."

Malcolm had the grace to look ashamed, but it didn't last long.

"Yeah, I meant to visit," he said as he stepped back and rubbed the back of his neck with one hand. He tweaked the corner of his mouth in a shrug. In the ring behind him, the two kids scuffled and battered each other with padded fists. "But, well, you know how it is. After you fucked up that last job the way you did… writing was on the wall. Boss wanted you to learn your lesson."

A sour mix of anger and resigned amusement sat in the back of Cal's throat. He did know how it was. That was why he hadn't come back around since he got out….

"What else could you do?" he asked.

"'xactly," Malcolm said. He bobbed up onto his toes and threw a mock one-two punch flurry at Cal's stomach. "My hands were tied."

Cal palmed Malcolm's forehead and shoved him back a step with a snort and a grin. There was no point in being pissed off at him. It wasn't the movies. Thieves robbed from the rich because that was who had the good shit, and they gave to the poor to get their car washed. No one hung out with crooks because you figured they'd be loyal and upstanding. Fun, sure. Cal could still remember the giddy rush the night he and Malcolm boosted the lawyer's flashy BMW. They hadn't even sold it on, just driven it into the Serpentine and left it to the swans. Best night of Cal's life up to that point, and the lawyer who'd fucked over Malcolm's dad had deserved it.

But once the adrenaline faded, that memory wouldn't even get a round in. When the shit hit the fan, it was Boy Scouts like El who'd stick around. They might not be fun, but neither were prison visits.

"Is Van in?" he asked. "I need a word."

Malcolm waved a hand at the bar. "Gwennie can buzz you up," he said. For a second, the happy-go-lucky front slipped and Malcolm tugged on his earlobe. "There's other car thieves on the books, Cal, and time served don't mean shit anymore. Don't be picky. Take what you're offered."

He didn't need to put the rest into words. They both knew what he meant. Break a few knees, shake down a couple of shop owners, shed a little blood to buy yourself back into favor. It was the sort of work Cal had always sidestepped. He'd never had the stomach for it.

If that was the price of entry, maybe there was more than one reason for Cal to go straight.

"See you around," Cal said with a last slap to Malcolm's shoulder as he turned away and picked his way through the tables to the bar. Behind it Gwennie polished a salt-glazed glass with a grubby cloth as though she'd ever get it clean and waited for Cal to ask, "I need a word."

Gwennie fished the key to the back out of her cleavage and handed it over. It was about as warm and damp as Cal expected.

"You know the way," she said as she grabbed a beer from under the bar. Only the one. She held it out. "Take this up with you, would ya? My knees aren't what they were."

Cal shrugged and took the beer. He was—technically—still on call. If Joe decided he wanted a midnight run to the coast, Cal needed to be sober for it.

"Sure," he said. "I get the tip."

Gwennie smirked at him with apricot-painted lips. "Yeah, I've heard that about you."

She flicked her cloth over her shoulder and strutted down the bar to pour a round of shots for some nervous, sweaty kids about to do something stupid. Cal remembered being them, but he'd *thought* he'd grown out of it. Apparently, he mused as he bounced the beer in his hand, not so much.

He let himself through the battered old door behind the bar and creaked his way up the back stairs to Van's office. His weight on the steps squeezed the stink of stale booze and old blood out of the carpet and soured the air. He stopped on the landing. There was no door, so he rapped his knuckles on the old wallpaper instead.

It wasn't much of an office. A leather sofa and a wide-screen TV took up most of the space, with a scarred old Formica table stuck in the corner of the room to do double duty as a desk. The desk was covered with paperwork, and Van was slouched out on the sofa as he watched *EastEnders.* He looked up at the knock and mugged surprise, as though he hadn't expected anyone.

"Caught me slacking," he joked as he swung his bare feet off the cushions and stood up. Honey-brown hair, gray smudged back from his temples, stuck up messily behind his ears, and his shirt was wrinkled. He spread his arms out wide and grinned. "Cal. Damn, I've missed you, man."

There'd been a time….

Cal ignored the "bring it in" spread arms and instead leaned against the raw plaster where the doorframe used to be. He studied Van and waited for the old twinge, the "hell, maybe" that you couldn't quite beat to death with a rock.

Unlike the rest of the old gang, Van hadn't grown up around there. He was a rich kid with the sort of bad habits you can't indulge on a part-time basis. For a while, when they'd been stupid kids, one of those habits had been Cal. He hadn't been Cal's first time or his first love, but it had been the first time he'd played the bit of rough to scandalize the parents.

It hadn't lasted, and that had been mostly down to Van. They'd stayed friends, but that had been mostly down to Cal. Not that he picked that up until it was too late. It turned out a year in jail was a good tool to kill the maybes.

"I need a favor," Cal said.

Van dropped his arms and hooked his thumbs in the pockets of his jeans. He hung on to the smile.

"From me?" he said. "Now see, I heard you turned over a new leaf. At least that's what your brother said. Apparently you didn't need the likes of me dragging you down. I should put that on my Christmas cards this year, give my parents a giggle."

“They taking your calls again, after you stole your sister’s wedding fund?”

The quick flash of anger painted red over Van’s cheekbones. He liked to play the gangster, not the strung-out junkie who’d steal from his own family. The truth was somewhere in the middle, but it was still an easy hook to catch him on.

“Like your parents want to hear from you,” he said.

“Yeah,” Cal admitted as he held the beer out. “But that doesn’t bother me.”

The chilled bottle dangled from his fingers. After a second, Van faked a laugh and took it from him. He used one of his rings as a makeshift bottle opener to pop the cap off the beer, and froth spilled over his fingers.

“What do you want?” he asked as he licked his fingers clean.

Cal glanced away and scratched his jaw. Over it didn’t mean entirely past it, apparently. Old memories poked at him until his cock twitched. It had been *fun* with Van. Everything had back then… until it had all gone wrong.

“I need to find a kid,” he said.

“Yours?” Van asked. He sat back down on the sofa and slung his arms over the back of the couch. The base of the bottle tapped against the cushion and left a wet stain on the leather. “Prison changed you, man.”

Cal reached into his pocket and pulled out the flick knife the kid had dropped before he ran. The flash of metal between his fingers made Van stiffen with sudden wariness. He shifted his weight and licked his lips.

“Now, Cal,” he said. “Let’s not—”

“Grow up,” Cal said as he tossed the knife to Van, who snatched it out of the air with one hand. “Some little thug tried to jump one of El’s clients at the city graveyard yesterday. Tried to stab me when I jumped in. He’s about five eight, wears a Slipknot hoodie and a skull bandana, and there’s a good chance I broke his wrist. That’s the knife.”

Van took a swig of beer and then put the bottle down by his feet so he could turn the knife over in his hand. He hooked his finger into the hole and tugged the blade out. It was hardly an antique, handed down from father to son, but it was a nice bit of kit. The blade was short and curved, with the logo etched into the blade, and the handle had been roughly etched with symbols and latticework—better than the knock-off ninja shit that most kids started out with. Someone would have envied it.

"What makes you think I'll find him?" he said.

A slow, humorless smile curled Cal's lips. His mouth was so dry he could feel his lips stick to his teeth. "Everyone has a mate that'll sell them out," he said. "Once word gets out you're looking, someone will dob him in."

Van stood up and prowled over to Cal. He stretched up as he did so, to prove the half inch in height he'd always claimed to have on Cal. His smile was pointed and challenging as he poked the point of the knife against Cal's collarbone. The scrape of it was cold as it scratched at the skin as though it were looking for an itch.

"Naw," he said. "I meant why would I fucking bother? What's in it for me, now you're Mr. Right Side of the Law?"

Cal grabbed Van's wrist and pulled it to the side. "You owe me."

"Your brother broke my nose when he came round," Van spat. He relaxed his fingers under Cal's grip and let the knife drop to the ground. "I let it go. When you got out, I stayed away. I could have talked you round. I always could, but I didn't. So anything I owe you, I figure I paid off."

He wasn't wrong. If he'd come round with a good idea for a heist and a bottle of Jack to plot it over…. Well, it wasn't as though Cal was good at being an upstanding citizen. His first instinct was always to take what he wanted and make himself scarce before anyone could complain.

That's what he should have done if he wanted to wipe the slate clean, but he hadn't.

Cal tightened his fingers on Van's wrist and twisted roughly. Muscles tightened in Van's arm as he fought to take his arm back, but it didn't work. Cal braced his thumb against the back of Van's hand and shoved him back over to the sofa. The backs of Van's knees hit the cushions, and he toppled over backward.

"How about this, then," Cal said. "I owe you."

"Get off me," Van said through pinched lips. His wrist was pushed back at an awkward angle until his fingers nearly touched the inside of his forearm, and his elbow was twisted painfully. "You think I can't touch you because you're sticking to legit work? All it takes is a couple of calls—"

His voice choked into a groan of pain as Cal bent his wrist back another millimeter. The color, what Van had of it, drained from his face as he writhed against the leather. Cal used his weight against the lever of Van's arm to pin him in place.

"A couple of calls. That's right," Cal said. "That's all it would take for me to give it legs. Van Davies sold me out to the cops. Pass it on."

"You wouldn't dare."

Cal waited. After a second, Van grimaced because he knew better. He pulled his leg up and kicked Cal in the thigh with a bare foot. It wasn't enough to hurt, but Cal backed off.

"Get off me," Van said as he got his wrist back. He pointedly massaged the joint. "I'll do it, all right? Jesus, all you had to do was say fuckin' please and thank you. Beg a little. Not you. You gotta take it too far. No wonder your mum's embarrassed to introduce you to her new family."

Cal shrugged. "She says the same about El," he said. "And El's got manners."

Something nasty flashed through Van's eyes, and Cal knew to brace himself. Like a rat backed into a corner, Van liked to make sure that even if someone won they walked away bloody from a fight with him.

"Yeah, but you're a package deal, aren't ya?" he said. "She can't have El without you. He'd never go for that. One more thing he can't have because he's got a fucked-up, dumb-as-dirt little brother."

That cut deeper than the knife had. Cal swallowed it and shrugged. "Find me the kid that jumped me. Once you do that, I have no reason to come round here and tell anyone the truth about who told the good Detective Kincaid what."

Van reached down with his good hand and grabbed the beer by the neck. He slouched back on the couch and took a swig. His throat worked as he swallowed.

"I'll see what I can do," he said. "Now fuck off, Cal. You bring the tone down."

Chapter Six

FIRST THING in the morning and there was another message from Kristen on Joe's phone. He didn't have the heart to delete it, but he couldn't bring himself to listen to it either. To be honest, he didn't need to. It probably didn't differ much from the twenty other messages she'd sent him since they broke up—either promises that they could fix this if they tried or pointed, precise anger as she cursed him up one side and down the other.

He didn't blame her.

Edward's disapproval was palpable as Joe banished the voicemail to languish with the others in the saved file.

"Kristen's beautiful. She's clever. She's accomplished," Edward said as he sat down on the other side of the small round breakfast table. He laced his hands together around his chalkboard black mug of tea, old scars a lacework of threads over his knuckles and the backs of his hands. "You could do worse."

"Maybe," Joe said as he set his phone facedown on the table, in case an email came in that he didn't want Edward to see. "*She* couldn't have, though."

"Maybe you should have let her decide that," Edward said as he took a drink of his brew and made a disappointed face. His preferred cuppa was black Yorkshire tea, bitter as something cooked up in a boot. He always said he'd developed a taste for it while he was in the Army, along with curry too hot to taste anything but regret. Apparently the hotel's tea bags weren't old and papery enough for him. He set the cup back down on the table and looked at Joe. "She loved you."

She did. Joe knew that.

"And I liked her," Joe said. "That's not enough."

At the far end of the suite, the main door parroted its usual "welcome back" message as Cal let himself back in. Joe glanced around and listened to Cal slam the door and then go into his bedroom. He'd been out last night, and he'd come back late and kept to himself. Joe had thought about another text, another late-night tumble, but he… hadn't.

The first time had been a Hail Mary, as likely to get his teeth knocked in as anything else. This time they would have both known what Joe expected, and that wasn't a good look. Joe knew what he'd think of himself, and he didn't want Cal to see him that way.

"Maybe you should have tried harder," Edward said, and the rough edge of his voice dragged Joe's attention back to their conversation. It took Joe a minute too long to realize that Edward still meant Kristen, not Cal. He didn't feel good about that. "Lust isn't love, Joe. Don't throw away what you had, what made you happy, to chase some… itch."

Itch. That's how it had always been done in his house—anything difficult was never said out loud, never faced up to. Things like his mother's death, the fact that Joe was not quite the son his dad expected, were brushed under the carpet and never mentioned again. All that was left behind was expectation and disapproval, like ghosts.

Joe had learned to stitch everything *untidy* away behind a composed facade. He could ride elevators without sweating, even as his stomach clawed itself raw with the conviction that he was going to die, and he could convince people he was happy with Kristen—even himself for a while, until he found himself in the back room of some club or hotel bar with a man.

To be honest, part of the reason he wanted to find out the truth about his mother wasn't even about her. He didn't remember her, and no one had told him stories about her that he could stitch together and pretend were his. She was a blank form in his head, a few dreams that were as much wishful thinking as anything real, but she was something *untidy* of his dad's that Joe could throw in Harry's face.

"Edward, I appreciate that you've been with my father for a long time and you think you know me," Joe said as he pushed away the remnants of his omelet. "You don't, and who I fuck isn't your job."

Silence for a second as Edward took a long drink of his tea. Then he set the cup down on the table and glanced at his watch.

"Six twenty-five. I'm not on the clock yet, Joe," he said. "All I am right now is an old friend of the family, who doesn't want you to make a mistake you can't take back. Kristen could make you happy, give you a family, a place where you felt at home."

Edward glanced away from Joe as though he could see Cal through the heavy, hotel walls. It looked like he was going to bite the bullet and actually talk about what they both knew had happened. Joe waited, a nervous prickle of anticipation on the nape of his neck. Instead Edward got up and walked to the sink to toss the oversugared dregs of his tea down the drain. He flicked on the tap to wash the sludge away.

"I don't have your itinerary for next week yet," Edward said. "What are your plans?"

The hollow space that cracked open in Joe's chest was either relief or disappointment. It was beyond him to identify it. He rubbed his hand over his face. The scuff of last night's stubble was still rough on his jaw.

"I'm taking the week off," he said. "I haven't been to England since I was a child. I want to see some of the sights before I go home."

Edward paused midrinse of his mug. Water spilled over his fingers and into the sink for a second before he finished the job. He set it down to drain and turned around.

"Do you have time?" he asked. It sounded casual. "You have to wind up all the company's business dealings in the UK by the end of the month. You've only *got* three weeks left."

Joe sat back in his chair and studied Edward's face for a second. In the long run, Edward would back whatever decision Harry made, but how much did he already know? Edward had worked for Harry back then, although he always said he never met Joe's mother.

"I'm going to spend a few hours at Buckingham Palace," Joe said. He fastidiously wiped his hands on a napkin and then crumpled it. "Or the Tower of London. Not take a hike to John O'Groats. If an emergency arises, I'll be available to deal with it. If my dad has a problem with that, tell him he can call me."

Edward gave him a disapproving look. Let him. Joe tossed the ball of his napkin into the bin and got up from the table. He paused on the way out the door.

"I don't want to talk about Kristen again," he said bluntly. "If you're so worried about her love life, find someone to set her up with when we get back."

"How many times did you cheat on her?" Edward asked.

"Too many," Joe said. Four times, four different men, but he doubted Edward wanted that information. "Now are we *done* on this topic?"

Edward looked thoughtful, but he nodded without further argument.

OLD PHOTOS. Old postcards. Harry had once had a sense of humor. Letters addressed to Mrs. Bailey, filed in yellowed envelopes with brittle cellophane windows.

Joe didn't know what he expected to find in Harry's old safety deposit box, although the part of him that had binged *Blacklist* on the flight over had its fingers crossed for a collection of fake passports. Instead it was just a box of memories Joe had missed out on.

Most of them anyhow. He lifted a newspaper clipping from the box, the paper yellow and rough under his fingers, and studied the low-res photograph. Three men and two women stood shoulder-to-shoulder outside a hospital, fund-raising buckets clutched in their arms. The caption identified the tall, awkwardly smiling woman on the far left, captured as she scratched her eyebrow, as Abigail Bailey. It wasn't the first picture Joe had seen of her, but most of them were contextless portraits where she smiled blandly into the camera. This was the first where you could see something of… her… in it.

It was also the only picture Joe had ever seen where he was in it with his mother. Even if she might have only known about him for a few weeks at that point.

He supposed he should feel something about that, but it was a smudged black-and-white photo of a stranger in a local paper. Maybe he wouldn't have liked her if he ever got to know her. Or maybe she wouldn't have liked him. It didn't feel set in stone that they'd have loved each other.

Right then it didn't feel as though he'd found his mother, all he had was another clue in a treasure hunt. If he wanted to find the next, he had to solve the first.

The beep of Joe's phone interrupted him, and he glanced at it. A reminder about his afternoon appointment at the lawyers sat on the screen accusingly, as though it knew full well that he'd forgotten and didn't really care. Joe closed his eyes for a second as he tried to find the person who, a year ago, would have eagerly embraced the responsibility of divesting the firm of their UK holdings. It should have been hard, with everything else on his plate, but if Joe were honest, it didn't take long.

He might not like his father much, but he was still Harry Bailey's son, and he still wanted to prove he deserved everything he inherited. Besides, he'd always been good at his job.

The meeting was a few hours away, but if Joe left now, he could get lunch first. Joe pulled his jacket on and, after a moment's hesitation, tucked the clipped story into his pocket. He wasn't sure why. Maybe it seemed like what someone would do in that situation, the same way he looked sad when he talked about his mother's death—habit and a desire to look like everyone else.

He brushed his hand down his front to listen to the muted crinkle of age-softened paper and then went to find Cal.

He should have knocked, not that Joe could quite bring himself to wish he had. He paused in the doorway and watched Cal finish a set of sit-ups. Tight bands of muscle clenched across Cal's stomach, pronounced under inked, sweaty skin, and his old gray sweats had slid dangerously low across his stomach. His steady pace faltered midrep when he caught sight of Joe in the door, and he grabbed his knees to steady himself when he stopped.

"Sorry," Joe said through dry lips.

Cal thought about that and then leaned back onto his elbows. His knees were still bent, feet flat on the floor, and they framed the long, lazy sprawl of his body.

"You sure about that?" Cal asked as he licked sweat off his upper lip.

A few scenarios flickered through Joe's mind. All of them ended up with both of them on the ground, Cal's legs over Joe's shoulders, and his cock in Joe's mouth. The fantasy was potent enough that when Joe imagined the tug of Cal's fingers in his hair, it sent a prickle of pleasure through his scalp and down the back of his neck.

"Well," Joe admitted in a voice that sounded a lot smoother than he felt, "I was enjoying the show, but I have some business today. The lawyers we were at the other day, Atkins, Kinsella, and Beattie."

Cal snorted and scrambled to his feet. He grabbed a discarded T-shirt from the bed and casually wiped the sweat off his torso with it. Joe felt a twist of mixed lust and regret as he wished he'd crawled onto Cal when he had the chance.

"Give me five minutes," Cal said as he chucked the T-shirt to Joe. It smelled of Cal and sharp, salt-fresh sweat. "I'll be ready to go. Stick that in the laundry bag, would ya?"

Joe hung the shirt over the handle of the door. "You give all your employers orders, Mr. Tate?"

"Naw," Cal said as he hooked his thumbs into the waistband of his sweats. They slid precariously lower, the sharp angles of his hip bones and the trail of fine, tawny hair that arrowed down from his belly button somehow more sexual than full frontal would have been. "Only the ones that wanna watch me undress."

Joe cleared his throat and chuckled dryly. He looked down at his feet. "Now that makes me sound like a pervert."

"I didn't say I minded," Cal pointed out.

In the corner of Joe's eye, he saw the gray sweats hit the ground and Cal step out of them. He left them crumpled on the floor, and Joe wondered how long it would take until that got on his nerves instead of making him hard. He shook the thought away before it could settle, because you got annoyed at clothes on the floor in a relationship, not… whatever you called a one-night stand that dragged on.

He let his eyes track up Cal's legs to his cock, half-hard at being admired, and then up over his chest to his face.

"You sure about it?" he asked. Joe was aware he was a lot of things that weren't particularly nice—a cheat, a liar, cold—but he didn't want to add predatory to that. "I do pay your wages right now. If you want me to back off—"

"Fuck off. I told you, I don't need you to say please in private." Cal licked his lips and reached down to give his cock a lazy tug. "Thank you will do."

He smirked and turned his back as he swaggered into the bathroom. Joe watched the tight curve of his ass, the bunch and play of muscle as he walked, until Cal swung the door shut behind him. It felt like something *gave* in his chest. He wasn't even sure what it was, but it was done.

Call it any expectation he had of leaving there in time to get to his meeting.

The water turned on in the bathroom, and Cal hummed off-key to himself. Joe took his jacket off and tossed it onto the bed. The lawyers were paid well enough. They could use some of the billable hours they overcharged for and wait for him. He followed Cal into the bathroom.

If Cal had expected company, he showed no sign of it. He stood under the stream of water, eyes closed and head tilted back. Soap trickled down his body in sudsy rivulets, very white against the red splash of color on his ribs, and his hand rubbed at his stiff cock with lazy interest.

Not a cold shower, then, at least.

Joe opened the door and stepped into the steamy cubicle. Water splashed against his face and spotted wet across his T-shirt and jeans. Cal turned and grabbed his shirt in one smooth, violent motion, and as Joe's shoulders hit the tiles, he thought he'd misstepped. Then the immediate threat of violence faded from Cal's face and was replaced with surprise and amusement.

"What the hell are you doing?" he asked with a laugh as he wiped water out of his eyes.

Joe glanced down at the fist knotted into his now-soaked T-shirt.

"Either I'm going to get my ass kicked, or…." He curled his hand around the back of Cal's neck and leaned in to brush a careful kiss over wet, soapy lips. It was supposed to be quick, an invitation rather than the start of anything, but Joe couldn't resist that mouth. He caught the lush curve of Cal's lower lip between his teeth and chewed the kiss into it. Then he explored the softer bow of the upper one with tongue and lips. Finally he pulled himself back and admired the soft, well-bitten flush of Cal's ridiculously pretty mouth. "That."

Water dripped down Cal's face as he blinked and then laughed. There was nothing practiced, nothing flirtatious about it. It was an incautious splutter of amusement.

"You're a nut," Cal accused as he leaned in for another kiss. It was… sweet. The corners of his mouth were still curled with warm humor and the water warm and flavored with lemon. That wasn't something Joe usually looked for in his one-night stands. His hand slid down Joe's side to his hip, and he hooked his fingers in the waistband of his jeans. "If you get a chill, Edward's gonna have my balls on a plate."

Joe licked water off Cal's jaw. He slid his hands down wet, slick skin—his thumb caught a thread of scar tissue buried between ribs and lost in the spread of red ink petals—and round to the curve of Cal's ass. "You'll need to keep me warm."

He kissed his way down Cal's throat to his chest. The flat, pink bud of Cal's nipple, framed in dark hair and black ink, puckered under the scrape of Joe's teeth. A groan rumbled out of Cal's throat, and he laced his fingers through Joe's hair, callused fingertips rough where they pressed against his neck. Joe flicked his tongue around the nipple and sucked at the flat disk of the aureola.

"I like that people can't see your tattoos," he said as he went down onto his knees. The water swirled around his legs and soaked into his jeans. He had others. Joe brushed his thumb over the scribbled star on the thin skin over Cal's hipbone. The ink had been worked in roughly enough that he could feel where the scars had lifted under the black lines. "It's like we have a secret."

"People have seen them," Cal said raggedly. His cock lifted toward his stomach, the foreskin pulled back from the wet, slick head as his cock hardened.

Joe huffed out a laugh and scraped a bite over the taut, flat plane of Cal's stomach. "Do you have a romantic bone in your body, Cal?"

"There's one," Cal said pointedly as he looked down.

"Still no ink?" Joe mocked him.

"Maybe I'll let you pick something," Cal said. "Fancy your name on there?"

The idea was hot enough to grab Joe's balls and twist, but no… not his name. It wasn't a serious offer, but Joe slotted it away to daydream about later anyhow. He ran his hands up the back of Cal's thighs—all rough hair and corded muscle—and leaned in to press an openmouthed kiss to Cal's balls. The fine skin was suede soft under his lips and tongue. Joe pushed Cal's thighs apart as he sucked and licked at the tender sac. He pushed his tongue along the taut, nerve-rich thread of skin that ran back from Cal's balls toward his asshole.

Cal moaned and braced his hand against the wall, his fingers spread wide against the damp, marbled tiles, His body was pulled into one long, brutally elegant line that ran from fingers to shoulders and down toward his thighs.

"I bet I could get you to put anything I want on it," Joe said as he finally turned to the hard curve of Cal's cock. He feathered light, breathy kisses along the length of it, from base to the taut ridge of the head. "Right now."

Cal dragged in a ragged breath. His fingers flexed and relaxed against Joe's neck. "I wouldn't want to take that bet right now," he said. "How d'ya think I ended up with the rest of these."

For that, Joe slid his hand up and gave Cal's balls a rough tug. It made Cal twitch, the muscles in his thighs clenched rock hard, and his fingers squeaked over the tiles as he shifted position. Joe ignored the stubborn gnaw of what wasn't jealousy—because he never *got* jealous—and wrapped his lips around Cal's cock.

It was slippery with water and precome, salt and lemon on Joe's lips. He slowly sucked his way along the thick shaft, his tongue flattened against the ridged base, and squeezed Cal's balls with each bob of his head. The pulse of the shower battered against his back and plastered his hair flat to his scalp as Cal scruffed the back of his neck.

Cal pushed his hips forward in a jerky, unsteady thrust. The head of his cock rubbed over Joe's tongue and bumped against the roof of his mouth. Joe pushed his tongue up, and Cal squirmed. His hand squeaked against the tiles as he slipped, and a choked noise that could only be called a whimper scraped out of his throat between eager, unsteady murmurs of encouragement.

The thickness of Cal's cock in Joe's mouth, the weight of it against his tongue, made Joe wonder what it would be like to be under Cal. Joe's hands braced against the headboard, Cal's weight on his back, and the mutter of encouragement against Joe's throat as his ass stretched wide around Cal's cock.

His stomach tightened with the thought, and his ass clenched. Hunger balled low in his stomach—a hot flush of want that tugged at his ass and his balls simultaneously. His jeans were uncomfortably tight as his cock pressed insistently against the zipper.

He pulled back until only the head of Cal's cock was caught behind his lips. The taste on his tongue was heavier as the salt and copper of sex overwhelmed the left-behind hint of soap. Joe ran his tongue along the flared underside of the head and then pulled it up over the top. He lapped at the slit to taste the musky richness of the precome.

"God, Joe," Cal groaned out. He tightened his fingers on Joe's neck and then pulled away and pushed both hands back against the wall to steady himself. "I'm gonna come."

Joe growled his satisfaction around Cal's cock and sucked the thick shaft back into his mouth. His throat spasmed as Cal's cock hit the back of it, and Joe pulled off a bit. He wanted to taste it. The weight of Cal's balls in his hand shifted as they pulled up toward his body, and Joe gave them one last squeeze.

He wanted his name in Cal's mouth, the syllables rough as it was squeezed out through gritted teeth, but all he got was a grunt and the sticky pulse of come as it spilled over his tongue. It smeared stickily over his lips as he let Cal's cock slide from between his lips. It dropped against Cal's thigh, spit and spunk washed away as the stream of water poured down his body. He was slouched back against the wet walls, one arm cocked over his head with his hand cupped around his skull and his lower lip chewed raw between his teeth.

Joe stood up, clothes drenched and plastered to his body, and cupped Cal's jaw in his hand. He was already so hard he hurt, and the zipper was rough against his eager cock, but when Cal opened his eyes, the heavy, dull ache in his balls sharpened to hungry pain. He looked satiated, almost dazed, and there was an unguarded vulnerability to his face that made Joe want to fuck him again. No smirk, no cleverness—not that Joe didn't like that. Cal's sly bluntness was oddly charming, but this was… this was *his.*

He leaned in and kissed Cal hard with come-sticky lips as the water hammered down on them.

"Swallow," he said in answer to yesterday's question as he broke the kiss.

Cal blinked at him for a moment, and then his expression sharpened with that familiar, guarded humor. He laughed and reached back to slap the shower off. Without the steam that filled the shower, Joe's clothes quickly chilled, and were soon clammy against his back and balls. He shivered, and then Cal pulled him back into a kiss.

"Your turn," he mumbled against Joe's mouth as he pushed the shower door open behind Joe. They both stumbled—over each other, over towels on the floor—toward the bedroom. Cal pushed Joe, wet clothes and all, onto the bed. He unbuttoned his jeans and pulled them down Joe's thighs, wet denim reluctant to peel away from damp skin. His mouth was hot around Joe's cold cock.

Chapter Seven

THEY WEREN'T a birthmark. Cal lay tangled in cotton sheets and rich boy and brushed his fingertips carefully over the red marks that dripped from Joe's forehead down to his eyebrow. The skin was raised slightly and rough to the touch.

"What happened?" Cal asked.

Joe turned his head and gently—then not so gently—bit the heel of Cal's hand. He stretched out on the narrow bed—Cal's room only had a single—and tucked one arm behind his head.

"You want to get to know me now?" he asked.

Cal shrugged and dropped his head back against the pillows. He closed his eyes. That wasn't the sort of thing you fucking admitted, even to yourself, even if it was true.

"My nanny splashed boiling water on me when I was a kid," Joe said after a moment. "I had a lot of surgery apparently, to minimize the scars, and that's all that's left. He never fired her. She was with us until I was, like, eight and Dad sent me to boarding school."

Cal winced. "Sorry."

"I don't remember it." Joe shrugged. He nudged Cal's thigh with his knee. "What about you? What happened to your ribs?"

"Nothing."

Joe walked his fingers—finally warmed up—from Cal's hip to his ribs. He poked his fingers right into a ticklish spot, and Cal swore as his nerves twitched an overreaction.

"Don't," he grumbled as he opened his eyes. "I know where it is."

"So do I," Joe said. "I showed you mine."

Cal glanced sidelong at Joe, at the red flush of old scar tissue, and tried to decide if story for story was a fair trade. He begrudged that he had to admit it was. It wasn't a secret, but he didn't want to talk about it.

"I got stabbed."

Joe waited. So did Cal, as he watched ready sympathy bloom on Joe's face and then quickly fade into wary suspicion.

"Edward said you had a record," Joe said bluntly. That was for the best. Cal appreciated that he didn't beat around the bush. "Is that why you got hurt?"

"Figured he would tell you," Cal said. He scratched his ribs. There was an inch of skin on either side of the scar that he couldn't feel. "And no. I stole cars. People didn't even know they'd been robbed until the valet couldn't find their Bugatti. Never even got a black eye on the job, never mind stabbed."

"So what happened?" Joe asked as he moved his hand away.

"I'd only gotten out of jail, and I went on a bender with my brother," Cal said. "We were both drunk, and some kid came to the bar to find his girlfriend and her friend. Or his friend. I don't remember. She wasn't there—smart girl—and since he'd walked all that way, he didn't want to go home without stabbing *someone.*"

It sounded almost funny. At the time it hadn't been. Cal didn't even remember the kid until the moment he nearly staggered over him. He'd been skinny and strung out, visibly at the end of something. Cal had put his hand on the kid's shoulder, easygoing with beer, and apologized for the near collision.

That still pissed him off. He'd said "sorry" to the man who was about to stab him in the side.

He hadn't actually felt it at first, not really. The knuckles had thumped against his side, and then he'd felt what felt like a cold stitch between his ribs. It was only when he saw the blood soak through his shirt that he registered it really hurt and he couldn't quite breathe.

"What did you do?"

Cal paused and glanced sidelong at Joe's narrow, elegant face and dark, wary eyes.

"He stabbed me," he said. "I bled a lot and yelled for help."

It was the truth. It wasn't 100 percent of the truth. It skipped the bit where Cal got twenty stitches and an orange juice, and the stabber spent two weeks in intensive care. Cal didn't like violence, but he'd grown up too pretty not to be good at it, especially when he was drunk and full of anger about the year he'd pissed away.

"Sounds sensible," Joe said. It was hard to tell if he was skeptical or impressed.

"It wasn't serious," Cal said. He untangled himself from Joe and the sheets as he sat up, the floor cold under his feet. "It hurt like hell, but

I wasn't going to die. It… made me realize some stuff, and I thought a reminder would be a good idea."

If he'd died, there'd have been one person who gave a crap at his funeral, and even El would have been better off. Cal hadn't wanted to go back to jail before that, but that was the first time he really wanted to clean up his act.

"Well, I like it," Joe said. The mattress creaked as Joe propped himself up. He tucked his chin into Cal's shoulder and wrapped an arm around his waist, fingers spread over the ink. "It suits you."

It felt real, for a second. Joe's weight was sprawled lazily over Cal's back, and his breath was warm and ticklish against his ear. But it wasn't, and Cal didn't feel ready to deal with that. He swallowed, his throat dry, and squirmed out from under Joe's arm.

"Didn't you want me to drive you somewhere?"

Joe pushed his still-damp hair back from his face, the loose curls defiant as they caught around his fingers. The white sheets tangled around his thighs in a poor attempt at modesty, and his cock was soft and stuck to his thigh. It made Cal want to crawl back into bed with him, even if his cock wasn't up for another round yet.

"Yes," Joe said. "I have to approve the sale of some of our local assets. I'd reschedule, but I have plans for next week."

Cal shrugged and tossed Joe his clothes. "No need," he said. "That's why you keep me around."

THE ONLY lawyers Cal had ever had dealings with wore suits, comfortable shoes, and depression. Bea McGuire, Joe's lawyer, wore a yellow dress with frilled, three-quarter sleeves and a flirtatious smile. The difference between a duty solicitor and business law, Cal supposed.

He glanced into the rearview mirror as she slid into the back seat, the flash of her knees deliberate as she artfully arranged her legs.

"Where to?" he asked.

She didn't look up. "There's a lovely bistro," she said as Joe folded his long, elegant body into the car. Her hand fluttered out and rested on his knee. "The tapas is to die for. The Minsk in Hay's Lane?"

Joe moved her hand. He glanced at Cal and raised his eyebrows. "Do you know where it is?"

"I'm sure he has GPS," Bea interrupted. She sighed and rubbed her hand along the leather in the back seat. "Although it is a shame to hook something like that into an old dame like this."

Maybe she was all right. Cal threw the car into first. "I know where it is," he said. "It won't take long to get there."

He glanced at Joe in the mirror again, just because. Then he pulled out of the car park and eased into traffic. He let Joe and Bea out at the Minsk, where the street in front was cluttered with well-dressed people who smoked with one hand and swigged wine with the other.

"We'll be an hour or so. I'll call when we're done here," Joe said as he paused next to the driver's door and stooped to look through the window. He brushed Cal's shoulder and paused long enough to be pointed. "You can take me home."

That was literally his job, Cal reminded himself as he watched Joe escort Bea through the crowd to the propped-open front door of the Minsk. No underlying meaning needed, but the nerves under his skin didn't listen.

He found somewhere to park and walked down to Queen's Walk while he waited. There was a spray-painted van on the corner that sold fusion ice cream in squid-ink cones. He got himself a Starbucks inside and called El from a bench that overlooked the river. Not that he could make out much of the Thames through the eddied crowd and the vendors with their packs of tat and quick patter.

"You got a few?" he asked when El picked up. No niceties; this was family. "I got you a coffee."

Half an hour later, El jogged up Queen's Walk in shorts and sweat-soaked T-shirt. A woman with an *Up* style canopy of mylar balloons fumbled the transfer between her and a small pink child as she clocked him. The kid wailed as the balloons drifted away, and he had to be consoled with two.

"Two birds with one stone," El said as he bent over and braced his hands on his knees. His grin flashed white and smug from between his elbows. "Anyone look?"

"A couple," Cal admitted. "Probably worried you were going to stroke out right in front of them."

El snorted and sat down on the end of the bench. He wiped his hand over his dense, short-cropped curls and huffed out a breath as he slouched back. Heat seeped out of his body.

"You reek," Cal grumbled as he shifted away.

"You're getting fat," El countered. He stretched his legs out in front of him and fanned his shirt. The flash of tight brown abs made a passerby in a nicely fitted suit stumble over his own feet. "Coffee?"

Cal hitched his hips up and pulled a fiver out of his pocket. He handed it over. "I left it in Starbucks. It would have got cold."

El took the fiver, folded it, and stuck it into the waistband of his shorts. He pulled his hand down his sweaty face and tilted his head back toward the sun.

"Why did I start running again?" he asked as he squinted his eyes shut.

"To make your wife think you had someone you wanted to impress," Cal said. "Not sure the show you made of yourself would impress anyone."

To be fair, not that Cal ever would be out loud, El didn't need to run to impress. He had a few streaks of gray in his curls and some wrinkles around his eyes, but whoever their dads had been, they'd passed down some good genes. Unfortunately, how he looked wasn't the problem with his marriage.

"You wanted to talk," El reminded him as he dragged his hand down his sweaty face. "What's up?"

"How'd Grandad get to know Harry Bailey?" Cal asked.

It wasn't the question El had expected. He opened his eyes and gave Cal a curious look. "Grandad? He didn't, far as I know."

"You said it was a legacy client."

El rolled his eyes. "Is there any point in giving you the client files?"

"No."

"It wouldn't kill you to read them."

"You don't know that."

El unhooked his arm from the back of the bench long enough to flick Cal on the ear. "I know you're not stupid or lazy, so stop trying to convince me. If you had read the file, you'd know that Bailey wasn't the legacy client. That's Edward Dexter, their head of security."

That was a surprise. Cal paused and thought of Edward's hard eyes, granite, deeply lined face, and the ice in his voice as he confronted Cal that night. Maybe not *that* much of a surprise.

"He was a crook?"

El scratched under his ear with his thumb. Grandad hadn't exactly kept detailed records about his clients. He probably wouldn't have even if they'd been legit clients. He'd been an "IOU on the back of a betting slip" sort of man. Of the two of them, El had been old enough to have a fifty folded into his hand and get sent to put a bet on or buy a bottle of Jack. He remembered more.

"Dexter was a cop, Cal," he said.

"So yes on the crook thing?"

There was a pause, and then El lifted his hand and wobbled it from side to side. He ended the gesture with a shrug. "Maybe. He went out with our mum, and you know what terrible fucking taste she had."

"The fuck?" Cal said as he sat up straight on the chair. "I don't remember that."

"You'd have been… what, five?" El said. "Four? Grandma was still alive, and she didn't want us around any of Mum's men. I saw them come around a couple of times, but Grandma would give me some cash and send us down to the shop to get some ice cream. Dexter got on with Grandad, though. He used to come around and they'd talk cars while they smoked cigars out in the garden. Sometimes Gran would let me sit and listen for a bit, but you know what she was like."

Cal nodded. Their gran hadn't trusted men around little kids—not teachers or neighbors or strangers. Hell, now that he was grown and looked back at some of her careful questions about what he'd done that day, she hadn't even trusted Grandad completely. Someone she'd trusted had burned Grandma at some point, and she'd been gun-shy for the rest of her life. As fucked-up as their mum had been, Cal had always kinda figured it had something to do with her.

"So what happened?"

"I don't know," El said. "He'd been in an accident in the Bentley—Grandad had loaned it to him to take Mum out for the day, and he brought it back all smashed up—but Grandad didn't seem that pissed off. I think Dexter paid for it, anyhow. A couple of weeks after that, though, he didn't come round again. I think he left town. Or, well, if he's working for the Bailey Group, I guess he left the country. Whatever happened, though, Grandad kept his name in the legacy file when he handed it over."

"Give 'em a good price, do a good job," Cal said, his accent thicker than usual as he mimicked his grandad's Tottenham twang. "Don't ask questions."

El nodded. "Why do you want to know, anyhow?" he asked. "Most of the time, you don't want to know anything about them other than where they want to get to. Is this about your rich boss, the one you didn't plan to sleep with?"

"No," Cal lied dismissively. If El found out what was going on, he'd definitely spill the beans to Edward. It was his business on the line. "He's a dick."

El pushed himself off the back of the bench and leaned forward, his elbows braced on his knees and his eyes trained on the scuffed toes of his trainers. He flexed his hands, spread his fingers, and then clenched them into fists.

"Is it about Van?" he asked as he glanced sideways at Cal.

"What?" Cal spluttered. His head had been full of misgivings over whether he should keep Joe's secrets or not. The sudden injection of his ex caught him off balance. "The fuck it is. Why would you ask that?"

"Someone said you'd been down at the Dobbins's the other night," El said. "Look, I know it's your life, Cal, but fuck sake. Is it worth another stint behind bars to drive fast in someone else's car?"

Probably not, but Cal was pretty sure that most people would have said definitely. He shook his head.

"Who?"

"Malcolm's auntie said that he'd seen you." El shook his head and pushed himself up off the bench. He crossed his arms as he looked down on Cal—something he hadn't been able to do normally since Cal hit sixteen. "It's… it took me a while to get used to the idea that you, you know, liked men that way."

"Fucked them."

El glanced behind him and grimaced an apology to the scandalized woman who hustled her giggling son away.

"Yeah, that," he said. "Maybe if I'd talked to you about it more, encouraged you to go after—fuck, I don't know—some nice kid from school."

"To be fair," Cal interrupted, feeling awkward as the conversation suddenly felt real, "I never went to school."

"Shut up," El told him. "You're a piss-poor adult, Cal, but you're trying. That matters. And, like I said, maybe I should have told you this more often back then—you deserve better. You need to find someone who treats you well, makes you feel good about yourself, not some version of our mum with a dick attached."

It was El's turn to get a stare from a passerby, although the woman slowed down instead of sped up. Cal supposed he couldn't blame her.

"Jesus," he said. His skull felt hot, and the skin across his shoulders tight, as if this were about to turn into a fight. He grimaced and crossed his arms as he tried to squash the sense that he was under attack. "I'm not—my life has nothing to do with our mum. She was never even around."

"Yeah," El said. "And that has absolutely nothing to do with why you hook up with people who think you're their dirty little secret or why I married the first girl I ever dated, even though neither of us were finished people at that point, so I didn't bounce from relationship to relationship like our mother."

"Yeah, you're screwed up," Cal said. He'd always liked Jane. She was smart, pretty, and mean enough to keep it fun. But they'd been at each other's throats since they were sixteen. "I was having fun. Nothing… psychological… about it. And I'm not chasing after Van either."

"So why were you there?"

"I needed a favor. He owed me," Cal said. "That's all."

"What favor?"

"That's my business."

Frustration twisted at the corners of El's mouth, but he let it go, that small bit of it anyway. "If you want, I can see if anyone knows more about Dexter and what went down back then."

Cal thought about it for a second and then shook his head. "If you can," he said, although he didn't know if there was any point. He'd thought that Harry Bailey might have a shady past, bad enough that someone had passed their grudge down onto his son. It was still possible, but less likely the answers were in their grandad's old records. Still, it might turn up something through Dexter. "I wondered how Grandad knew him."

El looked away for a second, his profile backlit by the sun. "You know, I know when you're lying," he said. "Fine, don't tell me. But don't go back. Van and that lot, even Malcolm, they'll drag you back in. You're better than that."

Cal scowled and squirmed in place as though he'd been caught on a hook. His ears were too hot, and he still wanted to punch El—an easy outlet for the hot-wire scratch under his skin. Most of the time, people accepted that he would live down to their expectations.

"Yeah, well…." He scratched his head and felt like an idiot as he shrugged. "Don't know about that, but I'm done with Van. He looks like hell these days."

El rolled his eyes. "Sure," he said. "That's the reason. If you change your mind about Dexter, let me know. Take care of yourself, little brother. Or find someone who'll do a good job at it."

The incongruity of that made Cal snort as he stood up. He gestured at himself. "Do I look like I need taking care of?"

"Naw," El said. He pulled Cal into a rough, sweaty hug and muttered into his ear, "But you do. I know you."

One last, back-slapping squeeze and El took his leave. Cal watched his brother's back disappear into the crowd with that scratchy mixture of annoyance and affection. He loved his brother, but El was wrong. Cal had never needed anyone.

Maybe, a quiet, stubborn voice whispered in the back of his brain, he *wanted* someone.

He ignored it.

Chapter Eight

THE EXCELLENT tapas sat, barely touched, in a collection of eclectically decorated bowls. The oil had started to separate into a thin film and puddled in the gaped shells of mussels.

"The Bailey Group isn't going to do business in the UK anymore," Joe said as he lifted the glass of wine. Bea had refilled it with the deceptively easy-on-the-palate sweet red… three times. He paused for a second, the rim of the glass cold against his lip, as he weighed the wisdom of another drink. His drive home was already arranged, and Cal could carry him in if he needed the help. The thought if it—Cal's arm around Joe's waist, his throat bare to Joe's eager mouth, and the eyes of the hotel on them—curled heat in Joe's chest. He took a long swallow of wine to quench it, not that it worked, and gave Bea a thin smile. "We won't need a law firm on retainer."

She leaned back in her chair, her arm braced on the low, curved back, and gave a careless, one-shouldered shrug. Her perfectly red matte lips curved in a slow, easy smile. "You'll still do business in Europe."

He gave her a dry look. "And how much use will an English law firm be for that?"

The practiced charm of her expression slid into genuine amusement as she tilted her head to the side in acknowledgment of his point. She reached over the table and plucked a spiced olive from the bowl to pop between her lips. At a nearby table, hunched over a tablet, a thin woman watched the show through her long, auburn hair with discreet interest. At least, Joe thought dryly, someone appreciated the moment… but not enough to distract her from her work as she tapped her fingers over the keyboard on the bright screen.

"I understand," she said. "Your father's made his position clear. What about yours?"

Joe raised his eyebrows at her. "What makes you think it differs from his??"

She paused as she studied him from under her lashes and licked the oil from her fingertips. "Because your father has had a stroke and would rather divest business holdings than turn over control to you," she said. "I did my research when the partners asked me to court your father back, Joe. You've proven your value to your father's company over and over, with negotiated mergers, hostile takeovers, headhunted investment opportunities. Yet here you are, left to put the chairs up and lock the door behind him. I'd have, let's call them feelings, on that."

She wasn't wrong. Joe had tried for years to impress Harry, had tried to prune away all the bits of him that he thought would keep that approval away, and the last few months had proven it hadn't worked. Harry didn't trust Joe with the truth *or* the business.

"The plans to close our British holdings were already in progress before my father's stroke. If anything, that delayed the process," Joe said. As if on cue, his phone buzzed in his pocket. He fished it out and checked it with a quick glance down at the screen. Then he turned his attention back to Bea. "And I had my own reasons to want to come to the UK."

It was another text from Edward. Joe wasn't in the mood to deal with them.

Bea raised her eyebrows at him as though he'd admitted something. "See? That sounds like something I could help with."

Joe studied Bea over the neglected spread. There was something uncompromising about her colorful, glossy dress, a probably false sense that this was the real Bea and not a socially accepted lawyer suit that she presented to the world. It made Joe want to like her, to believe her offer of assistance. The fact that it wasn't selfless made it more convincing.

Or maybe that was the wine.

Joe put his glass down and gently pushed it away until it bumped into one of the bowls.

"Why don't you let me think about that," he said. "In the meantime, draw up all the required contracts for the sale of our properties. I have an engagement next week with the buyers, and I want everything ready."

"I's dotted and t's crossed?" Bea asked.

"Exactly."

She sighed and gestured her surrender. They chatted a few moments longer as she finished her wine and insisted the firm had the check, and then Joe finally got up to leave. He pulled his jacket on and the tailored fabric settled over his shoulders. Then he extended his hand.

"It was a pleasure to meet you," he said. "I'll keep your offer in mind."

She shook it briskly, the earlier linger of her long, warm fingers abandoned. "Do," she said. "I'm an excellent solicitor."

Joe turned to leave and nearly tripped over the red-haired woman who'd watched Bea eat. Her drink splashed down his shirt, red against the white. She caught his elbow with one hand and apologized as she swiped at his chest with a bundle of tissues.

"I'm sorry," she said. "I didn't expect you to turn around so quickly. God, I'm such a klutz. Send me the bill for the dry cleaning."

Her clumsy swabs at the wide, pink stain pressed against the bruises left on Joe's stomach from the graveyard. They had already started to fade and blur to green at the edges, but they still ached when poked. Joe winced and blocked her anxious attempt at cleanup.

"I'm fine," he said with an attempt at an easygoing smile. "It's fine. Don't worry about it."

The woman pushed her hair back from her face and frowned up at him. She was older than he'd thought, Joe realized with surprise. He was usually good at ages, but the hint of fine lines around her eyes and mouth made him revise her age vaguely up from his initial "same age as me" guess.

"It was stupid," she said. "I wanted to…. I saw Bea, but I didn't want to interrupt. So when I saw you were about to leave, I thought I'd nip over. Now look at the mess."

She poked her fingers against his stomach again in an odd gesture. Joe clenched his teeth and stepped back. He put the chair between them.

"Forget about it," he told her. "I should have been more careful."

Bea had cocked her head to the side. "I'm sorry," she said warily. "I don't…."

The woman balled the wine-stained napkins up in her hands and laughed nervously. "Oh, I was blonde then," she said as she tugged at a strand of hair. "Remember me now?"

There was a brief flicker of embarrassed panic in Bea's eyes as she drew a blank. She grimaced apologetically and slowly shook her head. "Sorry, I…."

"Kelly," the woman prodded with a nervous laugh. "I'm sorry. There's no reason for you to remember me. It was ages ago. Oh God, this is not a good day for me."

To Bea's credit she didn't pretend the "Kelly" was enough of a prompt to jog her memory. Instead she gave a slow, red smile and waved her hand at Joe's abandoned chair.

"Sorry," she said warmly. "I have a terrible memory for anything that's not work-related—the plight of a solicitor. But join me. I can get to know you again."

Startled color pinched Kelly's cheeks, and she bit her lip on a return smile. "I should… I shouldn't interrupt anymore," she said. "You have business."

Bea angled her wrist to check the time on her watch. "I think I can go off the clock now," she said. "And Mr. Bailey is on his way out."

Kelly glanced down uncertainly at her tablet and then relaxed slightly. "Okay," she said as she tucked the pad into her bag. "I guess."

Joe nodded to both and took his leave. He stepped outside and moved down the pavement, away from the smoky no-go zone that spread out from the door. It was still warm, but there was enough of a chill in the air to make his soaked shirt unpleasant. He fastidiously plucked the damp red fabric away from his stomach as he texted Cal to come and pick him up.

The pulsing dots of an answer in the works popped up immediately. Joe watched it idly until a bike squealed to a stop in front of him, its skinny tires close enough to his toes that he jumped back on instinct. He looked up from his phone and saw a skinny bike messenger, all wood-hard legs and sweaty T-shirt, peer at him from under a perforated helmet and then check his phone.

"Joseph Bailey?" he asked as he looked back up.

"Yeah," Joe said, the acknowledgment out before he thought better of it. The image of Cal's arm flashed into his head, the curved slash of red that laid his forearm open, and he took another step back. "Who's asking?"

The messenger shrugged his pack off and efficiently unzipped it. "Don't know. I just got a message for you, mate," he said. "Sign here."

He stuck out the phone, signature block maximized on the finger-greased screen, and waited. Joe glanced around at the crowd in front of the bar. A tall woman in a summer dress drew a wave of laughter as she punctuated a story with a wild gesture and knocked the cap off another drinker's head. On down the pavement, two hikers sat outside, hips perched on the narrow shelf of a window, and ate something with their fingers while their dog snoozed on the ground.

Plenty of witnesses if the messenger did anything. Joe took the phone and signed it quickly, and the smooth, digital line skipped where the grubby screen misread the swipe of his finger. He handed it back, and the messenger traded it for a fat envelope he pulled out of the bag.

"Have a good day, Mr. Bailey," the messenger said as he swung his bag back over his shoulder. He hitched himself back up onto the bike and took off. His bell jangled a warning as he cut through the edge of the crowd and then bumped down the curb and onto the road.

Joe turned the envelope over in his hands. It was soft—whatever was inside gave and shifted under his fingers—and securely taped up. His name was printed on the front in neat, anonymous block letters. He pinched the bridge of his nose between his fingers and tried to decide what was worse—that this was the stalker or that he'd been served again.

Either way, he thought with bitter humor, he knew better than to sign something after two glasses of wine. Last time he'd ended up in court for a month over a copyright issue.

"Mr. Bailey?" Cal's voice interrupted Joe's thoughts. "Joe?"

He looked up. The Bentley was parked at the side of the road, the engine running. Cal leaned out the window, his expression curious with an edge of worry.

"I'll sit in the front," Joe said as he tucked the envelope out of sight in his jacket and cut around the front of the car. The last dregs of his earlier good humor, sweaty-sweet afterglow, had hung on this far. He wanted to keep them until he got back to the hotel and had to deal with this, even if it meant he let himself pretend it meant more to Cal than a paycheck and sex to pass the time. He climbed into the soft leather front seat and slammed the door. "Do you ever listen to music?"

There was a pause, and then Cal shrugged. He poked the phone he'd hooked into the stereo system, and a low, practiced voice cut in midsentence.

"Podcasts," he said. "But I can turn the radio on if you want."

It was about travel. The voice thrilled with the delights of Saville. Joe shook his head. "No, I like it," he said. He could pretend he was somewhere hot with a half-naked—or fully naked—Cal. There were worse ways to prolong a good mood.

THE BEAR sat lopsided on the clean, white counter in the small kitchen and stared at the world through melted plastic eyes. It had started life as a small cream bear with black eyes and paws that had shaped leather pads stitched to them. That was before someone had taken a blowtorch and left the thick fur matted into scabs and the stuffing melted in hard, charred lumps. It had been dunked in water after, and the smell of wet fabric and stale smoke oozed from it like body odor.

It was a nasty little present from a nasty little mind. Joe didn't know why it made his throat close up and his heart race.

"Look, you have to tell Edward about this," Cal said as he poked the dead bear with a spoon. "He can probably track it back through the delivery company or something, find out who sent it. Sick weirdo."

The bear toppled listlessly onto its side, unbalanced by an arm charred all the way up to the shoulder. Joe flinched inside as though it were a dog or a child, with that wash of empathy. As it toppled over, he saw the folded wad of paper stapled to its underside.

"I thought we had an understanding," Joe said. He sounded cold again, his voice filtered through a layer of tamped-down emotional noise. He reached for the bear. "You drive. I decide what Edward needs to know."

"And the fucking?" Cal asked.

The bear had been in the envelope for a while, stuffed into the bag against the messenger's sweaty back. It still felt damp where it wasn't rough or scaled with char. Over-the-top revulsion bubbled up out of Joe's stomach until he could taste the acid of it against the back of his throat.

It was a burned toy, he thought with irritated clarity. That was all. What was *wrong* with him?

"You drive me to that," Joe said as he pulled the bit of paper loose. Shreds of it were left stapled to the bear. "I decide when Edward needs to know about it. See? It's a perfect system."

There was an edge to Joe's voice that.... It wouldn't be fair to say he didn't mean it, because he did. But he could still wish it weren't there. The low snicker from Cal cut through Joe's mood like a dash of lemon, straightforward and amused.

"You're lucky you're pretty," Cal said. "Because you're a bit of a dick."

"I don't remember you complaining," Joe pointed out with a flicker of humor. It guttered and died out again as he unfolded the note.

The handwriting scratched over the paper in an unexpectedly loose script, all bulges and fat, exaggerated curves on the rounded letters.

DID YOU MISS ME?

Joe twisted the paper up between his fingers and tossed it toward the bin. "It would be easier," he said impatiently, "if they'd at least lay out why they hate me. It would help to narrow the field of suspects. And shut up, Cal."

"What?" Cal asked as he stuck his hands in his pockets and slouched, hip-shot and lazy, against the table. It wobbled under his weight, and Joe steadied it with one hand. He opened his mouth to say something and stopped himself, the side of his tongue caught between his teeth.

"You should go," he said instead. "Take the afternoon off. I'm not in the mood to be good company, and I'd rather you *didn't* join the ranks of those who want me to fuck off and die."

Cal shrugged. "I've got a thick skin," he said. "And you look like you saw your own ghost."

"It's frustration," Joe lied. It wasn't as though he could tell the truth. He didn't know why the bear had gotten under his skin. "They seem to know everything about me, down to where I have lunch, and I know nothing about them."

He voice cracked at the end of the sentence, and with a spike of anger, he swiped the bear off the table. It flew over the room, smacked into the wall, and bounced to the floor, scattering bits of burned plastic over the floor. Maybe it wasn't exactly a lie. He took a deep breath and let it out down his nose.

"I don't seem to know much about anything," he said. His voice sounded brittle, even to him. "Not my parents, not my past, not the stalker… nothing much at all."

Cal shifted and rubbed the back of his neck, visibly uncomfortable. "I'm kinda out of my depth here, Joe," he said. "This sort of thing… you want a professional."

It wasn't, Joe supposed, the sort of thing Cal had signed up for. A basket case in the middle of a meltdown wasn't exactly hot. He brushed his hands together fastidiously to get the last traces of ash and mildew off his fingers and pulled a stiff, humorless smile out of his lips.

"A therapist?" he asked.

Cal scowled. "Now you sound like my brother," he muttered and then shook his head.

Joe *wanted* to ask, but under the circumstances, it seemed hypocritical. Before he could work out a way around it, Cal forged on and he lost his chance. "Whatever rattles around your head and what you need to do with it, that's your business. Not mine. I meant like a private detective or something. Whoever did your background check on me."

"The one who makes 75 percent of his income from my father?" Joe asked. "Besides, I didn't think I'd need it. I thought it would be easy to find out what happened. Part of my job is to find out things that people don't want me to, and the dead don't get up too much."

"Whereas the living…"

"Disappear," Joe said. "She's not online. Her parents died when she was a teenager, and the aunt who raised her died before I was born. I don't know who her friends were…. I don't know where to start digging."

Cal reached over the table and put his hand on Joe's shoulder.

"You'll find her," he said. "But I don't want this nutjob to find you first, Joe."

He squeezed down around Joe's upper arm and ran his thumb across the wing of his collarbone as though he weren't sure if they were mates or lovers right then. Joe made that call on his own as he turned his head and pressed a kiss against Cal's bony, scarred knuckles. The press of his lips, the damp swipe of his tongue, made Cal suck in a quick breath that trembled in the back of his throat.

It felt… strange. Heady as whiskey. He'd fucked plenty of men, but simple affection was—

The front door to the suite beeped its usual interruption, and his thought derailed as he heard two familiar voices speak over it.

"I don't know if he's back—"

"I don't mind. I can wait."

The slow drunk of infatuation fizzled into nothing as old habits shouldered their way to the front of Joe's mind. He took a smart step back, out from under Cal's hand, and gave his jacket a quick tug as though a careless fit would betray more than he wanted. For a moment Cal's hand hung in the air, and then he curled his fingers to his palm and let it drop to his side. He looked amused as much as anything, his mouth tucked up wryly at the corner, but it was the detached smirk of someone who wasn't surprised.

"Get rid of that." Joe nodded at the bear as he straightened his tie, the lavender silk cool under his fingers. "Keep your mouth shut."

Cal snorted as he bent down to get the bear. He shoved it roughly back into the envelope and then stuffed the package into the back of his jeans.

"Don't worry," he said as he backed up to lean against the sink. "I know my place."

Joe gave him a frustrated look. It wasn't like that. Still bad enough on its own, but not that. The urge to apologize, explain, or order caught in Joe's throat at the same time and stuck there. He didn't know which would win, because Kristen swept into the kitchen before he could get anything said.

"What the hell, Joseph?" she demanded as she threw her handbag at him. The heavy, purple leather pouch bounced off his forearms as he raised them to guard his face. "You don't get to dump me and leave the country. What was I supposed to tell people? Why was *I* supposed to tell them?"

Because he was a coward, Joe thought viciously. He tried not to look toward Cal, reluctant to see the guarded *lack* of expression on Cal's face.

"Kristen," he said as he put his hands in his pockets and straightened his shoulders. "This is unexpected."

"I ran into her downstairs," Edward said. He never spoke fast, but the measured cadence of his speech sounded more arch than usual. It was the sort of voice that thought it knew something you didn't. "She came to find you."

"I came to *kill* you," Kristen corrected sharply as she dragged her coat off.

It was a bad choice of words, under the circumstances.

Chapter Nine

THERE WAS a trick Cal had learned when he was a kid—when you couldn't have what you wanted, don't want it. In fact, if you could convince yourself you'd *never* wanted it, even better. Then it didn't hurt and no one could use it against you.

Cal had never wanted, not even for a wistful fucking moment, more than the occasional sweaty hookup with Joe. Never even entertained the thought.

"You are such a bastard." Kristen flung the words at Joe. "You can't ghost your fiancée, Joe. It's not what happens. You owe me better than that. I deserve better than that."

After the conversation with El on the bridge, Cal couldn't resist a quick look at Edward. He didn't know what he expected to see. Whatever Edward's relations with Cal's mum had been, it had been a long time ago, and Cal couldn't imagine his mother as the love of anyone's life. Either way, Edward's face was as harsh and unreadable as ever.

"Why don't we do this in private, Kristen," Joe said. He waved a hand to the door. "The study is—"

"I remember. We stayed here before. And I have nothing to be ashamed about. If Mr.…" She paused expectantly and glanced past Joe at Cal. "Sorry, who are you?" she asked.

"Mr. Tate," Joe said before Cal could open his mouth. "He's my driver, and this isn't anything to do with him."

Kristen shrugged. "Fine." She turned on her heel and stalked out of the kitchen. Joe lifted his chin, his neck stiff all the way down into his shoulders, and didn't look around at Cal as he stepped over the purse on the floor and stalked out after her—not that Cal expected him to. This was a familiar enough ride.

"Awkward, isn't it," Edward said as he stooped down to pick up the bag. "When you have to face reality. Joe and Kristen come from the same world. They share the same friends. They have the same bank. What do you have, Mr. Tate?"

Cal hoped the slow grin he gave Edward was as filthy as it felt. It must have come close, because Edward gave him a disgusted look as he put the bag on the table. To Cal's surprise, Edward popped the clasp and stretched the mouth of the bag open. He peered inside as though there might be a trap in there and then dipped a hand in.

Cal crossed his arms. "Pro tip, Ed, petty theft works better if you don't have witnesses."

A humorless smile skimmed over Edward's thin lips. "Who'd believe you?"

It was a good point. Cal watched Edward search the bright purple Birkin bag for a moment and stack neat piles of half-wrapped candies, filched sugar packets, and loose vape cylinders on the table.

"Didn't you look into her already?" he said. "Isn't it always the ex?"

"She wasn't the ex then." Edward *tch*ed in disapproval as he came up with a scratched bottle of pills and then tucked the bag under the table so he could sweep everything back into it. "I only found out recently that she had… other reasons to be angry with Joe."

"Like?"

Edward fastened the bag and hung it over the back of a chair. He gave Cal a sour, almost eager look. "I hate to disabuse you, but you weren't Joe's first dalliance."

Cal snorted as he pushed himself off the counter. "And thank fuck for that."

Was he supposed to care? No offense to virgins, but Cal had never had the patience. He'd rather have someone who knew what they wanted and what they didn't at the start of the night.

"I do not understand you," Edward said as Cal walked past him. "This… thing… isn't going to go anywhere. Even if he's… not straight, Joe can do better than you. You aren't his type. You're a distraction."

The jibe didn't draw blood, but it hit the target. Probably, Cal thought sourly, because it was true.

"I never expected to be anything else," Cal tossed back over his shoulder as he walked away. "Guys like us, Ed, we don't end up at the altar."

For a second, Edward didn't say anything, and then a quiet, bitter "Go to hell" followed Cal to his room. It didn't make Cal feel any better. Well, not much better.

He shoved the bear in a drawer and flopped down on the bed, arms folded over his head. It was harder to hang on to the "don't give a damn" lie when you were alone. The tangled sheets and flattened pillows still smelled of sex and Joe's cologne, and that didn't help either.

Was this progress, Cal wondered, that he wasn't only a feral idiot with his cock but with his heart too?

It didn't *feel* like it.

He lay there and listened to the sound of Kristen and Joe arguing as it drifted through the walls. When it got too much, he rolled off the bed, grabbed his phone, and headed down to the bar.

TWO DAYS of Kristen had worn the sheen off Cal's brief infatuation. It was hard to pretend there was anything real happening when the evidence that there wasn't stamped around in expensive shoes and demanded answers. The relationship showed no sign it was about to be resurrected, but that wasn't the point. Kristen didn't know why Joe had broken up with her when all Joe wanted a bit of rough in his bed before he went back to his real life. Fair enough. It wasn't as though he'd promised anything else.

Cal sat in the greasy spoon a few streets back from St. Pancras and brooded out the window while he waited for his breakfast to arrive. A homeless man huddled in a sleeping bag in the chained-up doorway of an abandoned travel agent opposite, his hands wrapped around a bottle of gin as though there were any warmth in the drink. On her way past. a woman with her heels in a plastic bag over her shoulder and sensible trainers on her feet tossed a handful of coins into the cup in front of him.

It would be easy for Cal to end up there. He took a drink of bitter coffee with a film of grease from the kitchen on the liquid and grimaced sourly at either the taste or the thought. There were only so many chances you could expect from life, and El had already gone above and beyond. In the end, though, he ran a business, and if Cal fucked it up for him, he'd have to let him go.

No one else was going to hire him. He was an ex-con who'd scraped resentfully—on his and the teachers' parts—through school. He could go back to stealing cars, but…. Cal sat back and rubbed at his ribs. Habit made it easy to find the scar, even though the poke of his fingers didn't make it ache anymore.

The waitress yawned her way over to the table with his breakfast, last night's makeup still smudged in glittered lines around her eyes.

"Here you go," she said as she slid the plate in front of him. "Enjoy your breakfast."

She didn't wait for an answer as she headed back to the counter and topped up her massive cup of coffee. Cal rubbed rusty-water spots off his knife and fork and cut into his eggs, the yellow yolk bright against the scraped white plate as it puddled under the bacon and beans.

Breakfast was free back at the hotel, but it was also muesli and yogurt with the occasional boiled egg. In Cal's mood, a greasy fry-up sounded a lot better. It meant he didn't have to see Joe or Kristen either. He broke a corner off his toast and sopped up the mixture of egg and tomato sauce. He took a bite, and then the bell over the door behind him jangled and the tired waitress looked up from her coffee.

"Sit anywhere," she said. "I'll be with you in a minute."

Heels clicked on the linoleum, and Kristen sat down opposite Cal. She put her bag on the table in front of her and crossed her hands over the top of it. Probably the best idea—the bag cost more than anything in the shop and the floor was sticky. She didn't say anything as she studied his face with wide brown eyes that showed, despite skincare and artfully applied makeup, evidence of tears and sleepless nights.

Cal gave his mouthful of sodden bread a good-faith chew, quickly swallowed it, and washed it down with a gulp of coffee. He wiped his mouth on a napkin and glanced around to see if Joe was behind her.

"He's in a meeting," Kristen said. Her voice sounded measured and thoughtful, different when she wasn't midrant. She glanced over at the waitress. "I'll have a cup of tea, please? When you're ready."

The waitress grunted and pushed herself off the counter to grab an old, stained teapot from the shelf behind her. While she filled it, Cal wiped his fingers and waited for something other than an update on Joe's day. He didn't get it. They sat there awkwardly as his breakfast congealed until the waitress brought the tea.

"Do you want anything to eat?" she asked as she put the tea down in front of Kristen. A splash of it tipped over the side and puddled on the scratched Formica. The waitress pointed a chewed fingernail at Cal's breakfast. "We do an English fry until ten."

Kristen glanced down at the plate and wrinkled her nose. "No," she said. "Just tea."

The waitress gave a "no skin off my nose" twitch of her shoulders and left. Cal glanced down at his plate, and his stomach rumbled. He shrugged to himself and dunked the toast back into the egg yolk. If Kristen wasn't going to say anything, he might as well eat while he could.

The silent stalemate lasted two sips of Kristen's tea—her stylishly plum lipstick bright against the china—and most of Cal's bacon. He stabbed the last bit with his fork and Kristen finally broke the silence.

"I think you should ask to be relieved," she said. Her voice was calm and lightly dismissive, but color flushed over her cheekbones and spread out to her ears. It made her discreet diamond earrings look very dramatic. "Another driver can step in. It's not exactly a skilled job."

That was a relief. Animosity Cal could cope with. Tears he wasn't sure. Reason would have worked, but nasty little jabs rolled off him. He'd had plenty of practice over the years.

"I don't work for you," he pointed out before he shoved the forkful of bacon into his mouth.

Kristen tightened her hands on the bag. "If you only *worked* for him," she said, precise and calm as her ears flushed redder. "I wouldn't have a problem. It's the fact you're… obviously not up for the job."

"Yeah?" Cal said as he leaned back in the narrow chair. He wiped his mouth on the napkin, crumpled it up, and tossed it onto the table. "I've never had any complaints before."

She looked away from him. Her gaze fell on the homeless man across the street, and she frowned as though he'd ruined her view.

"You think you're special, but you're not. This is cold feet, about the wedding. Until this we were good together. Once he's had time to think about this, he'll come back to me." She looked sharply back at Cal as she finished. "He always does."

"That's your business," Cal told her. "Nothing to do with me."

Kristen popped her bag open and reached inside. She pulled out a fat brown envelope and set it on the table between her bag and Cal's plate.

"I'm not naïve," she said. While she talked, Cal reached for the envelope. "I know that Joe is bisexual. I know that he's cheated on me. I know that he's a liar."

Cal paused, the flap of the envelope half-lifted as the crack of anger in the last word caught his attention. That had been the first thing the stalker accused Joe of, hadn't it? That he was a liar. He stared at Kristen as she took a sip of tea to compose herself, and wondered if maybe that old git Edward had been right to suspect her.

The mug clicked as Kristen set it neatly back down in the ring it had already left on the table.

"I also know he loves me," she said as she stubbornly lifted her chin. "People cheat. It doesn't mean anything. *You* don't mean anything. So… make this easier."

There was enough cash stuffed in the envelope that Cal flinched at the idea Kristen that had walked down the street with it. King's Cross was hardly a rough area, but she'd had enough money in her bag to make any commuter think about a quick side job.

"Not really my style," Cal said. He ran his thumb over the edges of the crisp, straight-out-of-the-bank notes and wondered how many it would take to hire some angry kid with a flip knife. Two. Maybe one. She'd need someone like Edward to *find* them, but… there was always someone like Edward when you had money. "Did he ever tell you about his mum?"

Kristen rolled her eyes and looked impatient as she shifted in her seat. "His mother? Is this some sort of psychoanalysis? Because I don't need some two-bit *Fast and Furious* rip-off for that. I have a therapist. I'm sure she'd be ashamed of him, though."

"Because he's gay?" Cal asked.

She smacked her hand flat on the table. It made a louder sound than Cal expected, and the waitress jumped and frowned in their direction as she weighed whether to intervene or make herself scarce.

"Because he *hurt* me," Kristen snapped. She flinched back from her own words and pulled back onto her side of the table. Pain lingered on her face for a second, but she tossed her head, took a deep breath, and glared at him as though she dared him to notice. "I'll forgive him. Once you're gone."

Cal tucked the envelope into his jacket and glanced at his watch to check the date. "Two weeks, then," he said. "That's when my contract is up. You should order a cake."

She looked annoyed. "Do you think this is funny?" Kristen asked. "This is my life. Three months ago we were going to be married, we were going to be happy. Then I went to see my father, came back, and I can have the apartment. Like I was coming out ahead now?"

"Lady," Cal said. "Is he really worth it?"

The question seemed to stump Kristen for a second. She took one last sip of tea, stood up, smoothed her dress down, and looked at him seriously.

"You've known him a few weeks," she said. "You've driven him around. You've… I guess… caught his eye, and you think you can say what he's worth? He's my future. He's all the plans we made. He's every time I swallowed *this* sort of thing. If he weren't worth it, that would all be wasted, and I don't waste my time. Goodbye, Mr. Tate. If you're smart, this is the last time we'll have to see each other."

Cal leaned back in his chair, the narrow back sharp where it dug in under his shoulder blades. "And if I'm not?"

Kristen slowly picked up her bag and hung it over her shoulder. She stroked the strap with absent fingers.

"Then I guess he'll get to break your heart as well," she said. Her mouth twitched in a tired smile. "It's not like he told me about you. He didn't mention you at all."

Cal could have said the same, but he didn't. After a moment Kristen shrugged and left. Cal didn't watch her walk out. He stared into his plate until he heard the door rattle and chime, and then he looked out the window. Kristen crossed the road, precarious in narrow heels on the deeply rutted tarmac, and crossed down to put something in the drunk's cup. The man emerged from his nylon cocoon to splutter and grip her hand with fervent, surprised gratitude.

Kristen looked embarrassed as she disentangled herself and stood up. The homeless man grabbed whatever was in his cup and stuffed it into his pockets. Cal resented the ability to be kind. It would be easier if she were a bitch.

He left one of Kristen's fifties on the table to pay for breakfast and make the waitress feel like the morning was worthwhile. As he walked down the street, he wished that what Kristen said was as easy to leave behind as her money.

He reached the outside of the hotel, the muscles in his thighs tight as he followed the curve of the drive up from the road, where he pulled his phone out of his pocket and dialed.

It rang through to the answering machine. The "after the tone" message gave Cal time to second-guess himself as he nodded to the doorman and ducked into the hotel. The tone finally went, and Cal supposed he had to say something.

"Hey, Doc," he said. "Cal Tate here. You going to ask me on a second date or not?"

He hung up. Doc called back before he reached the suite. At some point, Cal supposed, he was going to have to learn his name.

Chapter Ten

THE ENVELOPE sat in the middle of the coffee table. It looked innocuous, brown and wrinkled at the edges, but they both knew it wasn't. Neither of them wanted to look at it. Joe, at least, was tired of plain brown envelopes that threatened to ruin his life. He thought briefly about the coolness in Cal's eyes when he handed the envelope over—"it's all there"—but he couldn't dwell on that with something like panic.

"Kris," he said. "What the hell did you think you were doing?"

She looked at her nails and picked at the cuticle on her index finger. When she was younger, she bit them down to the quick—Joe had seen the pictures—but she'd broken herself of the habit. Ladies, she told him once in her sour impersonation of her dad's pompousness, don't have ugly hands. Now she picked at them instead.

"I don't like him," she said.

"You don't have to." Joe walked over to the whiskey and tapped his finger against the bottle. Too early to drink or did the fact he *needed* a drink make it a bad idea whatever time it was. "You should go home."

"You're my home."

Hell.

Joe twisted the top off the whiskey and poured a finger's worth into a tumbler. There was no ice, but neat would do what he needed it to.

"Stop it, Kris," he said. "This isn't going to work. What did you think was going to happen? That you'd pay off my driver and I'd have to ask you to chauffeur me around? Then we'd be stuck in traffic so long I'd fall back in love with you? There are Ubers in London, you know, and taxis."

She muttered something that he didn't catch. Joe took a swig of whiskey and then turned to look at her.

They'd known each other their whole lives, in the way that rich kids from the same city did. His best friend had dated her younger sister. They'd both driven down to a mutual friend's Halloween party in Balboa

Park every year, and they both had issues with their families. Not friends, but they'd known each other in passing.

Joe asked her out the first time because a friend had walked in on him and a man whose name Joe had never learned, half-naked in the back seat of a Hummer. He'd thought he could make himself what everyone wanted, and she was the first step.

It wasn't fair to either of them.

"I don't want to get married, Kris," he said.

"We don't have to," she said as she got to her feet. "If you've got cold feet, if that's what this is about, we can put the wedding off for now. Go back to how we were."

"I don't want to."

She flung her hands up in frustration. "Why not?" she demanded. "We're good together, Joe. We have fun, the papers all want our pictures, our parents are happy. I know we weren't… you know… passionate, but we were happy. So why not?"

It had been good, and Joe had thought it would be good enough. But it hadn't been or, at least, wasn't anymore, not when he knew what it was like to *not care* because a man was so beautiful you had to touch him, or to sit in easy, hazy warm silence and daydream about sand on tattooed skin.

Cal's beauty. Cal's skin.

"I wasn't happy," he said.

Kristen shook her head in denial. "You were," she insisted. "I was there. I could have told if you weren't. I loved you… love you. I don't care that you… had a few slips. Once we're married, it'll be different."

"It won't," Joe said.

"Fine," Kristen said defiantly. She shrugged and smiled glossily when he raised his eyebrows at her. "It's the modern way of doing things, isn't it? Monogamy is old hat."

Joe hesitated. He'd thought it was kinder to blur the edges of their breakup for Kristen, or maybe he hadn't been confident enough that he was done hiding. Maybe he'd wanted to leave himself the chance to walk that decision back.

"I like men," he said. It felt odd. True, but still odd. He wasn't sure if the tight, breathless feeling in his chest was anticipation or dread. "That's not something an open marriage is going to change."

She turned her mouth down in an expressive, impatient shrug. "So you're bi," she said. Her voice had gone brittle, as though her refusal to acknowledge it had started to crack. "I don't care, Joe."

He looked down into his whiskey. The swirl of amber blurred the world. "I'm not bisexual, I'm gay," he said. "I loved you, Kris, but I wasn't in love wit—"

Her hand cracked across his face and knocked the rest of the words back down his throat. The slap caught Joe off guard, and he bit the side of his tongue. The taste of metal and salt mixed with the tang of whiskey. He swallowed and turned his head back to Kris, and she looked as surprised as he felt, her eyes huge and hands trembling. He waited for the apology he would have to reject.

"I hope he leaves you," Kristen spat out instead. She took a step back, legs wobbly under her, and snatched her bag up from the chair. She roughly stuffed the envelope in, on top of the clutter of old lipsticks and Post-it note reminders she had in there. "I hope everyone fucking leaves you. Maybe that's why your mother left you. She could see what a waste of skin you'd grow into. Go to Hell, Joe."

She stalked out of the room and slammed the door behind her. Through the door Joe heard Edward's low, controlled voice murmur something.

"Ask him," Kristen snapped. "You think he's so great, and he's a fucking liar!"

There was a pause, and then Joe heard the door of the hotel slam behind Kristen. She'd stayed in an executive room a few floors down for the duration, but Joe supposed she'd check out now. He sat down on the couch and leaned his head back against the warm leather, eyes closed.

When Edward finally let himself into the room, it wasn't with the question that Joe expected.

"Have you seen this?"

Joe opened his eyes and clenched his jaw against the urge to flinch away as Edward thrust the charred bear into his face. Being stuffed unceremoniously in an envelope had done nothing for its looks. In addition to the burn scars, the stuffing had shifted in its head and one of the crackled eyes had pulled free. Smoke-stained cotton poked out of the hole.

"Where did you get that?"

"Tate's room."

"You searched his room?" Joe asked coldly as he pushed the bear out of his face. "Who, exactly, gave you permission to do that?"

"Technically the room was rented by Bailey Holdings," Edward said as he withdrew the battered stuffed toy. "As their representative, I don't need permission to go through one of our own rooms. Especially when I had suspicions he might be involved in an ongoing security issue. Where the hell did he get this?"

"From me," Joe said. "I asked him to get rid of it. My stalker sent it. I don't know why. Do you?"

Edward glanced down at the charred, malformed thing in his hand. The expression on his face hinted at the same sort of bile-sour horror Joe felt when he looked at it, although maybe there was less confusion mixed in for him.

"No," he said as he slowly unclenched his fingers and set the bear down. Upright. Gently.

"Then why did you think I needed to see it?"

Edward gave him a scathing look. "Look at it," he said. "It's what those of us in the business call a red flag. When did the stalker send this?"

"A few days ago." Joe drained the whiskey and set the glass down. He licked his lips and got up off the couch. "It was delivered by a courier. I didn't get the name."

"Why didn't you tell me?" Edward demanded as he followed Joe to the desk. "This is my job. If I'm going to protect you, protect your family's interests, you can't keep something like this from me."

Joe laughed dryly and held up a hand in halfhearted apology as Edward's face darkened with frustration.

"It's not funny, I know," he said. "But be honest, Edward. That's ironic coming from you, isn't it?"

"What?"

The truth was on the tip of Joe's tongue, but he swallowed before it blurted it out. It still made sense to keep Edward in the dark, at least until Joe had *something* probative to put his finger on. But he was tired of lies—a flat, spent distaste had left a bad taste in his mouth—so he stripped the details off. The bones of that old frustration had been where this started.

"What really happened to my mother?" he asked as he flicked through a stack of folders.

Edward blinked. Once. "What do you mean?" he said. "You know what happened. She died, it was—"

"Sudden," Joe interrupted, "and tragic. But how? Did she have a stroke? Heart attack? You worked for my dad back then. You must have known her."

There was a pause. Edward cleared his throat and nodded slowly. "Only briefly," he said. "I didn't get the chance to get to know her, but I think I would have liked her. Joe, this is something you need to talk to your father about. I didn't…. It's not my place to tell you."

"Tell me what?" Joe asked sharply. "I'm not a child anymore, Edward. I've no idea who this woman was. I barely know what she looked like. You aren't going to burst some bubble I've been carrying around. I want to know the truth."

Edward grimaced, a barely there twitch of his stern mouth. "People say that, Joe," he said. "But they rarely do."

"So there *is* something you're not telling me, then?"

"You're right," Edward said. He paused long enough that Joe braced himself for a confession. "You're not a child anymore and, maybe, your dad owes you some answers. I'll talk to him when we get back, once he's a bit stronger—"

"Or later," Joe suggested with tired disgust. "Or sometime. Tell you what, Edward, don't bother."

"Why does this matter now?" Edward asked. "Because of your father's stroke? He's doing well. The doctors are confident he'll make a full recovery with some physio."

It was a good theory, Joe supposed. The stalker had planted the seed before that, the suspicion that Joe wasn't the only one with secrets, but the idea of being an orphan…. Harry Bailey wasn't the sort of father to inspire sentimental think pieces, but he was the only family Joe had. His mother was dead before he was born, both sets of grandparents dead long before that, no siblings, and none of Harry's girlfriends had ever made it past a fling. It was strange to think of himself completely alone.

That was when he realized he couldn't marry Kristen. She only made him feel more alone.

"I told you, Edward, it doesn't matter," Joe said. "I'm just… that wasn't a particularly pleasant conversation."

Edward looked around, his attention aimed through thick walls toward the St. Pancras lifts, and made a dubious noise under his breath. This was when he'd usually urge Joe to have second thoughts. Not this time.

"What?" Joe asked. "Not going to tell me I've made a mistake?"

Edward pursed his lips for a second as he looked down at the bear. "What's the point. You're not going to listen," he said as he shrugged the distraction off and pointed at the bear. "Tell me about the bear. What happened."

It didn't seem as though Edward deserved an answer, not when he hadn't given Joe any. In the end, it was the thought of Cal that made Joe sit back down to dwell on the details. Since Kristen had arrived, Cal had been distant, and Joe supposed he couldn't blame him for that, so it might win Joe some brownie points if he actually did what Cal suggested and told Edward what had gone on. Some of it.

AN HOUR later they rode the lift down in stiff silence. The awkward chill between them was something Joe was more accustomed to with his dad.

"I have an event to attend this weekend," Joe said as they reached the ground floor. Massive, church-white candles burned in lanterns in alcoves along the hall, shadows long and unsteady across the black-and-white tiled floor. "A charity thing our nearly unretained lawyers thought would be a good PR move."

He left out that it was the charity named on the only picture he had of his mother, which he'd scanned and sent to Bea so she could arrange a meeting. Both his maternal grandparents had died from cancer, and Abigail Bailey had not only fund-raised for the cancer charity, she'd volunteered, campaigned, and served on the board. If she was still alive, she'd still be involved. She didn't seem like the sort of woman who gave up on things once she started.

Joe tried to feel proud of her, but it didn't work. She seemed admirable, but there wasn't that personal connection that made Joe want to go "she's with me." Sometimes Joe wondered if there was something a little wrong with him, deep down where the emotional connective tissue was.

He wasn't the first to consider that.

Edward grunted as he took his trench coat from over his arm and shrugged it on. The light cotton hung from his shoulders as he roughly cinched it around his waist. "Short notice," he noted. "Send me the details so I can vet it?"

"It's an established cancer charity," Joe pointed out, "not a roundtable on international diplomacy. I don't think it needs a background check."

"Or it's a cancer charity," Edward lobbed back to Joe, "so they won't have done a proper security survey on the premises. Don't worry, I'll be discreet. They won't know I was there any more than Mr. Tate will."

Joe winced at the reminder. He was coward enough to hope that was true, but he wasn't proud of it.

"Speaking of that," he said. "You can't unsearch a room, but in future, Cal's off-limits. Understand, Edward?"

Disapproval puckered Edward's mouth. He might have dropped the refrain of reconciliation with Kristen, but apparently not the notion that he had a proprietary interest in Joe's life. He knew—on some level he had to know—but it never seemed to set as a fact in his brain. That might never change, but Joe didn't care what Edward thought of his love life anymore.

He hesitated for a second, aware of the dull-bruise ache of regret in the back of his brain. So maybe he still cared. It was hard to stop when you'd spent years worried what someone would think, what they would pass on to Harry. But not enough to twist himself into knots. Not anymore.

"He's trouble," Edward said flatly. "Always has been. He's like his mother."

Joe snorted. "Maybe I like trouble," he said.

There was a pause as Edward straightened the cuffs of his jacket with scarred fingers. He cleared his throat and shrugged. "Yeah, that's probably what that doctor Tate's been dating thinks too," he said. "He's certainly eager enough. If I got ditched on a first date so someone could head to work, I don't know if I'd go to have dinner at their hotel. I guess Dr. Lawrence is a more forgiving man than me. He even turned up on time."

Disappointment caught like a stone in the back of Joe's throat. He knew he didn't exactly have the right. Neither of them had made any promises, and while Joe had broken up with Kristen before he left California, the fact he'd had to spend the last two days finalizing it blurred the moral high ground a bit. But it was still there, cold and rough with the expectation he'd fucked this up. Even if he didn't have a clue what this might be.

He wasn't about to let Edward see that. "Or," he said as he adjusted his collar with absent precision, "Cal's hotter than your dates. Hard to say."

"Not for me," Edward said. "I'm happy with my taste in women. It's a shame you weren't. I won't be at this thing tonight for more than an hour. I'll let you know when I'm back."

"No need," Joe said. "Have a good time. Enjoy yourself. I don't have any plans to leave the hotel this evening. And I promise if I receive another burned bear, I'll tell you first."

He sketched a cross over his heart with one finger.

Edward scowled at him. "Take it seriously, Joe. They're escalating and you don't want to end up with more scars, do you?"

Joe reached up without any real intention to do so and rubbed his finger across the scars dappled along his temple. Most of the time he didn't really think about them. They had been part of his face for as long as he could remember, as unremarkable as his nose or eyebrows. Now he thought about the bear's melted ear and charred cheek and wondered sickly how much that would hurt on flesh.

It felt like he knew the answer—not the easily assumed "a lot" but the actual, visceral raw-meat pain of it. He didn't remember when he'd been scalded, but maybe his nerves did.

"That's enough," he said, his voice dry and sticky in his throat.

Edward studied him with narrowed, ice blue eyes for a second as he seemed to weigh the impact his words had. After a moment he gave a brisk dip of his chin.

"Maybe it is," he said. "Finally. If anything happens, call me. Anything at all. Trust me, after an hour I'll want a graceful excuse to leave. Something like this goes from 'catching up with old friends' to 'bunch of old codgers complaining about how it used to be done back in the day' very quickly."

Joe nodded his agreement, and Edward turned to leave. He got a few steps and then turned around to look at Joe.

"I know I'm not your dad, Joey" he said. "I never tried to be. But you're still the closest thing I have to family, and everything I do is with your best interests at heart. Even if you don't see it at the time. I hope you know that."

Joe knew that Edward believed that, and he was tired of arguments, so he nodded. "I know you mean well, Edward."

There was enough room left between the words of that statement for everything else, from the fact that Edward had been the one to sit with Joe when they thought Harry was going to die to the fact that he thought only he knew best. Both of them knew that. After a second, Edward nodded and left, his hands shoved into the pockets of his coat.

Which left Joe with a decision to make. The plan had been to come down, cut through to King's Cross, grab a coffee from Starbucks, and then go back to run an eye over the redundancy paperwork for their local employees. It needed done, and it really wasn't his business what Cal did. Or who he ate with.

He still headed for the hotel restaurant. By the time he got there, he was sure he'd have come up with an excuse for why he picked tonight to eat at the hotel.

Or not. If Cal didn't owe him anything, he didn't owe Cal an explanation.

The restaurant was all dark wood and crystal lights. It was full of murmured conversation and the busy click of cutlery on good china. The host, her hair up in a bouncy blonde ponytail, a tailored gray vest buttoned snug over her stomach, smiled politely at him.

"Do you need to be seated, sir?" she asked.

Joe glanced over her head. He tracked across the tables until he found Cal's profile, half-lit by the candle on the table. The man opposite was short but solid across the shoulders. His blond hair was styled back from his face, and his mouth was open as he held forth about something.

It could be hard to tell what Cal was thinking, except for the times he cracked that goofy grin, but Joe thought he had the knack of it. The smile that tugged one corner of his mouth up didn't have the sly turn that his humor usually took. He didn't look at the other man—the doctor—the way he looked at Joe. If he had, Joe supposed that Dr. Lawrence would have already rented a room for them.

He smiled at the host and pointed across the room.

"In that booth over there," he said. "By the window."

"Ahh…." The hostess turned and ran her pen down the reservations book. "That should be fine. Follow me."

She led the way to the booth, handed him a menu, and assured him that the waiter would be with him soon. As she left, Dr. Lawrence chuckled at something as he sliced into his fish, and Cal watched him and drank his soda.

Joe waited until he'd put his order in. Salad and a glass of sparkling water. After the day he'd had, whiskey made sense, but this was already a bad idea. No point in more fuel for it. While he waited for the waiter, he typed out a brusque message to Cal.

The deal was 24/7 after all.

He hit Send and waited. Across the room Cal shifted in his chair and said something to Lawrence as he reached into his pocket. He studied the screen for a second and then slowly looked around to scowl at Joe.

"Fuck off," he mouthed.

Joe texted him back *No* and smirked.

Chapter Eleven

Asshole.

Cal shut his phone off and turned back around in his chair to grimace apologetically over the table. Doc frowned at him, blue eyes somewhere between irritated and disappointed behind smudge-free lenses.

"Work again?" he asked. "Who'd have thought being a driver was so demanding. I save lives for a living, but they still give me time to eat."

Cal had to give him the jab about drivers. At this point even Cal, who'd always kind of viewed dating as a contact sport, had to admit he was being a dick. Not to mention the fact that an hour into their second date, he still didn't know Doc's real name. Cal had never noticed before how rarely you said your own name in conversation.

Yet somehow the guy couldn't let five minutes pass without the reminder he was a doctor.

"Long hours, short contracts," Cal said shortly. "End of the month, I could be sitting on my thumbs."

The doc laughed. "Or mine," he said. "If tonight goes well."

Cal paused and gave him a dubious look. That was weird. Doc realized it too as he laughed nervously and jabbed his fork into a piece of fish. It disintegrated into the sauce.

"That, umm, came out wrong," Doc said.

"I noticed," Cal said. He glanced back over his shoulder to see what Joe was doing. Still spying on Cal's date was the answer. Cal glared at him in frustration and then tried to smooth his face back out as he looked at Doc. "Look, do you mind if I step out for five minutes?"

Frustration pinched Doc's mouth together in a puckered line. "Actually, I'd rather you not," he said. "Most of my dates don't feel the need for a breather."

Cal looked at him for a second, shrugged, and got up anyhow. He crumpled his napkin up and dropped it next to the half-eaten burger he'd ordered. First Kristen at breakfast and now this. Apparently there was a conspiracy that didn't want him to finish a meal.

"Up to you," he said. "Tell the waiter to bill the meal to my room."

Color spread across Doc's cheekbones, under the wire rims of his glasses. He put his knife and fork down on the plate.

"I don't appreciate this," he said stiffly. "And I don't deserve it."

"I know," Cal said. "That's why I'm covering the bill. See you around, Doc."

"You won't."

Cal thought about that for a second. "Seems fair," he said and headed across the restaurant to Joe's booth. He leaned his shoulder against the hard wooden edge of it and scowled down at Joe, who looked lean and elegant in a gray suit and lavender tie. His hair had wilted out of its quiff and fallen into loose dark curls around his face. Cal didn't think about what it would feel like to bury his fingers in them, because he'd decided that wasn't what he wanted.

Liar, a sly little voice accused from the back of his brain where he kept all the things he had to work at not caring about—his mum, being an ex-con, the fact he was built to be a dirty little secret—*you want all of it.*

It was, for once, wrong. Cal didn't. He wanted Joe, but he didn't want closed bedroom doors and plausible deniability in public. But Kristen was right—that was all that was ever going to be on offer. Not because of her either. Take her out of the equation and Cal was still the itch that got scratched on a dirty weekend, not the guy you brought home to Mum.

Hell, even his own mum didn't want that.

"I'm on a date," he said as he crossed his arms. "This couldn't wait?"

Joe leaned back in the booth and laced his hands together on the table. "Hmm, now you mention it, I suppose it could," he said. "However, since I guess the date's over now? Do you have anything better to do?"

"Do you? Because I had him to do," Cal said as he jerked his thumb over his shoulder toward the table. "So my night was all booked up."

Joe leaned out of the booth to check the table. "He's still there," he said. "I can wait if you want."

Shit.

The immediate, dismayed reaction made Cal wince. Okay, so the date hadn't gone great. He probably shouldn't be disappointed that the date hadn't already ended badly.

Cal turned to look and the table was empty. The plates with their half-eaten meal were abandoned, and Doc's wineglass had been drained to the dregs. Guilt tried to pinch at Cal's stomach, but it struggled to make an impact through the quick rush of relief. Maybe later.

"You're an asshole," he told Joe.

"Maybe," Joe admitted. "But you looked like someone had told you that you could have seconds of a shit sandwich, so don't pretend you're that annoyed I interrupted. What was wrong with him?"

"Nothing," Cal said sourly. So he hadn't enjoyed the doc's company that much, but Joe had still been a dick to interrupt them. Cal could ruin his own dates without any help. "You're paying for his dinner, by the way."

Joe didn't look bothered, or sorry. "I see," he said, as though Cal had given something away. "So he just wasn't me?"

The calm confidence in Joe's voice made Cal squirm as lust prickled under his skin and between his legs. It didn't really make sense. The doc's boasts about his medical degree had bored him, but Joe's arrogance turned Cal on. Maybe because, with Joe, it wasn't a boast, it was… conviction.

"Join me," Joe said as he pointed over the table. "I already paid for the meal. You might as well eat it."

The thing was that Cal wanted to say yes. He wanted to have dinner with Joe, go upstairs, and get fucked until he forgot all the stuff he wanted and couldn't have. But he had a feeling that, for once, that wasn't going to work.

"I don't think so," he said.

"Cal—"

Cal didn't let Joe finish. "The doc was pompous and a bit of a prig. But at least he wasn't so ashamed to be seen with me that he needed to pretend that dinner was a business meeting, not a date."

For the first time Joe looked as though he'd been caught off guard. "I just…. Look, what did you want me to do, come over and punch him?"

Cal pushed himself off the booth and tucked his hands into his pockets. There was a tight knot of words caught in his throat—the sarcastic admission that "it would have been hot" tangled with the raw "you could have asked me first"—but in the end, he didn't say any of them. What was the point?

"Why would you?" he asked. "Like you told Kristen, your love life is nothing to do with me. So return the favor."

The flustered expression on Joe's face had faded. It gave way to a cool, irritated expression. The muscles in the sides of his jaw clenched as he glanced around at the nearby tables.

"This is hardly the place to discuss this," he said.

"Yeah," Cal said. "Exactly. Look, I'm not complaining. We both got exactly what we wanted, Joe, and it was fun. If you want to fuck? Sure, you know where my room is. But don't try and pretend we're dating, as long as no one else knows about it. I don't deserve that sort of shit."

Joe looked frustrated. He still kept his voice down to a tight, discreet mutter. "So, to be clear, sex is okay but not dinner?"

"More or less," Cal said. He stepped back from the table and gave Joe an empty smile. "Forward me the itinerary you wanted to go over, Mr. Bailey, and I'll go over it tonight. Enjoy your salad."

He turned to leave and caught the eye of an elegant, gray-haired woman who'd obviously shamelessly eavesdropped on them over her soup. Caught in the act, she smiled at Cal with white, even teeth and winked.

"Smart boy," she hissed her approval at him on his way past her table. "Never take sex off the table. Or jewelry."

He laughed despite the fact he felt like shit, and didn't look back on his way out of the restaurant. The flash of humor got him all the way back up to the suite and then drained away as he closed the door to his room. He dropped his head back against the door with a thump and wondered what the hell had possessed him.

It had seemed like the right thing to do in the moment, but where had he gotten him? Now his cock thought he was an idiot, his heart ached, and his stomach didn't know why it had to suffer in all this. Cal rubbed his forehead and wondered why the hell he hadn't shut his mouth. He could have had dinner, had sex, and if his heart hurt later… well, it did *now.* So he didn't see what he'd bloody accomplished.

CAL WOKE up to the sound of the first train of the day leaving, muffled through the thick walls and triple-glazed windows. He growled under his breath and buried his face in the pillow, his arm hooked over his head.

His head felt muzzy with a mixture of embarrassment and exhaustion. Last night he'd stayed up, checked his phone every ten minutes, and realized two things—first, that he made himself look like a soft idiot when he spewed his feelings all over the restaurant last night, and second, that Joe might know where Cal's bed was, but he wasn't about to knock on the door. Or text.

Oh, and third, that he probably owed Doc some sort of apology.

"Shit," Cal muttered into the pillow. He waited a while longer, until he could taste the damp from his breath against the cotton, and then rolled over onto his back. Maybe he should have been more sympathetic to El about the divorce. He'd known Joe for two weeks, and he felt like crap. If it had been years, he'd probably drink himself into a grave next to his grandparents.

The thought made Cal grimace sourly at this own dramatics. He scrambled out of bed, showered, dressed, and was ready to go by seven o'clock. Since no one had come to get him, or fire him, he assumed he wasn't needed yet.

That gave him time to make a couple of calls. The first two were easy—a blunt apology to Doc and a blunt reminder for Van that he wasn't a patient man. It was the last call that made him hesitate, his hands sweaty and his stomach sour from more than hunger. He didn't even know what the point of it was now. He was pretty sure he'd burned his bridges with Joe last night. This wasn't going to fix that.

He dialed away. It went to voicemail. Of course it did.

"It's Cal. Caleb," he said. Although he supposed she would know who he was anyhow. "Can you call me? It won't take long. I wanted to ask about someone you used to know. El said you knew him anyhow. It's important."

Ten years ago he'd have offered her money. That had always been a surefire way to get his mum to answer a call. She'd always needed money. These days her husband could give her whatever she wanted. He was a dentist or chiropodist, or something.

"If I don't hear from you," he said, and it didn't feel good that that was the best lever he had to get her to do something, "I'll call back."

He hung up. They weren't the sort of family who lingered over sentimental sign-offs.

It was done. Now he didn't have any excuse to loiter in his room. Cal glanced at his reflection in the mirror and gave his collar a tug to hide the edges of his tattoo. For a second, the memory of Joe's mouth on his throat—as he traced the ink with tongue and teeth—was so vivid he could feel the heat on his skin.

Cal scrubbed it away impatiently with the back of his hand. People who second-guessed themselves weren't good drivers, or thieves, and Cal was both. He'd drawn a line. Joe had decided not to cross it. Time to move on.

Not only emotionally either. It might be time to do it literally. After he heard from Van and his mum, he'd ask El to swap him out with another driver. Until then Cal could act like an adult.

That was almost as good as being one.

IT WAS like the first time they'd fucked. You wouldn't know anything at all had happened from Joe's behavior. He sat in the back, immersed in paperwork, emails, and the occasional brisk phone call. They had driven from the hotel to the abandoned housing development that Bailey Holdings were selling. The red-haired lawyer from the other day—Bea, Cal thought—had been there with two separate folders and a grim-faced man who'd thrown his clipboard down and stalked off in a rage.

Not good news, then.

"What time is it?" Joe asked as he looked up from the file.

Cal gave Joe a look in the rearview mirror. His phone had been in his hand five minutes ago. "Nearly two," he said. "Where next, Mr. Bailey?"

"I need to be at Saville Row by half three," Joe said as he closed the file and tucked it away in his briefcase. "I made an appointment for a fitting."

Cal forgot himself for a second and snorted. "You need more clothes?"

The slip from coolly professional made Cal wince. He spun his map of the city in his head and plotted out the quickest route through the narrow streets. It would be tight, but with the sort of money Joe spent on his clothes, Cal supposed the tailor would be more accommodating than your average dentist. He flicked the indicator on and changed lanes, the sleek shape of the Bentley tucked between the bumper of a white van and a blue Mini driven by a woman with a nervous face and a death grip on the wheel.

"Nothing wrong with looking nice, Cal," Joe said.

"I do all right," Cal said. "And I don't even own a suit."

"No," Joe said softly. Something hot and dark curled through his voice. It stroked down Cal's back like a hand. "You look hot. There's a difference."

Cal risked a quick glance in the mirror, but Joe had already dropped his attention back to his phone. The itch of hunger that lodged under Cal's skin, down his spine and along his inner thighs didn't seem to be mutual. Cal dragged his attention back to the road and wished his grandad were still about to clip him around the back of the head—not that it had ever knocked sense into him as a kid.

The thought of it certainly did nothing to discourage the lustful notion that it would be kinda hot to see Joe get all fitted up for a fancy suit.

Forty minutes later Cal stood in front of a full-length mirror while a prim young woman with a pencil clenched between her teeth measured his inseam. At the end of the process, she spat it out and scribbled the numbers down in her pad.

Once she was finished, she sat back on her heels. "Okay. It's short notice, but we can find something on the rack and then tailor it a little to fit." Her eyes tracked up to Cal's shoulders, bare except for ink, and she pursed her lips. "Maybe a lot. Do you have any preference for color."

"Gray?"

"Navy," Joe corrected from where he stood next to a wall of fabric bolts. "Three-piece. Maybe something in herringbone?"

The woman tilted head her to the side thoughtfully, her eyes narrowed as she considered Cal, and then nodded in approval. "Good choice, Mr. Tate," she said as she hopped to her feet. "Hold on a minute."

She ducked out of the shop, between the ranks of blank-faced, well-dressed mannequins. Cal scowled at Joe.

"What the hell is this?" he asked.

Joe pinched a paisley-patterned bolt of cloth between thumb and forefinger. "I didn't say the fitting was for me."

"I don't need you to buy me a suit."

Joe leaned back against the heavy wooden table, years of use scarred into the polished surface, and crossed his arms. He tilted his head to the side. "You didn't need to take off your trousers," he pointed out. "But you did. So you can't mind that much."

It had been the "please," soft and damp against his jaw, and Joe's hand firm in the small of his back. By the time Cal remembered they weren't doing this anymore, his trousers had been over a hanger and the woman's tape measure had been looped around his chest. By the time he worked his way up to annoyance, she was already on her knees. Last woman who'd been down there had told him to cough.

"You're lucky I'm wearing briefs," Cal muttered darkly to Joe.

Joe grinned. "For now," he said. "I wouldn't get used to it."

Before Cal could ask if that was a come-on or something to do with his new suit, the woman was back with three suits draped over her arm and more shirts than Cal owned dangling from her other hand.

"Here." She thrust a dark blue cotton shirt at him. "Try this one first."

They stared at him expectantly and Cal gave in and pulled the shirt on. All those years and those people who tried to teach him how to behave, and all they'd needed to do was to make it uncomfortable to make a scene.

"It's a bit small," he said. The fabric was tight over his shoulders, and the collar pinched across his Adam's apple. "I feel like I'm wearing my brother's shirt to go to court."

The woman snorted at him and brushed his hands away from the buttons. She did them up, top to bottom, with brisk efficiency. "It's meant to be fitted," she said. "Did you really do all that work on those muscles not to show them off?"

She stepped back and looked at Joe with raised eyebrows. "What do you think?" she asked.

"Maybe something with a grandad collar?" Joe suggested. "Show off his ink."

"Oh, yes," the woman said. "Lean in. Good idea."

She disappeared again. Cal figured he didn't want to know what she thought he was meant to lean in to. He hooked his finger into the collar of the shirt and gave in to the absurdity of the whole situation.

"So what?" He winked saucily at Joe in the mirror. "You want to go the full *Pretty Woman* here? I could be into that, I guess."

"No." Joe pushed himself off the table and walked over to stand behind Cal, one hand casually on his shoulder. "You were right. No more pretending to go out. It wasn't fair. On either of us."

The collar of the shirt tightened around Cal's throat as he swallowed. It usually felt better to be right. He let the disappointment settle.

"So we're clear," he said as he twisted to look over his shoulder at Joe. "Sex is still very fair. You give. I take. We both get off."

Joe leaned in and kissed him. He tightened his arm around Cal's shoulder, knuckles tucked up under Cal's chin to hold him in place. Warmth spilled over Cal's tongue and down his throat and then spread through his stomach and down into his thighs. It made the heavy muscles tense and tremble in anticipation.

After a second, Joe leaned back. He was still close enough that Cal could feel his breath, the heavy rise of Joe's cock pressed hard and insistent against Cal's ass through the pointless barrier of thin cotton. There were people in the shop outside, sales staff and clientele, and the woman was going to be back any moment with the replacement shirt. The threat of discovery sparked off Cal's nerve endings and prickled his skin with eager goose bumps.

"I'm going to one of the fund-raisers my mother used to support," Joe said. "There's a chance they can point me in the right direction. I want you to come with me."

Cal frowned. He thought he might have missed something, but it was hard to focus with Joe's cock nearly—not nearly enough—in his ass.

"Well, how else would you get there?" he asked. "You don't drive, and I can't see your posh ass on the underground."

Joe rolled his eyes and kissed him again. A laugh trembled between their lips as their tongues tangled.

"I want you to come with me as my date, you idiot," Joe muttered into Cal's mouth, between soft, nipped bites. He strayed down to Cal's jaw and scraped his teeth over the freshly shaven skin. "Out where everyone can see. Where anyone can see."

"Even Edward?"

Joe rested his head against Cal's shoulder and sighed into the corner of his neck. "Edward doesn't want to see," he admitted. "He has to know, but he doesn't have to admit. Well? Do you want to go out with me, Cal Tate?"

It was the sort of answer that should have been easy. Cal wanted to. He wanted a nice life, stable, on the right side of the law. It was too good to be true. If you were too happy, there was no way it was real. It was the rug over the pit, ready to be yanked out from under your feet.

"So the suit's so I don't show you up?" he said roughly.

Joe pressed closer against his back. He slid his hands down to Cal's hips, spread across the bare flat of his stomach under the loose shirt. "Wear shorts if you want." He lifted his head and smiled wickedly at Cal in the mirror. "I want to see you in a nice suit and then take it off you. If it bothers you, you can pay me back for it."

"Fuck off," Cal snorted. He felt as though he'd stepped back onto solid ground. The precarious happiness was still there, but being a dick made him feel better about it. “I’m not paying for some monkey suit so you can get off on it.”

The curtain tugged back, and the woman, shirts dangling from both hands on hangers, stepped in.

“Here we go…. Oh.” Her eyebrows shot up as she got an eyeful and she quickly stepped back out. The curtain rattled shut behind. “Sorry, but that’s not—”

“I asked him out,” Joe said as he stepped back. He straightened his cuffs and collar. “He said yes.”

“That’s nice,” the woman said. “But you’re going to wrinkle the shirt, and we only have ten minutes left before my next appointment arrives.”

Cal glanced down at himself, his cock half-hard under black cotton and his balls aching. He didn’t want to have to zip that into a pair of slim-fit trousers.

“Give me the shirts,” he said. “And give me a couple of minutes, okay.”

She stuck her arm through the curtain, shirts hung from a hooked finger, and waited for him to take them.

“Five minutes,” she said. There was a pause and then a prim little reminder, “Don’t make a mess.”

Cal grimaced. He wasn’t about to jerk off on Saville Row, but he supposed some people would. Retail was hell. Instead he closed his eyes and thought about cold showers and the weak, wrung-out feeling when he got stabbed.

It was effective enough to make his ribs itch with the memory of it but didn’t do much to discourage his cock.

“Hope you’re happy,” he grumbled to Joe as he stripped the shirt. He put on one that the woman had handed in to him. It was still snug over the shoulders, but the collar fit better. When he looked at himself in the mirror, he caught Joe watching with a still, thoughtful expression. He paused, buttons down halfway up his chest. “What?”

“I am,” Joe said. He gave Cal’s ass a quick grope on the way past. “I’ll be happier later, when I can make a mess.”

Heat puddled in Cal’s stomach, a weight of it in his groin, at the low suggestion. His barely discouraged cock popped back up again to nudge against the waistband of his briefs. He swore and pressed it down with the heel of his hand, and the dull ache of it throbbed in his gut.

“Try your suit on,” Joe told him. “I’ll send Ms. Kettler back so she can mark you up for adjustments.”

He ducked out through the curtain and tugged it straight behind him. Cal snorted after him, finished up the buttons on the shirt, and then grabbed a pair of trousers at random. He didn't know a dart from a seam. He just wanted to be dressed when the tailor came back. The legs were shorter than Cal usually wore his jeans, bunched around his ankles or frayed where he'd walked on them, and the fit felt odd.

Still, Cal checked his reflection in the full-length mirror and rubbed his hand over his cropped head. He did look hot in a nice suit.

Chapter Twelve

UNDER NORMAL circumstances it wouldn't be a great start to the day. The coffee was bad, the breakfast had been lukewarm, and Lem Jeter, whose investment in a dilapidated hospital in Cornwall looked more a losing proposition than ever, hated Joe's guts. Today, though, none of that was sufficient to put a dent in Joe's good mood. He'd woken up with Cal in his bed, a full-size hot-water bottle with an arm slung loosely over Joe's hip and his face buried in Joe's pillow.

That was a first.

Joe wasn't sure if he wanted to let Cal know that, but he was sure he wanted to wake up like that again.

"You know what?" Lem said as he shoved his meticulous proposal impatiently into his briefcase. He lurched to his feet and nearly spilled all the paper back out again. A quick scramble got the briefcase clutched awkwardly in his arms as he glared at Joe over it. "Go *fuck* yourself, Mr. Bailey. All I needed was another year to finish the refurb, and I'd have brought money in. Now I'm going to lose the property. Do you *understand* that? None of us are going to get anything back on this."

Joe pushed his coffee cup away from the edge of the table. "My company won't lose any more money either," he said bluntly. The Cornwall project had never been his idea of a good investment anyhow, but Harry had an occasional weakness for a whimsical project well done. The problem with Jeter was that he'd let well done consume him year after year as he finished one quarter of the project to perfection. "I appreciate your passion, Mr. Jeter—"

Jeter spat on the table and stormed out of the cafe. The door slammed behind him, hard enough to make another customer look up from his laptop.

"Penny for your thoughts?" Edward asked as he produced a folded paper napkin and wiped up the clot of sputum. He folded the napkin with a distasteful curl of his lip and dropped it into the dregs of his tea.

For the first time in a while, Joe thought he might give an honest answer to that question. He studied Edward for a second over the coffee and wondered what his reaction would be once there was no more plausible deniability. Joe thought it would be okay, in the end. Or maybe that was more hope.

"That after this tour, you'll have to work double time to stay on top of the death threats," Joe said dryly. "You might need an assistant."

Whatever reaction Edward would have to Joe dating a man could wait. He had enough balls to keep in the air—the search for his mother, his responsibilities to the business, his stalker—that he couldn't afford to add Edward.

Although, it occurred to Joe, the latter wouldn't have the flesh and bone of Cal to offer up as evidence. Joe would be back in LA, and Cal would be back on the market for some doctor to pick up. The thought sank through Joe's lingering good mood like a cold stone, despite his attempt to brush it away.

It wasn't a tragedy—you had to know someone at least a year for their absence to be a tragedy—but that didn't mean Joe had to like it. He grimaced to himself as he lifted the bitter coffee to his mouth. There were too many feelings around lately. Joe was used to a more limited range.

"Speaking of that," Edward said. "When did the stalker first make contact again, the original emails that you didn't think were serious enough to escalate to internal security?"

"Earlier this year," Joe said. "March."

"There was a… vlog?" Edward asked. He wasn't computer illiterate. Cybersecurity came under his oversight at the company too, but you could still hear the air quotes he put around the word. "You said it was after that."

Joe took a drink of coffee. "It was one of Eric's starlets," he said, the mention of his least reliable friend enough to make Edward scowl. It wasn't exactly the story that Joe had told Cal either, so he supposed he wasn't so proud of the company he sometimes kept. "Antoni. She got stoned, Eric got pushy, so I got her out of there. Some man with a handheld camera jumped us outside, shouted the usual gibberish to try and piss us off. I ignored him, poured Antoni in the car, and drove her home."

Edward pulled his phone out of his pocket and pulled something off. When he turned it around so Joe could see the screen, it was the grubby street outside the bar with him and Antoni caught in an image-editing-program-enhanced spotlight. She had her face buried in his shoulder to avoid the camera, and Joe remembered he'd nearly choked on the floating, brown curls. But the blog had splashed an "actress caught in romantic clinch with property magnate heir" red ticker over the photo.

"Could Kristen have thought there was any truth to the headline?" Edward asked.

"Antoni wasn't who she had to worry about," Joe said dryly. It might not be the right time to shove Joe's orientation under Edward's nose, but he wasn't going to indulge Edward anymore either.

"Did she know that?" Edward asked. He turned around and raised his hand to catch a waiter's eye. He mouthed "tea" and held up one finger.

Joe frowned. "You think Kristen sent me those letters?" he asked dubiously.

"She had reason," Edward pointed out. "You didn't treat her well, and… she's had problems in the past. After her parents split up, she keyed the mistress's car and sent her hate mail."

"She was thirteen," Joe pointed out. Although he remembered when Kristen had told him about it, the real venom in her voice when she mentioned her stepmother's name. Age hadn't changed how she felt. The flicker of doubt made him feel guilty, and he struggled to think of something else to disprove the accusation. "And it wasn't anonymous."

"So she learned her lesson and kept her name out of it this time," Edward said. He paused as the waiter brought his refreshed tea and took away the empty cup. "It makes sense, especially how it escalated after you broke up with her. Not to mention that she arrived the same day the bear was sent in the post. I should have considered her originally, but I hadn't realized you were having problems."

That would be ironic. He'd thought the stalker knew some sort of dark family secret, but it was Kristen getting pissed off after a couple of glasses of wine. Of course Edward didn't know about the man who'd jumped Joe at the graveyard. Kristen had still been in California then, although Joe supposed that even two-bit English thugs had PayPal.

"The bear, though," he said slowly. Even the thought of the charred blue fur made the back of Joe's throat taste like bile. He washed it away with the bitter coffee. "It… disturbed me."

Edward snorted as he tasted his tea, made a face, and added more sugar. "It was creepy, right enough." He chuckled, scratched between his knuckles, and picked off a rough bit of old scar. "But maybe that got it out of her system? I'll keep an eye on it, but I think maybe the closure will help cut it off."

Part of Joe wanted to argue that it was more than that. The bear had made him feel the same way a lift did, trapped and skin-stinging hot. It was hard to get the words out. He never talked about his claustrophobia, about the sour sweat under his arms every time he had to ride in a packed elevator. Harry, Joe knew, assumed he'd grown out of it like a kid who was afraid of the dark.

So he changed the subject instead. "I have a meeting with Bea, the lawyer, in ten minutes," he said. "We're going to discuss continuing the company's support of some charities in the UK on an ongoing basis. Good publicity, in case we ever decide to expand back into the local market. Do you want to go and—"

"Do anything else?" Edward asked. He sucked down half his tea in one quick, mouth-scalding gulp. He glanced at his watch. "Since I doubt the young lady is going to pose a threat, I'll actually go and check in with Harry. He's not enjoying being out of the loop. Anything you want me to tell him?"

Joe smirked briefly as he entertained the idea of whether or not he could make Edward tell Harry that his son was gay. The notion had its appeal, but it supposed it was the sort of thing he had to do himself.

"I hope he's getting some rest," Joe said.

Edward nodded, placed a tip on the table, and left. Alone for a while, Joe collected his coffee and moved to a table in front of the window. He watched the tourists file over the road and queue for the British Museum. The selfie shuffle on the forecourt, as everyone tried to get a shot of the Museum with no one else in it, amused him until Bea arrived.

She jingled through the door with her arm around the shy red-haired woman from the other day. A quick kiss and the woman laughed—a surprisingly big, sweet sound—and headed for the counter while Bea came over to him.

"Perfectly professional," she told him with a sly smile as she slid into the seat, long legs in flower-patterned tights tucked under her. "Rosie actually works for someone on the board of the charity. That's how I scored your tickets."

Joe raised his eyebrows. "That's a coincidence."

"Not really. Our firm has worked with this charity before. The board member who Rosie works for is a client, and a few of the trusts that we administer include donations made to various hospices and respite programs that the charity runs." Bea set her laptop bag in her lap and pulled out a neatly bound set of documents. She pulled a rueful face at Joe over them. "Apparently that's how we met the first time, but I guess she wasn't as cute and flustered then. Anyhow, I had a look, like you asked, at all the legal filings and contracts that my firm has done for your… company. Which you currently represent and, therefore, have every right to access. The only thing that really stood out was this—for fifteen years, your father, through a blind trust, bought and maintained a small house in Reading *and* paid a monthly stipend to the owner."

"Could it be my mother?" Joe asked. Maybe his mother had some sort of mental illness. Harry wasn't a monster, but like Joe's claustrophobia, he expected people would get better from their anxiety or depression if they tried.

Before he could speculate too far, Bea shook her head. "The owner was a widower with a young daughter," she said. A quick flight through her files pulled out a photocopy of a newspaper article with a photo of a stocky, bearded man as he carried a little red-haired girl with bandaged hands out of a graveyard. Bea tapped the blurred faces with a well-manicured finger. "Keith Mantle and his daughter, Daisy. The stipend is still paid, actually. After Keith died, we were instructed to pay it directly into a new account that Daisy was given access to."

"What was the connection between this man and Harry?" Joe asked.

Bea pursed her lips. "Well, nothing obvious," she said. "But… his wife died in a car accident. The little girl was in the car with her at the time. It was apparently pretty horrific, although reports stated that there had been only one car involved in the accident. The papers interviewed a witness—a woman from London out for the night—and she said the woman was alive when the car started to burn. Awful. The payments started around six months after that. It sounds to me like a guilty conscience."

"Dad doesn't drive," Joe said. "He's got epilepsy. He never learned."

"Maybe your mum, then?" Bea said. When he frowned at her, she spread her hands in apology. "Sorry, but it feels like a payoff to me, and one this generous? That's a personal connection. Anyhow, here's everything we have about it."

She handed the file over, zipped up her bag, and gave him an inquisitive look. "If there's nothing else?" she said. "I'll see you tonight."

Joe riffled through the pages she'd given him. There were pictures of the house, a report from an insurance company, and nothing that proved anything.

"Nothing else," he said. "Thank you."

"Keep me in mind in future," Bea said as she unfolded herself from the chair and glanced at her watch. "Now if you'll excuse me, I have half an hour to enjoy my lunch date…."

She looked around and bit her lip in distracted appreciation. Joe followed her gaze and Rosie had balanced cake plates precariously on top of two different-sized coffee cups as she wove through the tables. Her hair was in a scruffy ponytail, and she was in jeans and a shirt decorated with little birds. Each, Joe supposed, to their own.

There were probably people who didn't think Cal was attractive.

NO. JOE watched Cal ruin the line of his trousers by putting his hands in his pockets. He'd been wrong. This had to be universal.

Cal smirked at him. "Hot as you hoped?"

Hotter. The dark blue was a soft contrast to Cal's pale skin and tawny hair, and the tailoring showcased the heft of his shoulders and then tucked in to expose his narrow waist and lean hips. He still looked like bad news, but Joe would have been disappointed if they'd styled that out of him.

"You look," Joe said as he pushed himself off the doorframe, "like we don't have to leave for a while."

He walked over and cupped his hand around the nape of his Cal's neck to pull him into a kiss. His cropped hair was stubble-rough under his fingers, and the compliant tilt of Cal's heavy muscled body toward him made Joe's stomach twist with sharp pangs of lust. Stubble still grazed along his jaw, a golden scruff that scraped Joe's lips and tasted like cologne.

Joe worked his hands under Cal's jacket, his skin hot under the thin silk of the shirt, and he started to shove it off his shoulders. Before he got it down as far as the elbow, Cal bit his lower lip and shoved Joe backward.

"You made me get all dressed up," Cal said as he shrugged the jacket back up over his shoulders. "Now you get to take me out. Unless you've changed your mind."

There was something expectant in the way he said that, like he figured Joe had. If it weren't for that, Joe probably would have dragged him back over to the bed. Joe licked his lower lip where it still stung from Cal's teeth.

"Next time," he said as he gave Cal a last, appreciative once-over. "You can wear jeans to the party and keep that for when we get back."

Cal snorted and rubbed his hand over his head. The tips of his ears had gone red. Joe would have never thought that Cal was insecure about how attractive he was, but apparently a compliment could still fluster him a bit.

"Are you blushing?" Joe teased. He put his knuckles under Cal's chin, tilted his head back, and stroked his thumb over his lower lip. "You know I think you're beautiful."

Cal snorted and moved his head away. "You want to get laid."

"I do. But it's not hard to get you into bed," Joe said. "It's persuading you that I like you that I have trouble with."

The ghost of a smile tugged at Cal's mouth. "Maybe I want you to keep trying," he said. "Now, you going to show me off to all your posh friends, or what?"

They took an Uber to Charing Cross. Joe claimed his usual spot behind the passenger seat. It hadn't been that long, but it was already odd to look up and see a face in the rearview mirror that wasn't Cal. There were compensations, though. Cal slid over the seat and slung a heavy, well-tailored arm over his shoulders.

"Would you be mad at her?" Cal asked. He watched the cars crawl by outside as the driver nudged and edged his way through the traffic. "If she's not dead?"

There was a question. "Maybe. I suppose I should be."

"You don't have to be. Nobody can make you feel something."

Joe had never considered that before.

The driver dropped them off at the venue, a huge bookstore lit up brightly even as the lights went down. Cal bumped Joe's shoulder with his as they went inside. A trail of bright, summer florals and well-tailored suits led up the wide, glass-railed stairs, past stacked walls of brightly colored books and the occasional customer who peeked around a *Sherlock Holmes* cover to admire the fashion on their way past.

Bea met them at the top of the stairs. Her dress looked as though it had been poured onto her, liquid gold that dripped down from the point of her shoulder to her tanned knees. The perfect arch of her brows rose as she glanced from Joe to Cal.

"So that's how it is," she said.

Habit made Joe bristle, his hackles up with defensive paranoia. It took him a second to remember that he didn't care anymore. Or, at least, that he aimed not to.

"Is Howson here?" Joe asked instead of a sharp denial.

Bea handed him two tickets and turned to glance across the crowd of bare shoulders and prosecco. Howson might be a well-heeled member of the board now, but twenty-seven years ago, he'd been on the streets with a collection bucket next to Cal's mother. Before Bea could point him out, Rosie slid up next to her. Her hair was piled up on top of her head, and she was in a simple dark green dress that made her eyes look nearly as black as Joe's.

"Rosie," Bea hooked her arm through Rosie's. "You remember Mr. Bailey."

The smile Rosie offered him was uncomfortable, but everything about her shouted that she'd rather be somewhere else.

"Yes," she said. "I spilled wine on your shirt."

"No hard feelings," Joe said. He turned to include Cal in the introductions. "This is Cal Tate."

Rosie gave them both a brisk nod of her head, squeezed Cal's hand when he offered it, and then turned back to Bea. "I have to go. My boss isn't feeling well. I have to drive her home."

Disappointment dimmed Bea like someone had installed a switch. "Oh," she said. "Couldn't she take an Uber? I really wanted to spend some time with you."

Rosie's face shone as she looked up at Bea, but then she bit her lip and tamped it down.

"It is my job," she pointed out. "And she's always been so good to me. I have to go. Call me, though."

Bea touched the side of her face. "Definitely."

One last, shy smile pleated Rosie's lips, and then she slipped away. Bea watched her go and shook her head.

"Oh, I like her," she said, almost dismayed. "She's lovely."

Joe cleared his throat. "Howson?"

The tail of Bea's dress swung out around her knees like a bell as she turned. "Over there," she said. "By the window."

She pointed across the room to a tall man who reminded Joe of nothing in particular.... He was a rather faded man in a well-cut suit that had probably been tailored to fit at some point.

"Thanks," Joe said to Bea.

She dismissed it with a flip of her last ticket. "Good luck."

The crowd wasn't too bad yet. It parted to let Joe and Cal through on their way across the room. Once he realized they were aimed at him, Howson looked surprised. He drained his glass of whiskey and dusted sausage roll crumbs off his fingers.

"I'm sorry," he said. "Do I know you?"

Joe caught his hand when it was offered. It was warmer than he'd expected and stiff. He shook it carefully. "Joe," he said. "We've not met, but I'm trying to get in touch with an old friend of yours."

"Probably dead, then," Howson said dryly. "At my age, most of them are. Or retired, which is much the same. The only difference is they complain more."

"Abigail Bailey?" Joe said. "It was years ago, but she worked with your charity. I have a picture of you at a fund-raiser with her in—"

"Brighton," Howson interrupted with a chuckle. "I remember that. Abby hates that photo. She says it gives her more chins than Jabba the Hutt."

Says, not *said*. Joe's chest felt hot and tight with the undefined smoke of something he couldn't accurately describe. It could have been fear or anger, but it felt as though he couldn't breathe. He swallowed the stickiness in his mouth. Cal put a hand on his back in mute support.

"That's the one," Joe said. "I've been trying to get in contact with her, but I've had no luck. By any chance, are you still in touch with her?"

Howson started to answer and then turned it into an awkward cough as he cleared his throat. He blinked and scratched the side of his nose.

"Actually, I'd rather not say," he said. When Joe raised his eyebrows, Howson made a twitchy gesture with his clumsy hands. "A few years ago, Abby had some problems with a... stalker? I don't know. It wasn't romantic but odd. Since then she prefers to keep a low profile."

Joe frowned. That was a coincidence. It didn't mean it was related, but... still. Maybe he should have defended Kristen to Edward after all.

"It's an inheritance," Cal said. He held his hand out to Howson, ready for an introduction. "My father recently passed, and he knew Mrs. Bailey. He left a few… sentimental… items, but we've had no luck trying to track her down."

"Well," Howson said. "She's not been Mrs. Bailey for, God, twenty years. She's remarried and divorced since then. Um, sorry to hear about your father."

Cal looked down at the floor and scratched the back of his head. He looked sad and uncomfortable with the fact. "He wasn't a good guy," he said. "I guess. But it seemed important to him that I do this."

"If we could have a quick word?" Joe cut in smoothly. "Inform her about Cal's father's passing and see if she wants any of the things set aside for her? It's nothing big, a few old gifts."

Howson looked sympathetic to the implied star-crossed romance, but reluctant. "Honestly, I'm not comfortable with it. Abigail would not appreciate me—"

"Could you give her my number?" Cal asked. "If she wants to get in contact, she can."

He held out a square of card with EVADE printed blunt and black across the front. It hung in the air while Howson stammered uncertainly until he finally gave in and took it.

"I'll do my best," he said. "If you could excuse me, I do have to work tonight. Again, sorry for your loss."

He tucked the card into his pocket and ducked away into the crowd. Joe watched him press hands and crane his neck to nod and smile for a few minutes. Then he glanced at Cal. "Follow him?"

"And hope he doesn't need a piss."

Joe snorted out a surprised laugh as the down-to-earth comment punctured the knot of tension in his chest. It felt easier without it. He snagged a glass of champagne from a passing tray and followed Howson's stooped, cashmere-clad shoulders.

It turned out that Howson didn't need the toilet after all. Joe caught up with him by one of the internal glass walls that looked down through the floors of books. He'd handed Cal's business card to a well-dressed woman with auburn hair and a pair of Coke-bottle glasses balanced on her nose. There was something of the girl she'd been twenty years ago in her face, but Joe thought he could have walked past her at the bar and never guessed who she was. She looked confused as she turned the white rectangle over in her fingers.

"Sorry," Joe said as he joined them. "I don't believe you actually know Cal's father. That was a trick, I'm afraid. I needed to speak to you."

Even from inside his own head he could hear Harry in his voice, in the coolly flip apology. He didn't want that, but at least he understood it. If he wasn't cold, he wasn't actually sure what to be. A few minutes ago, he hadn't been sure what emotion to feel. Now he seemed to have them all at once.

Howson blustered and *hmph*ed in annoyance, but after a moment, Abigail patted him on the arm, reassured him that it was fine, and sent him to find her assistant.

"Dermot has been a very good friend to me over the years," she noted once he'd gone. "I don't appreciate you making a fool of him."

"That wasn't my intent. I needed to speak to you."

Abigail laced her fingers together in front of her stomach and twitched her eyebrows toward her hairline. "Well, now you have the chance."

He couldn't. The words stuck in his throat as fear squeezed it shut. His whole life he'd thought that he didn't have emotional attachment to the idea of a mother, but maybe he did… or wanted to. He needed to the next few moments to play out right.

"This is Cal Tate, my…." Joe hesitated as he flipped through the options and tried to pick one. He could feel Cal behind him, unsurprised at Joe's fumble. It wasn't that he didn't want to call Cal something, but what? *Boyfriend*? *Lover*? Maybe Cal didn't want anything that… committed. He settled on, "Date. I'm Joseph Bailey. Your son."

Surprise softened Abigail's face, and Joe braced himself for her reaction.

"You look like your father," she said with a small smile. It faded into a solemn, not-quite-apologetic expression. "But, Joseph, I'm not your mother. I never had a child."

Chapter Thirteen

THE SOUND of the fund-raiser opposite filtered through the long, clean glass walls of the bookshop cafe in a white-noise mix of earnest conversation and elevator music. Cal stood at the counter and stared through the plastic at plates of sugar-glittered pastries, waves of lemon fondant, and a small pile of chocolate-covered marshmallow top hats.

Behind the counter the barista stifled a yawn and clicked her tongs impatiently. "What do you want, sir?"

Cal didn't know. What sort of cake did people have when they'd had an expected kicking? He knew they didn't have jammie dodgers, his grandad's choice of biscuit for hard conversations.

"Three doughnuts," he said after a second.

"Jam, lemon, or chocolate?" she said blandly, her tongs poised over the tray.

"One of each," Cal said with a glare. It didn't have much impact. She piled the doughnuts up on a plate and turned to finish the drinks.

Abigail drank chamomile tea. The cafe didn't have any, so she'd get lemon and honey instead. If she didn't want to drink it, she could sit and sniff it. Once the drinks were finished and awkwardly fitted onto the tray, Cal swiped his card and picked them up.

He walked in at the middle of Abigail's explanation. She stumbled to a stop as Cal handed over the coffee and sweets.

"Thank you," she said as she nudged the plate away. "But I'm not hungry. I think I ate something that didn't agree with me earlier."

She touched her stomach and pulled a small face.

"My dad always said you were my mother," Joe said. "Why lie?"

Abigail sighed and took her glasses off. She pulled the sleeve of her dress down and fastidiously polished the lens. Without them her face looked oddly unfinished, her eyes smaller than they looked through the frames.

"I couldn't tell you," she said. "Maybe he thought it would save on explanations. He used to tell a lot of stories that way—edit out the parts that distracted from what he wanted you to realize. In the end, though, that's something you have to ask him. I've not spoken to Harry in nearly thirty years."

Cal sat down next to Joe, close enough that their knees touched. "He also said you were dead."

"Even fewer explanations," Abigail said with a small, wry smile. She seemed less annoyed to have been relegated to the grave than Cal would have been. Then her mouth twitched and she gave Joe a guilty look. "Or maybe he meant your real mother. She died."

She waited for a reaction. Joe didn't give her one. He looked composed and his hands were steady as he lifted his coffee off the table. It wasn't real. There was a muscle that twitched below the hinge of Joe's jaw, and the leg pressed against Cal's under the table was clenched as though Joe was ready to run. Cal could tell that, but from the flash of judgment that passed over Abigail's face, she couldn't.

"What happened?" Joe asked.

Abigail wrapped her hands around her coffee cup as though she were cold despite the lingering heat of the day. Her throat worked as she swallowed.

"It wasn't a good time," she said. "I don't think about it often. I don't talk about it at all. I'm Mrs. Abigail Beranger now, Clement's widow instead of Harry's ex. Ask Harry."

Joe gave a small, bitter laugh. "We both know he'd not tell me," he said. "I know you're not my mother, that you don't owe me anything, but for the last month, I thought my mother was alive. Now I know she's not. So it would be *kind* to give me something."

"I've not got long," Abigail said. She glanced at her watch, shifted in her seat unhappily, and then nodded slowly. "Fine. *That* I, maybe, do owe you, Joseph."

It still took a second to collect herself. While they waited, Cal felt his phone buzz in his inside pocket. He fished it out quickly to turn it off and saw Van's number on the screen. He held down the power button to switch it off. He could call back later.

"I used to tell this story at fund-raisers," Abigail said as she took a sip of her tea. "How my mother died of breast cancer when I was thirteen, my dad of bone cancer when I was nineteen, how I got ovarian cancer at twenty-four, and the charity helped me through all of those things, whether it was hospice care for my parents or the nurse who came to sit with me at night when I was scared. The bit that wasn't their business was that I got married at twenty-eight to a man who said he didn't care I couldn't have a child."

"Harry," Joe said. "My dad."

It had been a long time. A lot of the bitterness had worn off, but there was still a hint of it in the corners of Abigail's tight little smile.

"I cared," she said. "In the end, I guess he did too, despite everything he said. He had an affair, he got her pregnant—I didn't know anything about it, it went on for two years—and he left me. Eventually. Maybe a month or two later, he turned up with you. You were only a baby and, God, you had terrible burns on your face and your little arms. Cried all the time. He told me your mother had died—in a fire and that's what happened to your poor face. He wanted me to take him back. Your mother's ex-husband wanted custody of you too, to keep the family together, and Harry said that if we were together he'd have a better case against the ex."

Joe's jaw was clenched so tightly that Cal didn't think he could get any words out. So he asked the question.

"But you didn't want to take on someone else's kid?"

"Oh no," Abigail said. She reached over the table and covered Joe's hand with hers. "I wanted to take you so badly. You were hurt and you could have been mine, but…. For a while I did, you know. But I couldn't forgive Harry. I couldn't forgive myself."

Joe pinched the bridge of his nose with his free hand. "I feel this has to be asked," he said, a grim tiredness to his voice. "Did you have something to do with the accident?"

She laughed—a startled squawk of humor—and shook her head. "No. God, no." She tightened her fingers over Joe's hand. "But it was what I wanted. My husband, a baby, and if this poor woman had to die to get me that… I was okay with it. I couldn't be that person. I couldn't take her baby. That's all I know."

"Who was she?" Joe asked.

Abigail shook her head. "I don't know. I never wanted to know. She was bad enough as an idea without being given a name and a face." She took her glasses off again and wiped the soft skin under her eyes with her knuckles. Tears filled the creases in her skin. "There was a man Harry had hired around that time. Afterwards. An ex-police officer or something. He might know. I'm sorry, but that's all I can give you."

It wasn't much. Cal gingerly put his hand on Joe's knee, uncertain of how welcome it would be. Joe didn't slap his hand away, but then, he didn't seem to have noticed at all. After a moment of awkward silence, Abigail glanced over at the still-in-swing party. She nodded briefly and raised her hand in an a-minute-please gesture.

"I'm sorry," she said as she nudged the chair back to stand up. "I have to go. Tell your father I… I hope he's well."

She gave Joe a last, desperate look and then walked quickly away. Her heels clicked against the floor with each step. Cal squeezed Joe's knee, but Joe still didn't react. He sat and stared down into his coffee, his hands white-knuckled where they clutched the cup.

"You know, in hindsight," Cal said as he looked at the untouched puffs of fried sugar and dough on the table, "I should have gotten something that didn't ooze."

It didn't get a laugh, but Joe snorted and relaxed his fingers. He pushed the cup away. "I think this was more of a shortbread conversation really."

"You okay?"

"Not the conversation I expected," Joe said. He stared at Abigail's chair for a second and then abruptly stood up. "But I got the answers I wanted, so we should celebrate, right? What's the hottest gay club in town? The place to be seen?"

That wasn't exactly Cal's scene. He'd dropped off a couple of soap stars at a club a few weeks back, to screams and camera flashes from the crowd.

"Kiss, Kiss," he said as he stood up. Joe gave him a look and he grinned sheepishly. "That's the name. It's five minutes down the road."

Joe grabbed the lapel of Cal's jacket and pulled him forward into a quick, rough kiss that made—from the clatter behind them—the barista drop her tongs in surprise. After a second, Joe leaned his forehead against Cal's, his breath warm against Cal's mouth.

"Let's go somewhere I can show you off, then," he said. "Somewhere I don't have to think."

Somewhere, Cal thought wryly, Joe's lying dad could be scandalized by his son's bad choices in men. It stung a little, somewhere he didn't think he *had* a soft spot, but he supposed if anyone had earned the right to spite his dad, it was Joe.

THE CLUB was packed, bodies pressed against each other from one side of the raw industrial space to the other. Music pulsed from the speakers, loud enough to rattle the exposed pipes on the ceiling, and hips and shoulders bumped and pressed as people moved to it.

Cal steadied himself against the tide that tried to push him one way or another. The air smelled like sweat and booze. Joe pressed against him, one hand under his silk shirt, his mouth hot against Cal's neck, and his muscles tight as wires under his skin. Cal could feel the tension under his fingers as he cupped the back of Joe's neck.

The beer that dangled from his fingers had done nothing to loosen him up, and every time someone bumped into or pressed in around them, it made Joe flinch.

The song faded out on a skirl of electronica and frenetic movement as the dancers slowed down and broke up. A girl, all glitter and hair, laughed and stretched her arms to the ceiling. Her underarms were fuzzy with pink hair.

Cal grabbed Joe's shirt in both hands and pulled him off the dance floor. They stumbled around the corner of the bar, their reflection caught in the stress of polished and shaped steel, and into the narrow hall that led to the VIP area. It was strung off tonight, a heavy velvet rope pulled across and a chalkboard No Entry sign slung from it.

Cal pushed Joe up against the stripped-down chipped concrete and old-plaster wall. He slanted a hard kiss over Joe's mouth, the taste of beer and salt ripe against his tongue. Joe hooked his fingers into Cal's waistband and yanked him closer.

"You're not having a good time," Cal said as he lifted his head. The flicker of the lights in the club cast long blue shadows over the wall.

Joe smirked darkly and arched his hips up off the wall. His cock pushed against Cal's thigh, hard and insistent. "You sure about that?"

"This?" Cal snaked a hand over Joe's hip and cupped a handful of ass. He pulled him forward and ground their hips together. Pleasure ached in his thighs and shot, hot and electric, along his taint to the tight pucker of his ass. "Yeah. That out there? Not so much. If you want a headline on TMZ, I can grope your ass on the way out."

Joe growled under his breath and cupped the side of Cal's face. He tucked his thumb under Cal's chin to push his head back and spread his fingers along his cheekbone.

"This isn't about Harry," he said roughly. "You're the one thing in my life that's not about him. Asshole."

Cal twisted his head around to plant a wet-tongued kiss against Joe's palm. "Sure," he drawled against the wet patch. "That's why you wanted everyone to see us?"

"I wanted people to know you were with me, that I knew what this was." Joe slid his hand down Cal's neck and traced the lines of ink with his fingertips. "And that I'd be the only one who got to see it tonight."

A shiver sparked under Joe's fingers and ran down Cal's spine to his tailbone. There was a sweet bloom of warmth in his chest that he didn't trust. It was easier not to get hurt when you didn't care. Last time he'd cared, it had been Van, and look how that turned out.

And *that* had never felt like this.

"So then why pick here?" Cal asked. "You were on edge since we came through the door."

He almost got an answer. Then Joe tilted his mouth in that sparse, arrogant smile that had hooked Cal on the first night. He brushed a kiss over Cal's mouth and ran his hands down his stomach to tug his shirt out of his trousers.

"Maybe I changed my mind and decided that I shouldn't waste you and this suit on anyone else." Joe shut up for a second as he creased the thin, silk fabric between his fingers. "I don't want to think about anything except you tonight."

Even Cal—fucking feral ex-con Cal—knew that probably wasn't a good idea. But he couldn't resist it.

He shoved Joe back against the wall and claimed the kiss that Joe had teased him with. It was hungry and eager, but not desperate. Both of them knew they'd get what they needed tonight. Cal lost a handful of the expensive buttons on his shirt as Joe impatiently pulled it apart. He spread his hands over Cal's stomach, across the ridges of his abdomen and up to pinch the flat buds of his nipples. A moan scraped up out of Cal's throat and slid between Joe's lips.

The heavy, almost physical pulse of the music tangled with the heady pulse of hunger and heartbeats.

Cal dragged his mouth reluctantly away from Joe's. Undeterred, Joe bit and licked along Cal's jaw to his ear. While he sucked on Cal's earlobe—his mouth wet, his tongue busy, and the memory of wet skin and Joe's mouth around his cock vivid in Joe's mind—Cal reached out and unhooked the velvet rope. It dropped and the heavy metal hook clanked against the wall.

"Come on." Cal pulled Joe toward the stairs. "If you *don't* want up in the gossip rags, we should go somewhere a bit more private."

Joe saw the unhooked rope and laughed. "Look at that. Even in a nice suit, you're still a bad influence."

"Yeah, that's the one GCSE I got," Cal cracked dryly as they hit the stairs.

Joe stopped on the first step and tried to tug Cal back down. "Don't do that," he said. "You're not stupid."

He sounded like—Cal made a deliberate detour around a comparison with his brother and got stuck with what that really meant—someone who cared. That didn't mean he did. People got sentimental when they wanted to get laid. It still pulled Cal up for a second. He swallowed the jag of it.

"And you don't like crowds," he said. "You really want to get into this now?"

Joe looked frustrated for a moment but eventually shook his head. "No," he said. "Later."

Cal pulled him up a step, tangled a hand in Joe's styled curls, and grinned at him. "If you remember."

They scrambled up the narrow stone steps, clumsy with lust and unwilling to let go of each other. Cal guided himself up the stairs with one hand on the narrow metal banister and his other arm wrapped around Joe's waist. Joe kissed bruises down Cal's throat and ran his hands over Cal's back and down to his ass.

They finally tripped over the last step and into the long crescent curve of the VIP lounge. The walls were bare except for pink-and-blue scenes of anime porn, from fully colored sex scene panels to storyboard sketched outlines with scribbled arms and motion lines. Low pink-and-blue velvet sofas were discreetly angled around the room, and the anime girl oversaw a chrome bar. It was empty, booze relocated downstairs until they needed to restock, except for two jars that were full of theme-matched condoms and dental dams, respectively.

Joe smirked against Cal's jaw. "I guess they really do want us to kiss." His hand was between Cal's legs, his palm pressed against the hard jut of an erection that strained against the freshly tailored zip. Heat stirred like honey in Cal's stomach, hot enough to stick and sting as his nerves twitched and fired under his skin. "I'd hate to let them down."

"Oh," Cal said raggedly. "I don't think that's going to be a problem."

He dragged them both down onto the nearest couch, tangled together on the plush, fuchsia-pink velvet. Kisses bumped off lips and along shoulders as they fumbled at each other's clothes. Cal's jacket got tugged off and discarded, the navy silk of his shirt creased and plastered to his dance-sweaty skin. He hitched his hips up off the cushions to unbutton his trousers and laughed raggedly as Joe impatiently pushed his hands out of the way to do it himself.

Cal stroked his hands down Joe's back, traced the sharp jut of his shoulder blades and then down to his lean waist and the taut curve of his ass. He squeezed the firm rise of muscle and flesh and tugged Joe down against him. His cock pressed against the hard muscle of Joe's thigh and made his balls throb with hot tight pleasure.

"I bet I could make you stop thinking." He licked a kiss over the scarred skin at Joe's temple and smirked. "At least, stop thinking about anything but me."

Joe pushed Cal down into the cushions and leaned back, his hands braced against Cal's shoulders.

"If my father taught me anything, it's never bet on a sure thing," Joe said. He lowered himself down until his lips almost touched Cal's. His breath tickled Cal's skin as he spoke. "That first night, at the pool, your mouth on its own nearly made me forget how to swim."

Cal aimed a mock-bite at Joe's mouth. His teeth skimmed the elegant curve of it. "It's a good thing you didn't," he said. "I don't think you would have made quite the same impact on me."

"Liar."

The flickered memory of wet skin and scant black trunks flashed through Cal's brain. And yeah, Cal was.

Joe closed the feather-width of distance between them and kissed him, slowly and deeply. It left Cal breathless and aching. He groaned when Joe tried to move away, and he pulled him back down. The pulse of music from the club thumped up through the floor, vibrated through the couch and up into their skin.

A man's voice, pure as a bell and raw with experience, growled about the Devil and deals over the wicked skirl of guitars.

"… my Satan said with a grin." The lyric caught in Cal's brain like a hook. His Satan had always been a fast car and a bad decision, but maybe he'd traded up. Although the singer had one advantage over Cal. "Come with me and we'll make Sinner's Gin."

Joe was never going to ask him to go with him.

It didn't matter. Cal finally ended the kiss and let Joe pull away from him. This was enough.

Liar.

Cal ignored the drawled echo of the accusation and watched Joe shrug his jacket off and toss it aside. He dropped his hands to his trousers and tugged at the zipper with impatient fingers. Lust flushed his narrow, elegant face and made his eyes look even darker. His tie was pulled loose, a twisted knot of silk, and his collar hung open to expose the long lines of his throat. Faint marks faded toward purple on his skin, like Cal's mouth had given Joe his own ink.

Yet he called *Cal* beautiful. It made Cal wonder how Joe did his hair in the morning without looking in the mirror.

"You going to watch?" Joe asked as he freed his cock from his trousers. The fabric hung from his hipbones as he wrapped his fingers around the heavy shaft. "Or you going to roll over?"

"Is that a please?" Cal mocked as he stretched out to his full, tailored length.

"No," Joe said. He stroked his fist along his cock in rough time to the underscored drumbeat. "It's a choice."

"And if I pick watch?" Cal asked.

Joe narrowed his eyes. "I still get off."

Cal smirked and ran a hand down over his stomach, muscles tight under his skin, to his waistband. The calluses on his fingertips scraped the tender span of skin between his hip bones as he put off gratification.

"Me too," he said as he raised a knee. His trousers gaped open and he slid his hand down farther. "But if you use one of those pink condoms, I might change my mind."

Joe looked over at the jar and its garishly colored contents. He snorted.

"They could have been there a year," he said.

Cal grinned, he could feel the wicked in the edges of it. "They ain't dusty."

Chapter Fourteen

THE PIECES of Joe's life had come apart like a dropped jigsaw. It was all unmatched edges and lost corner pieces, unanchored and unsolvable. Even though the idea had *always* been that Harry had lied, somehow the evidence of it had knocked the wind out of Joe.

And like he always did when the pressure built up at the base of his skull, when he felt *trapped* even without walls, he wanted sweat, sex, and control, not novelty condoms and childish dares.

So the only excuse for the smile that tugged at the corner of his mouth was Cal's ridiculous, infectious grin. It was the sort of squint-eyed, odd-angled grin that didn't bother to be attractive but was full of humor.

"You want me to steal a condom?" he asked.

Cal raised his eyebrows and nodded as if it were a serious question. His tongue was tucked into the corner of his mouth.

"A pink one," he said. "Dare ya."

Joe took a deep breath of air that smelled like yesterday's pine cleaner and fresh sex. What the hell, he decided. Half of his life he'd spent turned inside out to please people who, it turned out, didn't have his best interests at heart—law school, engagement parties that all the right people turned up to, and a job that got done even when everyone hated him.

He could wear a pink condom if it amused Cal.

The foil crinkled between his fingers as he gingerly—although he supposed they restocked after each party—grabbed a packet from the tip of the pile. He pinched the notched corner between thumb and forefinger and ripped it open. The latex was slick with lubricant as he pinched the tip and then rolled it down over his cock, from head to his balls. The plastic squeeze of it was familiar, the vivid, angry pink shade less so.

Cal cracked up. "Didn't think you'd do it," he wheezed out between giggles as he got up onto his knees. He cupped his hands together and held them out, a grin still on his face. "Toss me a blue one."

"I believe the agreement was I get to fuck you," Joe said as he dipped his hand into the jar. They were all new, shiny, specially branded packets, fresh from the factory. He flicked it over to Cal, who grabbed it out of the air. "Not the other way around."

"Your loss," Cal mumbled as he ripped the packet open with his teeth. "I'm not going to leave a mess for whatever poor bastard has to come and clean these up."

He spat the foil out and rolled the blue latex down over his cock to the base. Joe folded his lower lip between his teeth and stroked himself as he watched. Banked heat ached between his legs, twitched impatiently in his thighs. He wanted to be balls deep in Cal, the day's events shoved out of his head to make room for tight pressure, salt-sweat on his lips, and Cal stretched out, spread out, for him, but he wanted to have this too—if only for a moment, as he watched Cal's hand slide along his cock, the ridiculous blue stretched tight around the thick, flushed length of him.

In another week, if that, he'd be back in LA and Cal would have someone else in the back seat of the Bentley.

Ironically the reminder of why he wanted to take his time was one more reason he couldn't. Joe crawled back onto the couch with Cal and pulled him into a kiss. They fell back against the cushions, Cal's thighs clenched as he leaned back and their cocks squashed between their bodies.

"I don't think this suit is ever going to be the same," Joe warned as he pushed Cal's trousers down to his lean thighs.

He felt Cal's smile against his lips. "Not like I'm out of pocket. You paid for it."

Joe cupped the back of Cal's head, the crop short hair like velvet against his fingers, and bruised the kiss over his mouth. He finally pulled back, one hand braced against the back of the couch and the other in his pocket as he fished out his wallet. He'd only been a Boy Scout for a few months, but he still remembered how to start a fire and to always be prepared. The packet of lube had been in there since he woke up that first morning, the thought of Cal's lush mouth and rough hands still vivid from his dreams.

"Turn around," Joe said as he filled his palm with slick gel. Thankfully it wasn't pink. "If you want, I'll buy you another one."

Cal squirmed around awkwardly as their knees and legs slotted together in the limited space. He made a low, rough sound under his breath as Joe shoved him forward, his cock pressing into the soft, overstuffed velvet. Midnight blue silk pulled tight over his shoulders as he braced his elbows against the hard frame of the couch.

"If I'm gonna be a kept man," Cal drawled as he twisted around to look over his shoulder, "buy me cars instead of motorbikes. Or a puppy."

Joe laughed as he worked cool, slick gel between Cal's cheeks and into his ass. The clench of tight muscle around his fingers made his cock twitch with anticipation. He licked dry lips and leaned forward to kiss the corner of Cal's mouth.

"A puppy?"

"Always wanted a dog," Cal said. He broke off for a moment, eyes closed tightly as Joe worked him wider. He gripped the cushions. "Never lived anywhere that would let us as a kid."

Joe shut him up with a kiss as he pressed his cock into Cal's ass and buried himself inside him with two hard, eager strokes. A rough "fuck" growled out of Cal's throat as he dropped his head forward, the nape of his neck knobbed and vulnerable, and sucked in ragged, uneven breaths.

"You could have both," Joe told him as he ran his hands down Cal's clenched arms and wrapped his fingers around his forearms. He licked down Cal's throat and sucked a bruise into the tight skin over his collarbone. Each thrust buried him deeper in Cal's ass, slick and tight as it squeezed down around his cock. He buried his face in Cal's neck and breathed in the smell of his skin. "You could have anything you want."

"No," Cal said softly. "Some things it's best to stop wanting."

Joe wondered how you did that. He didn't know if he could. Some things he couldn't imagine not wanting.

His thighs slapped against Cal's ass, smeared wet with sweat and lube between them as he thrust in time to the music that throbbed up through the floor. The guitar caught at his nerves and dragged him along with it as it built toward a crescendo.

Need dragged at Joe's balls and crawled up his spine. It felt like the tight *almost-there* satisfaction of a long workout, the heavy burn that he knew would turn sweet in a second.

Cal reached back with one arm and grabbed Joe's ass. He squeezed the handful of flesh roughly with each thrust and pulled him closer and deeper. Joe draped over his back and hooked an arm across his chest. He shifted to drop one foot to the ground and buried himself inside Cal with fast, hard strokes of his hip. Cal choked out a groan as he was shoved hard into the back of the couch, his cock ground roughly against the cushion.

"God, Joe," he gasped out. "Please?"

His voice trailed off into a whimper and he twisted his fingers tightly in the cushions. The need in his voice caught in Joe's balls like a hook. He thrust hard into Cal with short, ragged jerks of his hips and felt the hot spill of come around his cock as it was caught in the condom.

"See," he said roughly against the back of Cal's neck. It was meant to be lighthearted, but once it got to Joe's lips, it felt like a promise. "Anything you want."

He sprawled back on the couch and pulled Cal with him, his cock still inside. He wrapped his fingers around Cal's rigid, blue cock, and the slow raw aftershocks of orgasm still fired along his nerves as he brought Cal off with a few rough strokes.

Cal groaned and dropped his head back as he thrust up into Joe's fist. The tip of the condom ballooned as he came and, fuck it, Joe would have paid to have the couch dry-cleaned. He would have paid for a new tacky velvet couch.

Next time, he thought as he nudged Cal's head around for a sweaty kiss. He wanted to see the mess of it as it dried on their skin.

A door slammed down below and bottles rattled loudly enough to be heard over the lull in music. There was a pause and then an irritated woman's voice yelled up.

"If there's someone fucking up there—or up there fucking—you've got ten minutes before I come back and chuck you out."

Heavy footsteps echoed down the hall and another door slammed.

"Fuck," Cal spluttered—half laugh and half groan—as he scrambled off Joe's lap. He hunched over as he stripped the condom off his cock with one hand and dragged his trousers up with the other. "That'd make the papers."

Joe didn't want to move. A small, mean part of him thought it would serve Harry right to end up in the gossip rags. A lifetime's adherence to keeping his head down squandered as his only son got dragged out of a club with a wilted, neon pink condom hanging off his cock. It would serve him right. A larger part wanted to pull Cal back down onto the couch and see exactly how much mess they could make.

"I could hire the room," Joe pointed out as he propped himself up on his elbows. His cock lay wet and pink across his thigh.

Cal gave him a wicked look over his shoulder as he buttoned his trousers one-handed. "Where's the fun in that?" he asked as he bundled the condom into a napkin and tossed it into the trash. "Come on."

He loped back over and dragged Joe up off the couch. It was, despite everything in Joe's head, hard to resist Cal's grin. He dragged Joe to his feet, kissed him roughly, and told him to "put his dick away" while Cal picked his way over the buttons he had left on his shirt.

Joe peeled the condom off and tossed it. He hitched his trousers up over his hips and tucked his shirt tails in. There was a roll of fifties in his wallet, and he peeled off a handful and left them on the bar under the condom jar.

He might want to come back one day.

Cal tossed Joe his jacket and then grabbed Joe's arm on his way to the door. They snuck down the stairs as though they hadn't already been caught, two steps at a time as they muffled laughter. Two steps from the bottom Cal nearly tripped over the rehung rope and staggered to a stop, balanced on his toes at the edge of the riser. He muttered a curse under his breath, and Joe choked back a laugh behind his teeth. He glanced down the hall to the storeroom, where someone assiduously rattled bottles in a pointed stock take. It didn't seem as though they were in any immediate danger of being caught.

"I guess we're trapped," he teased Cal as he leaned back against the polished banister. "Lucky enough we have supplies."

"I don't think the condoms were edible," Cal said. His shirt was haphazardly buttoned in the middle, with a deep vee of smooth, inked chest showing and the occasional glimpse of his dented-in belly button. Joe admired the view while he still could. Finally Cal rolled his eyes and stepped over the rope. He held his hand out and wriggled his fingers when Joe didn't immediately follow him. "Come on. I don't want to piss someone off enough they call the cops. I used up my slaps on the wrist years ago."

Joe let himself hang back a second longer, and then a book slammed shut down the hall. He took the long step over the rope back into the real world. He would have had to eventually.

The tempo of the music had changed. The raw rock of the earlier set replaced by flashy, clashy electronica. On the main floor, the dancers twisted and hopped on the static-wrapped beat, all elbows and unpredictable moves. A short man with tiger stripes of glitter on his skin danced aggressively between Joe and Cal. His hands, encased in soft, brown gloves, stroked down his thighs in an unabashed come on. Joe snorted and dodged around him. "Your loss" drifted spitefully after him. The lights pulsed and strobed jerkily as the beams hitched here and there across the space.

Cal muscled through with a scowl to shift people where his shoulders didn't do the job, and Joe let him take the lead until they reached the pavement outside.

After the heat of the club, all sweat and hot breath, the air outside felt cold against sweaty skin. Joe shivered and wiped his hand over the back of his neck, sweat slippery under his fingers. Then he pulled out his phone to call a cab. Cars crawled by and the air smelled of diesel.

"So, did it work?" Cal asked as he nudged his shoulder against Joe's. "Are you the first man in London to successfully fuck his troubles away?"

No. They were still there, like the real world and his dad's lies. Joe still didn't know exactly how he felt about that… yet. Angry, yes, but the rest of it was a muddle of things he couldn't quite put his finger on. He'd expected more from Abigail than he realized—a child's fantasy of a reunion constructed in secret somewhere in his brain where he seldom looked. It had hurt to find her alive and then find out she wasn't anything to do with him. He thought—as he remembered the tears on her knuckles—that she felt something similar.

"It was worth a try," Joe said. "And as troubles go, there are worse. I arrived in London with a dead mother, and it turns out she's still dead. Probably. The only real change is that I don't know her name."

Or her face. He'd never pored over the few, posed shots of Abigail that Harry had kept, but he knew her without a second thought earlier. The fact he had no idea what his actual mother looked like felt lonely.

"Are you going to keep looking?" Cal asked.

It was a good question. He wasn't sure if it would be worse to know the truth or not. Maybe some secrets were best kept.

"I don't know," Joe said. "It doesn't sound like it will be a happy ending."

If Kristen had been the one behind the poison-pen emails, then the whole search had been a comedy of errors from the start. Maybe it would be best to put it back in the ground.

A taxi slowed on the way past, and a woman with a pale mohawk peered at them. Joe started to raise his hand, but she drifted past, and a tangled knot of drunk girls, interwoven and giggly in heels and spandex, poured themselves into the back.

Joe glanced down at his hand, still tangled with Cal's, and he supposed there was one thing that had changed since he arrived. He certainly hadn't expected to be standing on the curb, ripe with sex, stuck to his—*date*'s, he decided—hand while they waited for a taxi. It felt good. So maybe he'd just… fucked his troubles into perspective.

He could live with that.

The taxi arrived as the weather broke. Fat, round raindrops hammered the tarmac and bounced off the slick black curve of the cab's hood. It rained as though someone had dumped out a bucket, a hard splash of water that immediately soaked everyone on the curb. The huddle of smokers by the door tossed their butts down in puddles and squeezed back in through the door. Others, whose rides were still en route, swore and withdrew into doorways or under shared umbrellas. One woman laughed and turned her face up into the rain.

"Fuck sake," Cal grumbled.

He tightened his grip on Joe's hand, and they dashed through the rain to their ride. Oily puddles splashed up to soak their ankles and drench their socks. They toppled into the back seat, wet as though they hadn't bothered to run, and Joe shook his head to shed water like a dog.

"St. Pancras," he told the driver, who squinted at them sourly in the rearview mirror and nodded.

Cal didn't have to worry about wet hair. He swiped his hand over his sandy-brown crop and slouched back in the seat. His shirt gaped open over his bare chest and clung to his skin, hints of ink visible through the soaked fabric. Joe swallowed the lump in his throat—the only dry thing about him right then—and resisted the urge to crawl on top of him.

It was strange. Joe had come to London to look for the truth. Somehow, even as the lies piled up, it felt as though that was what Cal was. Joe's truth, anyway.

JOE WAS well aware that there was a tracker on his phone. He never turned it off, and Edward never questioned where he'd been. It was a silent game of digital chicken.

So it wasn't really a surprise to see Edward at the door of the hotel when they got back, dropped off on the wrong side of the street by a dour taxi driver who didn't want to swing back around. He was tucked back in the shelter of the door, out of the rain, with the doorman. When he saw Joe get out of the car, Edward flicked his umbrella open and stepped out into the rain under its shelter. He walked down the swooped drive toward the road and stopped at the curb to wait.

Cal slung an arm around Joe's shoulder, a comfortable weight, and tugged him down to plant a kiss on his temple. It was a half measure—intimate if Joe wanted it to be, friendly if he didn't.

"Do you think someone squealed on you?" Cal asked.

Joe turned his head and claimed a kiss from Cal's full, rain-wet mouth. "Probably," he admitted. "But I'd have to have this conversation eventually."

Edward had said he liked Joe's mother, even though he hadn't known her long. He could have meant Abigail, but maybe he meant Joe's real mother, the woman who'd gotten pregnant, broken up a marriage, and then died before she knew if any of it had been worth it. And *maybe* he was finally ready to tell the truth about it.

The rain plastered Joe's hair down over his face in wet curls and commas. He slicked it back with a faint flash of annoyance—the first week he'd been in London he'd carried his coat everywhere. There'd been an umbrella tucked into the back seat of Cal's car. In spite, the weather had stayed bright and hot—a late summer the news had complained about—until he forgot to be wary. It wouldn't change anything, but the fact he looked like a drowned rat put him at a disadvantage going into the conversation.

Cal's arm stayed slung over his shoulders as they jogged over the road. Edward's mouth was turned down at the corners as they reached him, and his nostrils flared as he ran a scathing look over Cal from head to unbuttoned shirt.

"Not exactly the consummately professional behavior your company boasts of, Mr. Tate," he said icily. "When I hired a driver, I expected a sober one. I'll convey my displeasure to your brother."

"Enough, Edward," Joe snapped.

Cal laughed and licked a kiss over Joe's throat. "He's my brother," he said to Edward. "He might rake me over the coals, but he's going to tell you to go and fuck yourself. Grandad might have liked you. Doesn't mean El is going to crawl."

Surprise and what looked like embarrassment flashed over Edward's face. He pressed his lips into a thin line and worked his jaw from one side to another.

"Don't forget who pays your wages, Mr. Tate," he said. "Joe might be stupid enough to have a soft spot for you, but his father does not. Nor do I. If you want the contract paid, I expect appropriate decorum."

Joe caught Cal's arm as it lifted, middle finger already extended. "I need to talk to Edward, alone," he said. "Go inside. I'll meet you upstairs."

"Indeed," Edward said dryly. "Run along, young man."

This time he got a finger jabbed in his direction, but Cal stepped away and jogged up the drive to let himself into the hotel. Joe's good mood went with him, and that left the rest for Edward.

"I told you, Cal's not your business," Joe said.

Edward extended the umbrella to cover him. "I don't want to see you get hurt," he said. Then he admittedly stiffly, "Either of you. Whatever you… whoever you love in the end, Joe, it's not going to be him, is it? An ex-con, dragged up in Tottenham, can barely even read? You're going to have him on your arm at the theater. Cut him loose now, before he thinks this means more than it does."

Joe walked away from the dry shelter of the umbrella. "He's dyslexic, Edward," he said flatly. Probably, he admitted to himself. He knew Cal wasn't stupid, that he had a library of audiobooks on his phone, and he'd seen how Cal blocked out addresses when he needed to read them. "And at least he's not a liar."

"He's a thief. Thieves lie, even if only by saying nothing. It's part of the job."

Joe turned around and stared at Edward through the veil of rain. "Is that how you did it?" he asked. "Held your tongue and never contradicted Harry? Lies by omission didn't taste as bad?"

The umbrella was tilted into the rain and cast a shadow over Edward's face that made it hard to read. Guilty or still a liar, Joe wondered.

"I don't know what you're talking about, Joe," Edward said. His voice was easier than his face, and the tight edge on it betrayed him.

"Did she call you?" Joe asked. "Or get in touch with Harry?"

There was a pause. "You have to talk to your dad. I think, maybe, Harry is ready to listen, but you need to hear it from him. I might have watched you grow up, but you're not my son. This isn't my business."

"Neither is Cal," Joe said coldly. "So remember that in future. You speak to him like that again, you're the one who'll be looking for a job."

"You think your father will let that—"

Joe took two long steps forward, back under the umbrella and into Edward's face. He could smell fried chicken and beer on his breath, see the heavy bags under Edward's eyes.

"If he doesn't, I'll quit," Joe snapped. "Either way, you'll be out of my life."

"Is he that good in bed?" Edward asked, his lip curled in distaste.

"Yeah," Joe said, and punched him.

It wasn't the best punch. Joe didn't have enough room or enough practice to get his shoulder behind it, but his knuckles caught Edward on the jaw and knocked him back a step. That might have been surprise as much as impact.

Joe shook his hand, realized he didn't have anything left to say, and walked away. His head was full of noise that meant nothing, and the tight, anxious aftertaste of lost control. He hunched his shoulder and water dripped under his collar and down his neck.

"Joe," Edward yelled. Joe tightened his jaw and didn't look back. "Joseph!"

The urgency in his voice caught in the nape of Joe's neck like a hook and yanked him out of his temper. He started to turn, but before he could, something hit him. He lurched sideways and tripped off the pavement into the road, and his elbow and hip cracked hard against the tarmac as he went down. His face caught the curb and he saw stars. The car, however, barely missed him. It slowed for a second and then bounced back down into the road and screeched away down the street.

Edward lay on the pavement where the car had tossed him, his body awkwardly angled and still. It was too dark and wet to see blood on the pavement, but it was dark and vivid against his skin.

"Edward!" Joe scrambled to his feet, awkward as his bruised leg didn't want to work yet. He limped over to the still body and stooped down to grab Edward's shoulders, although some vestige of common sense drew the line at any attempt to shake him awake. "Edward, *open your eyes*. Come on, Edward, *speak to me*."

He wheezed instead, and one eye fluttered open, although it didn't react as though he saw anything. Then it closed again. At least he was alive.

The doorman had run halfway down to them and stalled. "I've called the ambulance," he yelled. "The police. They're on the way."

People had stopped to watch. "You shouldn't move him," a man said with authority. "He could have hurt his neck."

"What happened?" someone asked

"Car lost control," the authoritative man said. "He shoved his son out of the way but couldn't dodge himself. Tragic."

Joe remembered the impact of hard hands in his back and flinched with guilt.

Then Cal was there, his jacket stripped off and tucked under Edward's head. "It'll be all right," he told Joe as the ambulance arrived. "C'mon. I'll get you to the hospital."

Chapter Fifteen

EDWARD WAS the sort of man who looked hard as nails even unconscious in a hospital bed. An IV was down in the crook of his arm, and electrodes were glued neatly to his chest to make the assorted machinery whine and beep.

He had a room to himself, and the doctor had actually come in to speak with Joe.

Cal wasn't sure if that was because Bailey Holding employees had good health care, or that Edward's condition was serious. He scratched his side. All he usually got when he was busted up was a gurney, a tired nurse with dissolvable thread, and a glass of orange once the stitches were done.

"I need to change," Joe said from the chair by the bed. He'd spent the night there, conflicted and mostly silent. He rubbed his hands over his face. "Call my father, let him know what's happened."

Cal pushed himself off the wall. "I'll drive you back," he said. "The hospital will call if anything changes."

"They wanted to know if he had any relatives," Joe said. "I didn't know. The things you don't know about people. I've known him my whole life but… he knows who my real mother is, and I don't know if he has a brother or a niece. I don't know whether to be pissed off at him or guilty."

"It wasn't your fault."

"I know. And yet."

After a moment Joe sighed and stiffly pushed himself upright. He put a hand on Edward's shoulder with awkward, obvious affection, and then walked past Cal and out into the hall.

"Thanks, for staying," he said as he paused in the doorway and put his hand on Cal's arm. "I know he's not your favorite person, but he'd appreciate it."

"I didn't do it for him."

"Then *I* appreciate it," Joe said. He briefly tightened his hand.

"Didn't say it was you either," Cal said with a shrug. He winced inside as he said it, but his skin itched to get it over with and screw up the moment.

Joe smiled and then winced as the expression creased the road rash on his jaw and cheekbone. It was raw and freshly cleaned, the yellow swab of iodine stained onto Joe's skin, but the nurse had decided not to bandage it.

"I have to speak to the police later," he said. "A detective is going to call at the hotel. Not sure if I should call my father before or after."

"After," Cal said. That reminded him of the missed call from Van that he still had to return. It would have to wait. He fell into step beside Joe as they left the room and walked down the hall. "Otherwise you'll have to call him again. Trust me, your family always wants to know what the police said to you."

Joe dredged a cool smile from somewhere. "You're the expert, I guess."

That comment would usually have made Cal smirk and crack wise, reassured in a weird way that he was right about how people saw him. It wasn't as though he could complain about it either—he brought it up.

"Not exactly something to be proud of," he said instead. The words felt rough in his throat, and he felt the back of his neck scald with embarrassment at being soft. Or… vulnerable. Cal cleared his throat and crooked the corner of his mouth in a smirk. "Maybe I should have stuck with stamp collecting when I was a kid, had another string to my bow."

Joe bumped his arm against Cal's. "I like you fine the way you are," he said. "I don't think stamps would have made a difference."

"Probably not," Cal admitted as he hooked his arm around Joe's waist. He leaned in to rub a rough, stubbled kiss up Joe's jaw so he could he confess into his ear. "Especially since when I say collected, I mean cut them off the letters old lags sent to my granddad from Spain… or Strangeways."

He still had them somewhere. Maybe. After Grandad died, most of his stuff went to El, boxed up and packed in the white van he rented. El offered Cal whatever he wanted from the house, but what would Cal have done with it back then? When he had money, it pissed through his fingers, and when there was no money, he didn't have a pot to piss in.

The vague idea of going to get them floated through Cal's head. Although he didn't have any idea what he'd do with them—frame them to cover the weird dent in his rented one-bedroom apartment? Before he could pick the idea to shreds, Joe snorted and pushed Cal away from him.

"If I ever need to send an emergency letter, I'll call you," Joe said. "For now, I need to talk to the nurses and make sure they have my contact details. Meet me outside with the car in fifteen minutes and we can go back to the hotel?"

Joe turned away without waiting for an answer. It wasn't a problem. The car was parked in the high-rise as the parking fees stacked up in twenty-minute increments. It was a bit high-handed—a *please* wouldn't have taken long—but under the circumstances, Cal could let it go. It was the *we* that made him hesitate, even if not for the reasons it would have two weeks before.

"Once I drop you off," Cal said, "I'll need to take a couple of hours personal time."

That made Joe turn to look at him. As easy as it was to read him sometimes, at others, Joe was still opaque behind that handsome, reserved face when he felt he needed to be. Joe was disappointed, maybe, or curious. Whichever it was, he didn't dwell on it.

"I suppose I'm lucky that my secret admirer hasn't scared you off entirely," he said. "Fine. I doubt I'll be going out anywhere this morning. If anything changes with Edward before that, I can get an Uber. That is, assuming you will be back?"

"Nowhere else to be." Or that he'd rather be, but even that made Cal squirm with discomfort.

Joe let a slow sweet grin slip through his reserve as though he'd heard it anyway. "Good to know," he said. "Until we get back to the hotel, though, you're still on the clock. I'll see you outside."

He headed over to the nurse's station, and Cal left him to sort out the details while he went to fetch the car. He supposed he could have told Joe what he had to do, but he preferred to keep it to himself until he knew whether or not Van had found out anything useful about the kid who'd attacked Joe in the graveyard… and if Cal trusted the information.

Van wasn't the most reliable man at the best of times, and Cal had blackmailed him.

Cal dropped Joe at the hotel and then called Van on the Bluetooth as he turned the Bentley toward his flat. He needed to change. There was a point where the smell of last night's sex became "the smell." It rang an unfeasibly long time before it finally cut to the answering machine.

"I'm busy," Van's recorded voice drawled. "Or you're not important. Try again later."

Cal didn't bother to leave a message. Ten minutes later the phone rang. It used to be that the sight of Van's name splashed over his phone would have given Cal butterflies. Even after Van fucked him over, Cal always half wanted the next call to be the one that made it better. Not that there had been many.

As he changed lanes and squeezed the Bentley past a double-decker bus—the tourists on top took pictures as he passed, in case there was someone worth a photo inside—he felt flat. No infatuation, no adrenaline kick in expectation of their next job, not even any anger.

It felt strange, but Cal supposed he knew why.

He answered the phone.

"You fall down a hole?" Van asked over a backdrop of cafe noise and the snotty gasps of someone in tears. "I called last night."

"I was busy."

"I saw that on the news," Van said. The line went muffled, Van's voice dim as he snapped at someone, "Would you give over? If I didn't want to keep fucking you before, I certainly don't now. You look like my mother after she's been at the gin."

A young voice spat a tear-snotty "Bastard," as a chair scraped back from the table.

"Thank fuck for that," Van muttered as he lifted the phone back to his ear. He didn't bother to explain himself. He didn't need to. It wasn't the first scene like that Cal had seen, or been part of, although he'd stuck to the insults and skipped the tears. "That guy who got knocked down at the Renaissance, I saw you with his boss in the photos. Cozy. Looked like you got yourself in there nicely."

That made Cal feel something, but he clenched his teeth on his temper. He didn't like the wet insinuation in Van's voice, but he still needed his information.

"It looked like it was none of your business," he said. "What did you get for me?"

Van's laugh was dirty. "Gotta tell you, after your little display the other night, a hard-on. It reminded me of what I'd missed. We used to have a lot of fun together. Remember?"

Cal botched an attempt to cut in front of a white van and had to tuck the Bentley back into its lane. It wasn't the come-on, it was how fucking transparent it was that Van thought he could use Cal to get something out of Joe. It was pathetic, and Cal used to fall for it.

"I remember," he said. "It used to be a right laugh in the cells at night when I told people how you'd set me up. We all thought you were a right joker."

Van clicked his tongue and dropped the act. "Still holding a grudge. All right. The guy you want is Logan Calle. He's seventeen, lives in a flat over a hairdresser's on Turnpike Lane. Him and his girlfriend had a sideline in rolling Johns for their wallets. That how you met him? We both know your new friend must like a bit of rough if he's into you."

"What hairdresser?"

"Loads of Locks," Van said. There was a crunch as he bit down into some toast. The thought of breakfast, despite everything that was going on, made Cal's stomach grumble. "Woman who runs the place is called Maggie Dee. She owes me one, but I'm not wasting that on you. So, if you want a favor, sort it out yourself."

The line went dead.

MAGGIE DEE was six foot two in heels and wore a headscarf pleated into intricate folds until it looked like a shell. She'd also a soft spot for scabby little oiks like the one she rented her flat to, and she wasn't about to tell some stranger with scarred knuckles anything about him.

"I'll tell him you called," she said as she plucked his card from his fingers with sharp, white-tipped nails. She looked down her nose at him. "If I see him, that is."

1970s pop played in the background, and the staff, at a loose end this early in the morning, eavesdropped as they made busywork at nearby stations. The only client, an old lady in to have her thin, white hair washed and set, didn't even bother to pretend she wasn't listening. She turned around in her chair and drank her tea while she watched them with interest.

"I'd appreciate that," Cal said. "Tell him that he ain't in trouble. I want to have a word about… someone he knows."

Maggie tucked the card into the waistband of her skin-tight trousers and gave him a thin, dry smile. "I'll tell him you called. Now, unless you want your hair cut—" Her eyes flicked to his close-cropped scalp and she pursed her lips in disapproval. "—you can leave."

His hair *did* need a trim. Cal suspected that Maggie would make a point to take it down to the wood. He shook his head and left her with one last assurance that it was important he talk to Logan. She didn't look like she cared.

Cal went across the road and two doors down, to a narrow little kebab shop. It was tiled like a bathroom and smelled like old grease, but they were open for breakfast. Cal handed over a fiver for a pita stuffed with meat, mushrooms, and onions with a fried egg slapped on top to leak through. He doused it with ketchup—the Aussie behind the counter made a face at that—and went out to wait for Logan to either roll in or out.

He was halfway through his breakfast and all the way to regret when the bus pulled up and a lanky teenager shuffled off. Cal hadn't gotten a good look the day at the graveyard, but the Slipknot hoodie was the same, and after the kid spat in the gutter and scratched himself, he headed in through the door to Loads of Locks.

Cal tossed the remnants of the breakfast kebab in the bin and wiped his hands on a napkin as he jogged over the road. He dodged the oncoming cars—one dented Nissan Mura with too many kids packed in the back nearly ran over his booted feet—and hopped up the curb onto the pavement. The chimes hung over Maggie's door rattled as he let himself in.

"… is she?" Maggie asked Logan as she pushed a mug of tea into his hands. Without the skull mask pulled up to his nose, Logan was a bony teenager with surprisingly good skin and heavy, blood-shot eyes. He dropped the tea when he saw Cal. It hit the black-and-white-tiled floor and splashed milky tea everywhere.

"What the fuck are you doing here?" he spluttered at Cal. Then he cut a suspicious look toward Maggie. "Did you tell him I was going to be here, Maggie? I *told* you it was a fucking accident."

"Don't be an idiot," Maggie snapped. She grabbed his arm and twisted her fingers into his hoodie. "I told him to go, but of course he was going to come back. You knew that. He found out your name. He wasn't going to shrug it off because you weren't in when he got here."

Cal closed the door behind him before Logan could make a break for it. He pushed his hands into the pocket of his jeans and tried to look unthreatening.

"I just want a word," he said.

"It was an *accident*," Logan spat at him. "I was only going to give the tall guy a scare, warn him off. Then you came out of nowhere and grabbed me. I had to defend myself, right? It wasn't my fault you got hurt. Maybe you should stay out of things that don't concern you, mate."

Maggie raised her hand toward Cal. "I don't want any trouble," she said. "Not in my shop. Don't—"

Cal ignored her. "Maybe you shouldn't push people into open graves," he said.

Whatever the kid had told Maggie, that hadn't been part of it. She dropped her hand and gave him a disappointed look. "Logan."

He flinched. Cal would bet there weren't a lot of people in the kid's life who cared enough he could disappoint them. So he'd never gotten used to it.

"You don't get it," he said. "I told you it was for a good reason. The guy had it fucking coming."

He pulled away from Maggie and left her with a handful of his shed hoodie clutched in one hand. Panic twitched over his face, and he lunged at one of the stations to grab a pair of scissors. He clutched them in his fist and jabbed the sharpened points at Cal.

"Get out of my way," he yelled, and his voice cracked.

"What are going to do?" Cal asked him. "Give me a bad trim?"

Maggie threw the hoodie at him. "Logan. Put those down, or I'll call the police."

That was one pressure too many for the kid. Logan threw her a panicked look and lunged forward at Cal. The point of the scissors caught in his T-shirt and poked the skin underneath. It didn't sting as much as the tattoo it scratched had when he'd gotten it.

Cal punched him in the face. He felt the crunch of cartilage under his knuckles, the familiar wet spit of blood over his fingers. It wasn't enough to break Logan's nose—probably—but he did drop the scissors as he staggered back.

"That hurt," he whined, the back of his wrist pressed to his dripping nose.

"So does stabbing people, Logan," one of the other hairdressers, a tiny woman with a crest of pink hair snapped. She handed Logan a towel to stem the bleeding and gave Cal a nervous look. "You okay?

Look, I know he's being a dick, but he's harmless. He's under a lotta pressure and…."

Cal pulled the neck of his T-shirt down. There was a red mark scraped through a line-work skull. A few drops of blood had oozed up from under the skin, but it had already dried up.

"I think I'll live." He glanced at Logan. The kid was at bay against one of the chairs, the towel still bunched up under his nose and his eyes on the door at the back of the room. "You run, I'll catch you."

Logan dropped the towel enough to sneer at Cal. "You didn't in the graveyard," he said. "Old man like you, all you'll catch if you run after me is a heart attack."

That stung. Cal wasn't *old*, but he had gotten to the point where he was too old for a lot of stuff he used to do—going to prison, playing gutter-trash arm candy, not caring that he was alone. He was not ready to be too old to intimidate scrawny little toughs.

"I found you, didn't I?" he growled. "If I have to find you again, I'll break your fucking kneecaps when I do. Now sit the fuck down. I told you, I want a word."

Logan stared at him, wire tight as he tried to decide what to do. It was Maggie who decided it for him. She gave him a shove toward an empty chair.

"Sit down and stop tracking tea and blood all over my floor," she said sharply. "Better to talk to him in here than whatever alley he runs you down in. He's not going to do anything to you in here."

Logan shot her a look over his bloody towel. "He punched me," he pointed out.

"You deserved that," she fired back at him. "Sit. Talk."

After a second, Logan reluctantly did as he was told, hunched up and sullen as a kid at school as his ragged, knock-off sneakers dangled off the floor. Maggie turned and headed for the door. She paused briefly as she passed Cal.

"Don't be too hard," she murmured. "It ain't an excuse, but his girlfriend is real sick. He's strung tight, is all."

She didn't wait to see if Cal cared. She strutted over to the door and locked it.

"I have an appointment in fifteen minutes," she told Cal. "You can talk to Logan until then. After that I'll call the cops and get him thrown out."

Cal turned one of the black chairs around, brushed clipped blonde hairs off the leather seat, and sat down. He leaned forward, elbows braced on his knees, and narrowed his eyes at Logan.

"Why did you attack Joe at the graveyard?" he asked.

Logan snorted, winced, and wiped bloody snot away on the back of his sleeve. "Joe," he mimicked in a sing-song sneer. "Like you're mates? I saw you at the graveyard—Mr. Bailey this and Mr. Bailey that. Him in the back like Little Lord Fauntletits and you going where you're told. You ain't mates, bro."

"I ain't asking for your opinion," Cal shot back. "Why were you there?"

"People go to graveyards," Logan muttered. He tossed the ruined towel over the arm of the chair and slouched back. "Maybe I wanted to get in early, get a good spot."

Cal leaned over and hit the height adjustment lever on the chair. It dropped and Logan yelped in surprise as he went with it. His hands flew up in surprise, and he winced as the impact jarred from his tailbone up to his battered nose.

"Dickhead," he snapped at Cal as he dropped his hands self-consciously.

"Answer the question," Cal said bluntly. "I don't want to dob you in to the cops, kid, but I will."

Logan shifted in the chair and tugged absently at his earlobe. It had been pierced once but healed over, and he rolled the scarred channel between his fingers.

"You're not going to be any good to Asha in a cell," Maggie chipped in from where she'd stood to sort her scissors and pretend she hadn't listened in. "Tell him what he wants to know."

The pressure made Logan screw up his face and fiddle more at his ear.

"You think you owe this person? Whoever put you up to it?" Cal said. "They pulled your fat out of the fire once, maybe, or they were nice to you sometime. Now you want to pay them back, show that you deserved their attention, right?"

In his case, with a shrug and a "whenever," Van had fronted him some cash when he needed it. Of course he had. The money didn't mean anything to Van. He didn't need it for his rent or his kid. He hadn't even sweated for it unless you considered the ten minutes it took him to empty his dad's wallet. But Cal remembered how desperately grateful he'd been and how relieved he'd been with Van later when he asked his opinion about something. A way to pay off the favor while he paid off the loan. Then Van had needed something from Cal, and even if Cal had wanted to say no—and he hadn't, he'd bought in 100 percent—he couldn't have done it.

Logan shrugged his opinion with a dismissive tilt of his shoulders. "She's not like that."

"She." Cal hadn't missed that. Maybe Edward was right, then. That would wake the harsh old man.

"What's she like, then?"

Logan rubbed his hand over the side of his face. "Good," he said. "Kind, like. Not to me, either, to Asha."

"His girlfriend," Maggie interrupted again. She looked around at Logan and pursed her lips sympathetically. "She has leukemia."

"It's the best sort to get," Logan explained brusquely. The words spluttered out of him on autopilot, something he'd learned by hopeful rote. "If you're gonna get cancer, you want this one, right? She's really sick, but she's gonna get better."

He said it like he needed to believe it.

"That's where you met this woman with a grudge against Joe?"

"She's his ex," Logan said. He scratched at his elbows as he shifted in the chair. He glanced up to give Cal a hard look. "He used to beat her up, this mate of yours. I've seen the scars. Then he came back, started threatening her all the time and sending people to watch her. He was a real perv. And she didn't ask me to do anything. I said I'd do it. I wanted to help her like she helped Asha.

"Scars?"

Logan held his arms up to show his forearms. "All up her arms, like he burned her or something."

Cal hesitated as he tried to pull the threads of the story into something that made sense. The ex part implicated Kristen, but how would she meet a kid with leukemia in London? She didn't have any scars that Cal had noticed either, and the description hardly fit someone desperate to turn up at her ex's hotel and tell him they weren't broken up.

But there was one person in the story who was involved with a cancer charity.

"Do you mean Abigail?" Cal asked reluctantly. He had liked her, with her massive glasses and careful sympathy, even if she wasn't Joe's mother. She'd seemed kind, but Cal had assumed that because she was at a cancer fund-raiser. "Abigail Beranger?"

"Naw,' Logan said with a flash of annoyance at Cal for not getting it. "Not Missus B. It was her daughter. Daisy. The redhead."

Chapter Sixteen

JOE SAT on the low, leather chair in his bedroom and stared blankly at his computer. The police had come, taken some notes, promised to call if they found anything, and gone again. It had taken all of ten minutes. Now all Joe had left to do was call Harry and fill him in. Skype was open on the screen, Harry's profile pulled up, and all Joe had to do was hit the phone icon. That was all he'd had to do for the last half hour.

He took a drink of coffee—the harsh, strong brew from the hotel room's machine somewhere between what he needed and what he deserved—and wondered what to say when his dad answered.

"Edward was hit by a car," Joe said aloud to the empty room. "I'm gay, and I found out my dead mother isn't dead *or* my mother. Busy week."

Maybe Harry would have another stroke, Joe thought bitterly, and die. Then none of them would have to deal with it.

Despite everything, the thought of Harry being dead caught at Joe's heart with a mixture of guilt and fear. Harry might be a liar, but he was still Joe's dad, the only family he had. Joe didn't want to call Harry, because he would actually have to ask him about all the lies, and he was scared about what the answers might be.

Before he had to bite the bullet and get on with it, someone hammered on the door. Joe knew it wasn't Cal, since Cal had a key, but his heart still jumped with anticipation. Maybe he'd forgotten his keys or had his hands full?

Joe knew he hadn't, but it was an excuse to slap the lid of the laptop down and go find out. He glanced at himself in the mirror and grimaced at the raw scrape, the edges bruised blue, along his jaw. He looked like a twelve-year-old who'd tried to shave for the first time, but there wasn't much to do about it.

He pulled the suite door open and stared in surprise at Kristen—not who he'd hoped to see, and he was used to the faint guilt of that, although he supposed it wasn't warranted now that they were officially exes. And she was not who he expected to see either.

"Kris—"

"You can go to Hell!" she blurted as she threw something small and glitter bright at his face. "And you can stick that up your ass."

Joe fumbled the ring out of the air. The edges of it cut into his palm as he clenched his fingers around it. His temper spluttered in confusion, ready to ignite but not quite sure where to go.

"What the hell are you doing?" he asked.

"You told the police I'd followed you to England? That I *stalked* you?" Kristen took a step back from the door and raked her fingers through her hair. It tangled around her fingers as she shook her head in disbelief. "I *loved* you. I came to England because I didn't understand why you didn't love me anymore. Maybe I'd have liked to get back together, if we could, but what I wanted was to understand why. That's not stalking. It's normal. It's fucking normal! How dare you try and make me out to be crazy when you're the one who lied and ran off and *cheated*!"

Joe glared at her. "You think the fact you got on a plane would make me call you a stalker?"

"What then? That I wanted you back? That I wanted you to talk to me?" Kristen shoved him with both hands in frustration. "You told me that you loved me, then you told me you never did. I needed an answer. That's not stalking, you asshole."

Doubt picked at the edges of Edward's theory. It had already been frayed when the police asked if he knew anyone who wanted to hurt him, but it had still seemed convincing. Now it had unraveled enough that it was on the verge of coming apart. What did Kristen have to gain from this little show of angry innocence? The breakup was done and dusted. He'd already told the police what he knew.

The hurt in her eyes seemed real. It made Joe feel as bad as it always had.

"You're saying you didn't send the letters?" he asked her. "Courier me the bear?"

Kristen blinked back tears. "What letters? What bear?" Her expression was curious as her eyes drifted over the lines of his face. Whatever she saw made her lips tremble before she pressed them together in a tight line. She took a step back from the door. "You think

I'd do something like that? Harass you? Fuck you, Joe, but thank you for my answer. You never loved me at all."

She turned on her heel and stalked away. The last threads of Edward's theory fell apart in Joe's head, and he was left with a handful of accusations and guilt.

"I'm sorry," he said.

Kristen jabbed the Call button on the elevator and then looked back at him. "For what?"

He put his hands in his pockets. "I shouldn't have listened to Edward. I should have known you weren't behind any of this," he said. "It was … at least if you'd done it, I knew something. I knew why."

"Is that all?"

"No. I'm sorry for a lot of things, for hurting you," Joe admitted. He glanced away from her and chewed the inside of his cheek. It might have been a lie, what they had, but it had been one Joe had convinced himself was true. "I did love you, Kris… like a friend, like a sister. I thought that would be enough. Now I know it wasn't even close. I'm sorry."

She wiped her hand over her face, tracks of tear-pink skin visible through her make-up. The elevator chimed softly as the doors opened.

"You can shove that up your ass too, Joseph Bailey," Kristen spat at him as she got on the elevator. She jabbed an impatient finger against the button to send it down. "I never hurt you. I never would. I hope you're happy, Joe, and I hope you know that you don't deserve it."

The doors slid shut before Joe could say anything. He leaned against the doorframe and listened to the soft growl of the elevator as it went down. Something itched at him, down under the guilt and embarrassment.

What did his stalker think they deserved? It had been easy to blame Kristen, because it at least made some sort of sense. He wronged her and she lashed out to let him know that his mother wouldn't have been proud of him—to get her own back, to have her satisfaction.

If it wasn't her, then all of this had, after all, been about Joe's mother's death and his father's lies. But Joe was the one who wanted to know the truth about that. His abusive pen pal already did, or believed they did. So they had to want something else out of it.

Joe avoided his room and the quietly expectant computer and went into the small, well-appointed kitchenette to pick through the room-service breakfast he'd had no appetite for until now. The chilled orange juice and hot coffee had met in the middle and settled on tepid. The scrambled eggs had congealed. The granola was still granola, but once he'd ladled in the yogurt and fruit, he realized he still had no appetite for it. He pushed it away.

Most of the time, he had a knack for this sort of task. It was a useful talent for a troubleshooter. People were rarely glad to see you turn up at their business, but once you knew what to offer them, that changed.

He usually had something to work with. He had done his due diligence on the business and employees and, more importantly, he knew what he could and couldn't do to get them what they wanted. All he knew about whoever sent him burned bears in the mail was that they were angry.

What was Joe supposed to do about that? Back then he'd been a baby. He couldn't influence what happened. And while hindsight was twenty-twenty, even if he had the full story, he didn't know what he could do to fix anything now.

Take a leaf from Harry's book and throw money at it. He poured himself a coffee.

He paused midpour, the french press dangling from his fingers as something finally clicked—the file that Bea had given him the other day. Joe left the coffee to cool and stalked back into his bedroom.

Yesterday it seemed like a distraction. If it was important, he'd assumed, then once he found Abigail, she'd be able to explain why. But it turned out she didn't know much more than him. That left this.

Joe unearthed the file from the drawer he'd tucked it into and emptied the contents onto the bed. He impatiently spread them out over the heavy quilt until he found the stapled-together report from the latest survey on the property.

The address was printed on the top sheet in rounded, careful block capitals, underneath a low-res photograph of the house itself.

Maybe Joe didn't know what his abusive pen pal wanted or imagined they were due, but for over twenty years, his father had thought someone deserved this white-plastered suburban house with the small, aggressively neat lawn. In the same way that Harry had put a roof over his own son's head, he'd made sure this family in Reading had room and board.

Maybe….

When Bea suggested it was guilt that motivated the regular-as-clockwork monthly deposits, Jack had dismissed it. He might have been wrong, although he thought Harry's guilt wasn't for what Bea thought it was. Maybe Harry and Abigail weren't the only family the affair had split up.

He texted Cal—twice. Nervous energy propelled him around the suite four times between the first text and the last. When he didn't hear back in ten minutes—his brain at odds between the bittersweet acknowledgment that Cal owed him nothing and the bitter grudge that Cal did owe him transport—Joe called an Uber instead.

The app gave him twenty minutes. He left his phone on the coffee table, the app open to watch the cartoon car jerkily etch-a-sketch itself along the rendered streets, while he pulled a jacket on over his dark gray T-shirt and laced up his running shoes. When he checked his phone, the estimated time of arrival had jumped. He had five minutes to get down in the elevator and through the hotel's long, bare corridors. And still no text from Cal.

Joe went to text him again but thought better of it and swiped between windows so he could call Bea.

She must have been sitting on the phone. It barely got half a ring out before it cut to her sleep-husky face.

"Joseph," she said, her voice soft. "What do you want?"

He let himself out of the suite and headed to the elevator. "That house in Reading," he said. "Can you meet me there?"

There was a pause, and then she cleared her throat. "What? I don't know what you mean. I… had a late night."

Joe snorted. He could hear the shower in the background, and the off-key warble of someone singing along to Adele cut in and out of the call. It sounded like Bea's night wasn't over yet.

"The house in Reading that the company bought," he said. "I'm meant to be divesting us of all our UK holdings, including that one. So I need to have a look at it. Can you make that happen?"

"It's the weekend," she said.

"It's important."

"Okay," she said slowly. "I'll make it happen. You know where it is?"

Impatience flicked at Joe's mood. He squashed it with the reminder that he had asked for a favor, a precarious one too, since he knew that the property was one that Harry had never expected him to find. He'd been given a list to work through, and Reading hadn't been mentioned.

"I have the files you gave me," he reminded Bea. "I'll be there in an hour."

The shower stopped, and Bea took a quick breath. "Me too," she said. "Let me get out of here. I'll meet you there."

She hung up.

Joe shook his head and flicked to the Uber app so he could check the car while he pressed the Ground Floor button. He couldn't judge. His first meeting with Bea had been delayed because of a shower, muscles, and a smirk.

The thought of Cal, and the memory of wet, clean skin under Joe's mouth made him lick his lips. He texted a quick update as the elevator opened and Uber reminded him they were already outside.

Most of Joe's life, he reminded himself as he tucked his phone back into his pocket, had been navigated without Cal. He should probably get used to it again. The car outside was a navy blue sedan that smelled of upholstery cleaner and children's sweets.

"Reading?" the driver checked as he looked over his shoulder at him. "That's a way, mate."

"Is it a problem?" Joe asked coolly as he put his seat belt on. "I can call another cab."

"Not a problem," the driver said. "It'll be expensive. You want me to drive you back too?"

Joe leaned back against the freshly cleaned upholstery. "No," he said. "I've a car arranged to pick me up later."

He wasn't ready to let Cal go yet, whatever he should or shouldn't get used to.

THE UBER dropped Joe off at the end of the street, eager to be on his way back to London. It was easy enough to find the house. It hadn't changed at all in the five years since the surveyor had snapped a photo of it. The flowers in the garden were still pink and yellow and perfectly lined up in rows. The curtains in the windows were still blue, and the mat at the door still said Welcome, although the bristles had worn down to the nubs.

Joe hesitated on the path up to the front door. He wondered if he'd ever been there before. It didn't feel like he had. There was no sense of déjà vu, no familiarity. Of course he'd been a baby. How old did you have to be to form memories?

Joe waited on the street for a while as he paced down to the chalk scrawl of flowers, faces, and impermanent graffiti about who wanted to kiss who. There was no sign of Bea, and no texts from her to update her time of arrival.

There was a missed call from Cal.

Something tight in Joe's stomach relaxed as he saw it. He tapped it with his thumb as he gave up on Bea and headed up to the front door. It couldn't hurt to speak to whoever still lived there, or try to. If they slammed the door in his face, at least he knew his lawyer was, supposedly, on her way.

It was a voice message. Joe hit Play and lifted it up to his ear. He caught the heavy growl of traffic and the tail end of a muttered curse as he pressed the doorbell. It bing-bonged inside the house.

"I found the kid from the graveyard," Cal yelled into the phone. "Someone hired him to beat you up and give you a scare, and they told him you were an abusive ex. It weren't Kristen, though."

A horn blared through the recording, and Cal told them to fuck off. Joe tilted his head away from the noise and flicked his attention back to the door as it creaked open. A slim woman in black jeans and a gray T-shirt, her hair pulled back in a loose ponytail, smiled at him as she held out her hand.

"Joseph," she said as he accepted the handshake out of habit. "I've been waiting."

"I know you," he said as the familiarity slotted into place. He'd been thrown by how she held herself, the twitchy mannerisms and ducked chin abandoned for new confidence. "You're the girl from the bar, Bea's girlfriend. Rosie."

"Yes," she said as she waved him into the hall past her. It was small, most of it taken up by the stairs, and had the faintly musty smell of somewhere not used much. "Bea asked me to meet you here while she crossed some Ts. I made us tea."

Joe hesitated as she pushed the door shut behind him. There was something wrong, he realized, even before the recording of Cal's voice warned from the phone, "It was Abigail's assistant. Daisy something. She claimed she was Abigail's *daughter*."

Joe ended the call and turned to look at Rosie. Or Daisy, he supposed.

"They're both flowers. It didn't feel like a lie," she said. The butcher's knife in her other hand glittered in the morning light as she lifted it. "Go into the kitchen."

He lunged at her instead and grabbed for the wrist. They struggled back and forth between the white-painted banisters and the neatly lined up striped wallpaper. Joe was stronger than she was, but Rosie refused to let go of the knife. She leaned forward and sank her teeth into his wrist.

Joe had been bitten before. The occasional lover had left a crescent-marked bruise on his skin, a blue-tinged souvenir that lasted longer than his memory of the man, and he'd been nipped by dogs and cats. This was different. The blunt pressure as she clenched her jaw made his bones ache, and her teeth tore instead of pierced his skin. He pulled away from her in surprise and his fingers loosened on her wrist. Rosie wrenched her hand free and lashed out with the knife.

The point of it, ground down to a scratched, uneven point over the years, caught him under the ball of his thumb and sliced him open to halfway up his wrist.

It didn't hurt. For a moment there wasn't even any blood, all he could see was his skin peeled back to flash wet meat and the struts of white bone and cartilage that was his thumb. He had enough time to suck in a startled breath, and then blood filled the injury and spilled down his arm onto the floor.

A sick dizziness hit Joe as he grabbed his forearm and dug his fingers down into the bloody sleeve. It hurt now—a sullen throb of pain that kept time with his heartbeat. He staggered back a step and leaned against the stairs. His feet had left bloody marks on the floor, worked the blood down into the soft nap of the carpet.

"I didn't mean to do that," Rosie told him in an oddly prim voice. When Joe looked up at her, he saw that her face matched the off-beat tone of her words. She'd stabbed him, but her face was set in purse-lipped disapproval, as though he'd walked mud into the carpet instead of his own blood. Only her eyes seemed to realize the seriousness of what was going on. They looked tight and twitchy as she kept the knife on him. "Why won't you *ever* do what you're supposed to Joseph? If you'd *gone away*, then none of this would have happened. Now it's all ruined."

She poked him in the chest with the knife to underline her point. Joe clenched his jaw at the small, smart pain as it dug into his skin. He swallowed, his mouth dry and sticky, and tried to pretend this was another business meeting. How many times had he sat down at the table to negotiate a deal where tens of thousands of dollars hung in the balance.

This was just a bit of blood and a ruined shirt.

"Why?" he asked. "You contacted me. You tracked me down. What did I ever do to you?"

"What you always do. Ruin everything. Take everything." Her voice was shrill and cracked as she singsonged her mockery at him. "Joseph needs to talk, go outside and wait. Joseph needs some paperwork, I can see you afterward. Joseph loves the bear, give Joseph the bear, Daisy."

The blue bear, charred and blinded by fire, popped into Joe's head. He still didn't remember it, but the thought of it made his stomach knot with sick tension and made pressure fill his head.

"If you loved it so much, why did you burn it?" he asked. Blood oozed between his fingers. It soaked his sleeve and had soaked the carpet under his feet. "If it was yours."

Rosie reached up and thumped the heel of her hand against her temple in exasperation.

"It wasn't mine, it was yours. Everything I wanted, you got. Everything I loved, you took away. It was my life. I never wanted you to come in and ruin it. *I* never wanted you. *I* never wanted to go and live with Harry. I wanted to stay with my dad, but no one listened to what I wanted, did they? Everything was about you, about what you needed. If you'd never been born, Joseph, my life would have been perfect. It would have been happy."

Joe wasn't in charge of his legs anymore. He tried to lock his knees, to stay on his feet, but he didn't get a say. His knees folded, and he slid gracelessly down the wall.

"You're my sister," he said.

She flinched away from that, or maybe it was the puddle of blood she stepped back to avoid.

"Half sister," she said defensively. "And that doesn't count. Everyone knows that. That's why Dad got me and *Harry* took you away. You should have stayed away. Everything was fine."

With a hollow thump, Joe leaned his head back against the painted wood. He swallowed and worked his tongue around his dry mouth.

"*You* emailed *me*," he reminded her.

She rubbed her eye with the back of her hand. The knife caught strands of her red hair and clipped them short.

"I was angry," she said. "Dad had died, and I hadn't seen you in so long and then I saw your name on Twitter, your *photo*. You looked happy—in love. Like you still got to have everything, and I got nothing. It reminded me of everything that happened. I'd wanted to forget about it. I needed to forget some of it, but how could I when you kept lying."

Joe's ears had started to ring. He worked his jaw from one side to the other to try and relieve the pressure. His ears popped, but he could still hear the bells. It was only when Rosie crouched down next to him and reached into his pocket that he knew what it was.

"Cal." She turned the phone and showed it to him. "He's worried about you."

Joe laughed bitterly and raised his arm. "He has a point."

Something soft passed over Rosie's face. It thumbed away the tension lines around her eyes and softened the brackets around her lips.

"Bea worries about me," she said. "I only wanted to delay you that day in the pub, so the courier could get there. Maybe I'd met her before, but I didn't remember it. I really like her."

"I like Cal," Joe said. He peeled his dry lips off his teeth and tried for a smile. "They're both going to worry today."

It was a joke. Not a very good one. Rosie sighed.

"I know," she said. "But… I realized something today, when you called. You're my Moby Dick."

Joe laughed raggedly. "That's what he said."

She gave him that prim look again. "Don't be crude. You're never going to go away. Neither of us will ever, ever be really happy."

"I was happy," Joe said.

"No," Rosie said. "And neither will they be. Bea and Cal. We aren't meant to be here, you and me. That's why it always goes wrong. That's what I wanted to explain, until you made me…."

She gestured at Joe's filleted hand and pursed her lips in distaste.

"If you wanted me to go back to California, all you had to do was wait," Joe rasped out. The phone rang again, a persistent chime from Cal, and Joe supposed that he might be lying… or not. He didn't know if he'd have stayed a while longer for Cal, and—more importantly—neither did Rosie. "My tickets are booked, and you'd have never heard from me again."

Rosie put the knife down on the sideboard and walked over to drag Joe back up onto his feet. She squirmed under his arm and grabbed the back of his jeans with one hand.

"It wouldn't have made a difference," she said calmly. Once he was up, she grabbed the knife again. "You've already spoiled everything. All Abigail could talk about last night was you—how handsome you looked, how she wished she'd have been able to let herself be your mother. I spent years with her, Joseph. I was the daughter she never had, and now she doesn't care about me anymore. And when Bea finds out, when she realizes I lied to her…. No. Children should have a mother, Joseph. We grew up wrong without her—selfish and broken. I think maybe you were right, that we need to find her."

Joe leaned on her shoulder as she walked him down the hall and into the kitchen. The table was set for two, but there was a layer of dust on the cutlery. The fridge hummed and rattled, but from the dead cartons of takeout stacked by the fridge, it wasn't used much. It didn't feel like a memorial, more like a squat—someplace you came and stayed but tried to leave no trace.

"I thought our mother was dead," he said.

Rosie nodded distractedly. "For years," she said as she tucked the knife into her jeans and unlocked the back door. "You wouldn't remember, even though it was your fault, because you were only a baby."

Had Harry, somehow, been responsible, Joe wondered? The thought stuck in his throat like a bone, but Rosie's conviction that this was all Joe's fault somehow made him wonder.

"Are we going to her grave?" he asked. The words slurred on his tongue, and he tightened his grip on his bloody arm. "I need to go to the hospital first."

"It's fine," Rosie said blithely. "It's only a scratch."

She pulled him out of the back door and down into the garden. A swing creaked gently as it swayed, and music played tinnily from behind one of the fences.

"Hey," Joe yelled, or tried to. "Help. I'm hurt!"

"Stop that," Rosie hissed. She pulled the knife and pressed it against his thigh, so close to his balls that he flinched. "Nobody is going to hear you anyhow. They're all old around here. Old people who mind their own business. But if you don't shut up, I'll cut you open. Then you won't ever see Mum again."

Joe bit the inside of his cheek.

There was a car parked at the bottom of the garden, parked on a half-crumbled concrete slip that let out onto a narrow alley. Rosie dragged him to it and opened the boot.

"Don't," Joe protested. The old fear hit him, sharp as knives and hot enough to burn, as he tried to pull away from her. She dragged him back, stronger than she looked, and shoved him awkwardly into the narrow space. An old pair of muddy boots dug into the small of his back and he couldn't breathe. He grabbed at the edge of the boot to try and pull himself out, but she rapped his knuckles with the butt of the knife. "Rosie. *Daisy.* Please, you don't have to do this. Okay? I won't tell anyone."

"That's what Mum said," she told him as she folded his legs in and up. "After we drove off the road, she told me that she wasn't angry at me, that nobody ever had to know I'd grabbed the wheel. That's what mothers are meant to do—protect their children. Except then she told on me when that policeman went to hand you to me, told him it was my fault. It was an accident, Joseph. That's what everyone said, a tragic *accident.*"

"Please?" he begged raggedly as his chest tightened up. "Rosie. Daisy. What did you do?"

She reached in and stroked the side of his face. "Nothing, didn't you listen? It was an *accident*," she said. "I never meant to hurt Mum. That's not why I grabbed the wheel. All I wanted was for her to listen to me for once. But then she couldn't even hear me because you wouldn't stop screaming. You always had to have all the attention—from Mum, from Harry, even from that policeman in his big car. If you'd shut up, maybe he would have saved Mum instead of you. Did you ever think about that? I could have grown up with a mum and been normal. Instead she died, and look at us. We're awful. That what I've realized, Joe. We should have both stayed in the car, with her."

Joe grabbed at her arm and left bloody prints all over her neat white blouse, but he wasn't strong enough to hold on. She pulled free and slammed the boot down.

"I was too scared back then," she told him through the metal. "But this time, we'll both go. Together. Mum will like that."

Panic closed in on him like teeth, a pressure against his ribs and hips, and he screamed as the car started. He kicked at the metal walls and sucked in lungfuls of air that couldn't be as hot as the claustrophobia tried to tell him it was.

It turned out Rosie was right. No one on her small, neat street wanted to get involved. Joe eventually—quickly?—ran out of steam. He rolled onto his side, the old boots tucked against his stomach, and tried to keep up the pressure on his arm.

Although he wasn't sure if that was a good idea or not. Maybe he should let it bleed out before Rosie lit the match.

Chapter Seventeen

"ANSWER THE phone," Cal muttered as the Bluetooth rang dutifully in his ear. He clenched his jaw as though frustration could reach down the line and complete the connection on its own. It couldn't, and Joe's voicemail cut in for the sixth time.

"What the hell are you doing, Joe?" Cal asked, his voice pitched to carry over the sound of traffic and the hiss of the wind. "If you get hurt, I'm going to kick your ass. Answer the fucking phone."

He ended the call and revved the bike. It growled between his legs and the vibration of it caught in his hipbones as he wove haphazardly between the fast-moving traffic. This time of day, everyone had gotten to work, no one had left work yet, and the only people on the road where stay-at-home parents and airport cabs. It made for a straight shot down, but worry gnawed at the nape of Cal's neck that he wouldn't be fast enough.

It was a good thing Joe had texted him the address in Reading before he left the hotel or Cal would really have panicked.

As opposed to this—he thought wryly as he passed a fat, bubble-shaped people carrier on the inside, close enough that their wing mirror caught on his sleeve—completely reasonable reaction.

He left the people carrier and the pissed-off driver behind as he gunned the bike and peeled onto the turnoff to Reading. It took him twenty minutes and one foul-mouthed rant at his bike's satnav to find the street that Joe claimed was important.

The heavy rumble of the bike as he rolled down the street twitched curtains in every few houses. A few cars flashed their lights as someone behind a door decided to check if they'd remembered to lock them last night.

Cal snorted to himself. Nobody who could afford his bike would go out of their way to drive out there and trade it for a hard-driven Nissan Leaf. The resale value was shit on the legit market.

The rust-pocked 45 screwed into the brickwork on one house finally caught his eye and Cal pulled up to the curb. It didn't look like the sort of place that had a dark secret behind the dusty lace curtains. It looked like a normal house, the sort of place Cal would have bought as his starter home if he hadn't blown all his money on whiskey, motorbikes, and bail.

He kicked the stand down with the heel of his boot and left the bike to cool down as he walked up to the front door. Instead of the doorbell or the slot of the letterbox, Cal rapped his knuckles against the door. No answer. He tried again and shifted his weight impatiently on the worn bald doormat—the Welcome blurred where years of feet had scraped over it—as he waited for someone to come down the stairs or yell from the downstairs loo for him to wait.

When neither happened he pushed the letterbox open with a finger and leaned down to peer inside. Some people might have mistaken the stain on the carpet for something else—tomato juice, mud, anything that excused them from having to acknowledge the ugliness—but Cal had cleaned bloodstains out of the carpet of his grandad's Rolls to earn his pocket money. He knew what it looked like.

"Joe," he yelled. "Joe, are you there?"

No answer. Fuck it. He stepped back and kicked the door. It was heavy PVC and the impact of his boot rattled it in the frame but didn't pop it open. He kicked it again and one of the panels popped at the side.

A window cracked in the house next door, and an old man poked his head out. "If you're after Daisy's gentleman friend, you've just missed him," he snapped. His lips folded in over his worn yellow teeth as he took a drag on a crooked cigar. "I don't know what this place is coming to. First that woman down the road gets that boy of hers a scooter—up and down the street like a demented bee at all hours—and now some fella around, yelling the odds at—"

"Where'd they go?" Cal asked.

The old man squinted at him from under the glasses he'd shoved up onto his high, bare forehead. "Don't see what right you have to know."

Cal put his hand on the fence between the gardens and braced his weight on it. "I can come and kick *your* door in instead, old man."

The old man pulled back into the house like a turtle into a shell and pulled the window in with him. "No one tells me where they're going," he spat out. “All I know is the car left from out back, him still giving her the worst word in his mouth. Nice friends you have, young man.”

“When?” Cal asked.

“Few minutes ago.” The words squeezed out through the gap in the window as the old guy latched it. “You can catch them if you run.”

“Fuck off,” Cal said.

He didn’t bother to ask what sort of car that Daisy/Rosie drove. It was a Volvo, the same one he’d seen at the graveyard and in his rearview mirror. His bike coughed in protest at being gunned back up so soon, but the engine smoothed out as he pulled into the street. Where was he going? Where would *she* go?

Bleak panic swelled in Cal’s chest. It was already there, ready to go, because he’d expected this all along. Even if he had been quick enough it would still have ended like this. Cal wasn’t someone who people stayed for. He was someone they left.

He stopped the bike outside a corner shop and felt the black, stupid compulsion to smash the narrow, fly-spotted windows. It wouldn’t help, but that had never stopped him before. There was a certain sick satisfaction in a failure that was so defiantly on your own terms.

Except this time it wasn’t the exams he knew he was going to fail at school or the faith that El put in him and Cal figured he might as well disappoint sooner than later. It wasn’t Cal this time—it was Joe.

Cal braced his foot on the curb, the weight of the bike against his thigh, tugged his helmet off, and reached into his jacket for his phone. Part of him wished this was something he could blackmail or bribe Van into sorting out for him.

Not that it made any sense to expect his mum to come through for him, but he called her anyhow, five times in a row, until she finally answered with the clipped, irritated “yes” that people gave cold callers.

“What happened the night Edward fucked up Grandad’s Bentley?” he asked.

It was a longshot, but how else would a mediocre London copper end up as the lifetime employee of an American millionaire and surrogate dad to the millionaire’s kid? The timing fit too. That didn’t mean it would help, but it was the only idea Cal had.

“That was a long time ago,” his mum said, her voice slow with surprise. It was the kindest her voice had ever sounded on a phone call with him. Not that it lasted, the usual edge of tension crawled back into it as she added, “And this isn’t a good time. Can you call back later?”

“No,” Cal said. “Either we talk now, or I fucking move to Newcastle. How much of a good time would that be?”

“Don’t be ridiculous.”

“This is important,” Cal said. It wasn’t the first important thing that his mum had missed, ignored, or ruined, but this time, if she let him down, Cal would actually follow through on his threat. “If you don’t talk to me, I will come up there and ruin my life all over your shiny new one. So answer me, what happened the night Edward crashed the Bentley?”

“He didn’t crash it,” his mom said sharply. There was a muffled pause and he heard her make the excuse of “insurance salesman” to someone. Then a door clicked and she came back. “We were on our way to Cirencester for the night. A band I liked was on, and this red Lexus veered across the motorway. It clipped the front of the Bentley, bashed up the headlights, and then hit the guardrail and went down the embankment. I don’t talk about this, Caleb.”

“Surprised you remember my name.”

“I picked it.’

“Whatever. Look, we both know you’ve seen worse than a car accident. Don’t pretend you’re some shrinking violet now. What happened?”

There was a pause. Cal wondered, with a touch of surprise, if his mother actually was upset.

“It wasn’t the accident,” she said quietly. “It was the screaming. It was a mother and two children in the car. The older child, a girl, crawled out of the broken windshield, but the other two were trapped. I called the ambulance. That’s what you’re meant to do. But by then the car was on fire. Edward went to help—his hands were ruined, all blistered from the metal—but the driver, their mother, wouldn’t let him help her. She told him to get the little boy out first, poor little brat. He wasn’t very old, still a baby, and I remember wondering if I’d have done the same for you. Maybe she was a better mother, or she knew that… well, they took her in two pieces later. I don’t think Edward could have helped her even if she’d let him.”

Cal swallowed the bitter taste in the back of his throat—he never learned where his mum was concerned—and focused on the fact he’d been right. The night Joe's mum had died and been carefully erased from his world, Edward had been there. He'd kept the secret and Joe close. Cal wasn't sure if he'd attribute that to Edward's self-interest or to some sense of responsibility to the baby he'd rescued.

Either way, thank God for his grandad's soft spot for ex-squaddies and his daughter's ex-boyfriends. It had been enough to make their firm Edward's first call when he needed a driver.

"Where did it—" he started to ask.

"It was the little girl, though," his mum said over him. He'd blackmailed her into this, but now she'd started to speak, Cal didn't think she even really knew it was him on the line. "She'd caused the accident—that's what the woman told Edward—grabbed the wheel and drove them off the road. Not even a teenager and so angry, just so… angry. She told Edward to put the baby back in the fire. That's when I decided to move up north, to make a clean break of it. It was better for everyone, because I was that girl. Every time I came and got you boys, took you away to play house until it went wrong, I put you back in the fire."

That hadn't happened. Cal had been five. He'd have remembered if he ever went to live with his mum for longer than a weekend in a grotty bedsit in Blackpool. Unless that had been it, the best she had to offer before it all went to hell again.

"And Edward went to work for the boy's dad, right?" Cal said, because that was something he could deal with.

"Yes," his mum said, her voice surprised. "He was a mess after it happened, he couldn't get over the fact he let that woman die to save the boy. PTSD, I suppose. Nightmares. Drink. I was gone for the worst of it, but friends told me about it. They thought it was because I'd left him, but it was her. That poor dead woman. He lost his job, and when the boy's father found out he offered Edward a job with him instead. In America. The last time I saw him, he'd come up to say goodbye. I don't know why he bothered. We were broken up by then, but maybe he didn't have anyone else to say it to.

"Where did it happen?" Cal asked. "What road? It doesn't have to be the address, just close enough."

He didn't expect much. This was a woman who had once forgotten not only his birthday, but Christmas. To his surprise his mother answered precisely, in a small, firm voice. Cal had heard people give evidence like that.

"The M4," she said. "It was past Pond Farm. I'd made a joke about it, said that Edward could buy it and raise pigs. He didn't think it was funny. That's why I remember. He usually thought I was funny."

Cal exhaled. It felt like the first time since he'd seen the blood. His mother's story wasn't much, and he still didn't know if Rosie was on her way back there, but it was something. It was enough that he mentally cut her free from a lot of things he blamed her for. This made up for it.

"Thank you," he said. "I won't call again."

She surprised him when she didn't hang up right away. "I knew you'd be okay," she said. "I knew that my mum, your gran, she'd be like that woman in the car. She'd have saved you boys without a thought. So I knew. I had to stop putting you in the fire."

Cal couldn't say anything. He'd spent too many years angry at her. It was easier to let her off the hook for her screwups than have to admit that maybe she hadn't made as many as he thought.

For the first time, Cal hung up on her.

Pond Farm. He'd driven past that a couple of times, enough that he could find his way back with no problem. If he was right, then he'd find Joe, and if he wasn't….

Cal tugged his helmet down over his ears and gave the top of it a smack to settle it in place. There'd been a lot of blood in the hall. If Joe wasn't at Pond Farm like Cal thought—if the emails and burned bears weren't Rosie reliving her bad deeds—then maybe Cal wouldn't find him at all.

HE CAUGHT up with the car about twenty miles from Pond Farm. Rosie's middle-aged sedan wasn't built for speed, and he didn't think she expected anyone to follow her. Cal tucked himself in behind her and called the police.

Cal had been in enough car chases on the other side of the line to know what a bad idea they were. If he could get the police out there to wear Rosie down, to toss their spike strips over the road to slow her down, Cal would take that.

He recited the license plate number to the chipper young policeman on the other end of the line, told them that Rosie drove erratically, and exaggerated the damage to the front of the car so they'd make the connection with the car accident at the Renaissance. It would take too long to explain the truth, and it was a bizarre enough story that he'd go through three sets of ears before someone believed him.

Ahead of him Rosie abruptly switched lanes into the fast lane, her bumper an inch from the car behind. She ignored the agitated blare of horns and let her speed drop as the car fell back. Cal held his place and kept an eye on her in the rearview mirror.

He was pretty confident she hadn't recognized him. They'd met for a minute at the event, and he'd been in a suit instead of jeans, and bare-headed instead of hidden behind a matte-black visor. There was no way she could know who he was.

But somehow she did. She abruptly switched lanes again in a hard diagonal that ended with the car on the hard shoulder. It juddered past Cal at panel-rattling speed, and he saw that she was the only person visible in the car.

Cal hesitated as he weighed his options. He didn't want anyone to get hurt, especially Rosie, since she might be the only one to know where Joe was, but he didn't want her to get away either. Habit made the decision for him. It was easier, after all these years, to go fast than slow.

So he stuck to Rosie's tail as they wove in and out of traffic. Three times she scraped him out with a desperate, ass-clenched move around one of the massive trucks that lumbered around the road. He caught up with her every time she sped out from behind the truck or fell back to try and mingle with the other cars.

Sweat itched under Cal's hairline, rubbed raw against the nape of his neck by the helmet, and he was ashamed to admit there was a little part of him that enjoyed the speed. A gray Porsche tried to keep up with them as he mistook the chase for a race, but it had to fall back with a squeal of brakes as a Sainsbury's delivery truck had to veer in front of him so it didn't rear end Rosie.

Cal could have caught her. In the end he was the better driver, with a better vehicle for the chase. The problem was that she didn't want to get away, she wanted to reach the right spot. Ten miles after Pond Farm—farther than his mum had thought—Rosie pulled the wheel to the right and bounced up onto the hard shoulder. Then she just went on over. Her bumper crumpled against the corrugated iron guard rail and the car took flight.

Only for a second. Then gravity caught it and smacked it back down into the ground. The windows popped and shattered by the pressure as the car scraped down the incline on its side and crashed into a fence post.

A handful of birds who'd been perched on the fence took off in a surprised flurry of wings, and Cal's stomach dropped down to his feet with dread as he pulled up onto the hard shoulder. He let the bike fall onto its side as he scrambled down the torn-up hillock of grass.

He raced toward the car as small, frantic hands hammered out the flexible sheets of glass shards that used to be the windshield. For an odd, surreal moment, he heard his mum's voice in the back of his head, her memory of the accident overlaid over this new one.

Rosie crawled out over the steering wheel and the hood of the car. She collapsed into the mud as she slid down off the bumper, her legs as weak as his had felt earlier.

"Where is he?" Cal demanded as he grabbed her arm and dragged her back up onto her feet. He shook her to make her eyes focus on him. "Where's Joe?"

She stared at him for a second. "He's… he's gone to be with Mum," she said. Her voice got more certain as she talked. "We'll be with her forever now. Like we were meant to be."

Cal shook her again, hard enough make her head snap back and forth. "You crawled out. Again. Where's Joe?"

Rosie stared at him for a second, and then her stubbornly prim expression gave way to wide-eyed horror. She opened her mouth and closed it again, her lips pressed together to stop the tremble that picked at the corners. Her only answer to Cal's question was to shake her head and screw her eyes up tight.

"What's wrong with you?" Cal yelled at her. He gave her a disgusted shove away from him, and she staggered back, tripped over a knot of grass, and fell down. She didn't try to get back up. "Why did you do this?"

If Rosie had an answer to that, she didn't want to share it with Cal. He left her in the mud and lumbered over the long, matted grass to the car. The particular smell of gas and brake fluid hung heavy in the air, a smell so thick it had a taste. Under the dented hood, the engine still rattled and spat.

Cal looked in the back seat of the car. No Joe. There was no sign of him in the car at all. For a second, Cal thought he had been wrong—not about the fact that Rosie had stopped being able to make good decisions a while ago, but that the bad decision she wanted to make was this.

If she wanted to relive that night, Joe would have to be here.

Something rattled in the boot. Cal froze, his hands pressed against hot metal. “Joe?”

Another kick, the double-punch of fists against metal, and the sound of a desperate, muffled voice from inside as Joe begged desperately to get out.

“Cal, please, get me out. Get me out! I can’t breathe. Cal… please!”

“Wait,” Cal yelled as he pressed his hands against the metal. “I’ll be back. Wait.”

He scrambled back up the bank on his hands and knees, fistfuls of grass used as handholds, to his bike. He’d promised El he’d behave himself when he got out of jail. But if he ever had to break that promise, he’d wanted to be prepared. Cal grabbed the heavy screwdriver from where he’d stashed it under the seat. It was nearly as old as him—stolen from his grandad’s shed when Cal was ten for… something, probably mischief—but it was still good enough for the job.

Another car pulled over. The driver rolled her window down and peered out. Purple hair quiffed up over a pale, earnest face.

“Is everything okay?” she asked and pulled a face as the question left her lips. “Stupid question. I mean, is anyone hurt? What can I do?”

“Call the ambulance,” Cal said. He glanced over at Rosie, who’d hidden her face in her hands. “And the police.”

She nodded and grabbed her phone from the holder. Cal left her to it as he started back down the bank. Halfway there the fire coughed itself into life on the undercarriage of the engine. It bopped there for a second, blue and meditative, and then made hungry, yellow inroads on the rest of the car.

“Shit,” Cal muttered. He staggered back from the rush of heat, one hand up to protect his face, and then stumbled around the car. The metal had been warm before. It was hot now, and he could hear Joe cough inside the drunk.

He jammed the screwdriver into the lock, gave the handle a whack with the heel of his hand, and then twisted it to core the locking mechanism out by force. The boot held for a second and then popped open. Cal blistered his fingers on it as he pulled it open and reached in to drag Joe out and away.

Relief and fear and guilt caught in the back of Cal's throat. He'd thought, for a few minutes, that he might never see Joe again, or that if he did, it would be in a box. There was probably something he could say that would cover that, explain it, but it was beyond Cal. Once they reached a safe distance, he dragged Joe into a rough, desperate hug and breathed in the smell of him mixed with smoke and old oil.

"You scared the fuck out of me," he rasped in Joe's ear. "You asshole. Don't bloody do that again."

Joe laughed. There was more wobble to the sound than usual. "I have no intention of doing this again. Once was enough." He leaned against Cal and cradled his arm to his chest. Blood had soaked through the rough bandage he'd made of his sleeve and dripped slowly from his fingertips. "She cut me. I think I need a doctor."

"The ambulance is on the way," Cal promised. He stroked Joe's hair back from his forehead, twisted his fingers in the soft, dark curls, and pressed a kiss to his scarred temple. "You'll be okay."

Joe nodded and relaxed carefully into Cal. He closed his eyes, clutched his forearm tightly, and rested his head against Cal's shoulder as they waited to hear the siren of thc ambulance. When they finally did, Joe lifted his head and glanced over at the crumbled Rosie.

"Don't tell them what she did?" he said. "Say it was an accident."

"Why?" Cal protested. "She tried to kill you."

"I know," Joe said as the ambulance pulled in and the paramedics spilled out. "But she's my sister, and I think I've taken enough from her, even if I didn't mean to."

The paramedics pulled Joe away, his arm up and bundles of gauze pulled out of packets before Cal could promise one way or the other. In the end, when the policeman asked what happened, he shrugged and lied about wildlife in the road. He'd passed enough furry corpses on his drive up from Reading to expect that to be believable.

Rosie wasn't his sister, but the sight of her huddled in the grass made him think she might actually have lost enough.

Although, if anything happened to Joe, he thought grimly as he watched the ambulance pull away, he'd have to rethink that.

Epilogue

IT TOOK two months for the doctors to finish the job on Joe's hand, to stitch the damaged nerves back into place, to chase the infection out with handfuls of pills, and to eventually chuck him back out onto the street. The minute he was out, the first place he went was the cemetery.

This time to the one his real mother was buried in.

Cal loitered back by a copse of oaks while Rosie, muted and grateful they hadn't told her lawyer girlfriend anything, showed Joe through the rows of the dead. It made Cal's nerves twitch under the skin to watch, but Rosie's breakdown at the scene of the accident seemed to have given her some peace. At the very least, she'd accepted she had a brother… like it or not. Cal didn't trust her—that was why he was there in Edward's place and with Edward's scowl—but she was Joe's sister. It was his call.

After a few minutes at the graveside, Rosie—she said she felt more like Rosie, that Daisy was the little girl at the fire—left Joe to it and walked slowly back to her new car. The insurance—after everyone had held firm on it being an accident—had paid out for her to replace the husk she'd left on the side of the road.

It was a good thing too, since she'd lost her job. Even without the full details, Abigail had enough information to decide that it was better Rosie get another position.

Cal waited until she'd gone. Then he walked up the hill to join Joe at the graveside. It was a small, simple gravestone with her name and date of death. Not much to tell you about a person.

"So, you found her," Cal said.

"Yes," Joe said. "I don't know if it makes any difference now. I'll never know her."

"She loved you," Cal pointed out. "She picked you over her own life. You know that. It's more than some people get."

Joe leaned into Cal and put an arm around his waist. "I guess."

They stood and looked at a dead woman's grave. Her given name had been Margaret, her middle name Jessica, but they didn't know what she liked to be called. Rosie claimed that she didn't remember. They all knew that was a lie, but Rosie had to live with the fact that she'd killed her mother, however accidentally. If it made her feel better to keep some secrets still, Joe had decided to let her.

After a second, maybe because Margaret had been brave, Cal finally asked the question he hadn't wanted to face until then. Two days before he had no choice.

"What are you going to do now?" he asked. "The doctors said you could travel again. Are you going to… go back to California?"

He couldn't imagine anyone would say no to that, and Joe didn't surprise him.

"Maybe," he said. Joe tightened his arm around Cal's waist as he rested his head on Cal's shoulder. "Not yet. I think distance is good for me and Dad right now. I know he meant well, that he wanted to protect that little girl from what she'd done and me from knowing what I'd caused—"

"You were a baby," Cal objected.

"I still feel guilty. My birth was what started all this, I don't know if I could have coped with that as a kid," Joe poked his toe at a stray weed by the grave. "Still, he nearly got me killed. It's easier to be kind from this side of the ocean."

It was stupid to be relieved. Joe hadn't said he'd stay forever, or even for very long. That didn't seem to matter. All Cal needed to know was that Joe didn't want to leave yet.

"And if I do go," Joe added. "You're coming with me."

The statement caught Cal flat-footed. He stumbled over his answer and found objections instead. "I've never driven in America before."

Joe lifted his head and gave Cal a wry look. "You know we're dating, don't you?" he said. "You're my boyfriend, Cal Tate, and even I'm not asshole enough to expect you to still drive me to meetings and wait in the car. You did know that, right?"

Actually Cal hadn't. But now that he knew, he… didn't mind.

He pulled Joe into a kiss and smiled against his mouth. "I think you're meant to ask me," he said. "But I suppose you can text me later."

It probably wasn't the most respectful place to kiss, at the foot of Joe's dead mother's grave. In the end, Cal didn't think she'd mind. Whatever she might think of Cal, she'd loved Joe.

So did Cal.

TA MOORE is a Northern Irish writer of romantic suspense, urban fantasy, and contemporary romance novels. A childhood in a rural seaside town fostered a suspicious nature, a love of mystery, and a streak of black humor a mile wide. As her grandmother always said, "She'd laugh at a bad thing, that one." Mind you, that was the pot calling the kettle black. TA studied history, Irish mythology, and English at university, mostly because she has always loved a good story. She worked as a journalist, a finance manager, and in the arts sectors before she finally gave in to a lifelong desire to write.

Coffee, Doc Marten boots, and good friends are the essential things in life. Spiders, mayo, and heels are to be avoided.

Website: www.nevertobetold.co.uk
Facebook: www.facebook.com/TA.Moores
Twitter: @tammy_moore

BONE TO PICK

Digging Up Bones: Book One

Cloister Witte is a man with a dark past and a cute dog. He's happy to talk about the dog all day, but after growing up in the shadow of a missing brother, a deadbeat dad, and a criminal stepfather, he'd rather leave the past back in Montana. These days he's a K-9 officer in the San Diego County Sheriff's Department and pays a tithe to his ghosts by doing what no one was able to do for his brother—find the missing and bring them home.

He's good at solving difficult mysteries. The dog is even better.

This time the missing person is a ten-year-old boy who walked into the woods in the middle of the night and didn't come back. With the antagonistic help of distractingly handsome FBI agent Javi Merlo, it quickly becomes clear that Drew Hartley didn't run away. He was taken, and the evidence implies he's not the kidnapper's first victim. As the search intensifies, old grudges and tragedies are pulled into the light of day. But with each clue they uncover, it looks less and less likely that Drew will be found alive.

TA
MOORE
EVERY OTHER
WEEKEND

Divorce lawyer Clayton Reynolds is a happy cynic who believes in hard work and one-night stands. He also believes that being an excellent lawyer means he never has to go home to the miserable trailer park where he grew up and that volunteering at a women's shelter will buy off the conscience that occasionally plagues him. So when Nadine Graham comes in with a broken arm and a son she desperately wants to protect, Clayton can't turn down their plea for help.

Taking the case means appealing to investigator "Just Call Me Kelly" for help. That wouldn't be so bad if Kelly weren't a hopeless romantic… and the hottest man Clayton's ever met.

Kelly has always had a crush on the unobtainable Clayton Reynolds. He agrees to help, even though he has enough on his plate with the motherless baby his widowed brother left him to care for.

As Nadine's case turns dangerous and the two seemingly opposite men are forced to work together, they discover they have a great deal in common—but solving the case and saving Nadine's life might cost Kelly everything.

www.dreamspinnerpress.com

Wanted – Bad Boyfriend

TA MOORE

Island Classifieds: Book One

His mother. His best friend. The barmaid at the local pub. Everyone is determined to find Nathan Moffatt a boyfriend. It's the last thing Nathan wants. After spending every day making sure his clients experience nothing but romantic magic, the Granshire Hotel's wedding organizer just wants to go home, binge-watch crime dramas, and eat pizza in his underwear.

Unfortunately, no one believes him, and he's stuck with lectures about dying alone. Then inspiration strikes. He needs the people in his life to want him to stay single as much as he does. He needs a bad boyfriend.

There's only one man for the job.

Flynn Delaney is used to people on the island of Ceremony thinking the worst of him. But he isn't sure he wants the dubious honor of worst boyfriend on the entire island. On the other hand, if he plays along, he gets to hang out with the gorgeous Nathan and piss off the owners of the Granshire Hotel. It's a win-win.

There's only one problem—Flynn's actually quite a good boyfriend, and now Nathan's wondering if getting off the sofa occasionally is really the worst thing in the world.

FOR

MORE

OF THE

BEST